A HENRY HOLT MYSTERY

BURN

JOHN LUTZ

HENRY HOLT AND COMPANY
NEW YORK

Henry Holt and Company, Inc.
Publishers since 1866
115 West 18th Street
New York, New York 10011

Published in Canada by Fitzhenry & Whiteside Ltd.,
195 Allstate Parkway, Markham, Ontario L3R 4T8.

Library of Congress Cataloging-in-Publication Data
Lutz, John.
Burn / John Lutz. — 1st ed.
p.   cm. — (A Henry Holt mystery)
1. Carver, Fred (Fictitious character)—Fiction.   2. Private
investigators—Florida—Fiction.   I. Title.
PS3562.U854B87   1995   94-32187
813'.54—dc20   CIP

ISBN 0-8050-3480-3

First Edition—1995

DESIGNED BY LUCY ALBANESE

Printed in the United States of America
All first editions are printed on acid-free paper.∞

1   3   5   7   9   10   8   6   4   2

FOR MIKE AND PATTY
OF TOAD HALL

With knowledge doubt increases.

—GOETHE

BURN

A HENRY HOLT MYSTERY

1

HE LOOKED a lot like the serial killer Ted Bundy, only older. Mid-forties, probably. Carver's age. He had Bundy's all-American, amiable features, complete with neatly arched eyebrows and small, chiseled nose turned up slightly at the tip; the same innocent blue eyes and a mouth always ready to smile, even when things were going bad. As they must be, or Joel Brant wouldn't be in Carver's office.

Brant sat down and raked his fingers through his dark, wavy hair, which was going gray at the temples. He was wearing pleated blue slacks and a gray sport coat over a white shirt without a tie. A thick silver neck chain winked in the light among dark chest hair where his collar parted.

"Morgan recommended you," he said. He looked worried; the sincere blue eyes held secret pain.

"I know," Carver said. "Vic called me about you." Vic Morgan's recommendation was the only reason Carver wanted to touch Brant's problem. Morgan was a retired vice cop, and a more savvy judge of human nature than a roomful of psychologists. He believed Brant, which went a long way with Carver.

"The police won't believe me," Brant said.

"You sure? Maybe they're just doing their job. A complaint's filed, and they go through a certain procedure."

Brant shook his handsome head. The neck chain glittered. "No, I can tell by their expressions they don't believe me. I suppose you can't blame them for that, though. I mean, it's the times, the way things are right now on the news and in all the magazines. Like the whole society's gone mad." He absently rubbed a finger along the chain where it disappeared beneath his collar. A nervous habit, maybe. "I doubt if you're going to believe me."

"You don't have to make me believe," Carver said. "You only have to make me curious."

Brant dragged a crumpled pack of cigarettes from his shirt pocket. Camels. "Mind if I smoke?"

Carver noticed Brant's hand was trembling. "Smoke away," he said. He wanted Brant to relax and talk freely. Besides, the smoke didn't really bother him. He smoked cigars himself sometimes after meals.

Brant stuck what appeared to be the last cigarette from the pack between his lips, then fished around in a pocket and withdrew a silver lighter. It took him three tries to get the lighter to work, then he sucked in enough smoke to burn away half an inch of the cigarette. He threw his head back and exhaled toward the ceiling. For several seconds he watched the smoke spread out up there, then lowered his gaze and looked directly at Carver. His eyes were calm now, but one corner of his mouth twitched slightly before he began to speak.

"I'm what could be described as a reasonably successful businessman, Mr. Carver. My company, Brant Development, is a small construction firm specializing in residential estate. You might have seen Brant Estates, our newest subdivision, off the highway west of town."

Carver nodded. He recalled driving past the spread of neat, medium-priced homes that were perched like a goal and a promise on the edge of the poorer section of Del Moray.

"I'm a widower," Brant went on. "My wife Portia was killed six months ago by a drunk driver. I'm not what you'd call a womanizer—in fact, I hardly have any social life at all. I spend most of my time working. After my wife's death, I got into that habit to try forgetting my grief." An expression almost palpably sad passed over his features, as if gravity had given them an extra tug. "I'm still doing that, I suppose, still trying, still not forgetting. So I was damned surprised when this thing started. At first I thought it was some kind of sick joke, then it continued and I knew the woman was serious."

"And the woman is?"

"Marla Cloy is her name. A month ago she called the police and accused me of stalking her. She told them I'd even parked across the street from her house and watched her through binoculars. She described my car and gave the police the license number." Brant leaned forward earnestly, like a salesman trying to close a deal. "I was nowhere near her house at that time nor any other, Mr. Carver."

"Where were you?"

"At home by myself. I can't prove it, though. How many people can prove when they were home minding their own business?" Brant decided he needed more smoke. He inhaled, exhaled, then studied the ceiling again for a second or two, as if there might be answers floating up there in the carcinogenic haze.

"Was your car parked in the street?" Carver asked.

"In the condo garage, out of sight. With the foliage around my unit, it's even out of sight from most of the neighbors when it's parked in my driveway."

"You should park it in the street from now on," Carver said.

"Make sure it's at least possible someone can verify it was there if the woman makes the same kind of accusation again."

"I thought of that," Brant said. "At first I didn't do it because I didn't see why I should have to change my life just because some crazy woman decided to persecute me."

"She says you're persecuting her."

"I hadn't even seen her when she made her original accusation," Brant said angrily.

"But now you have seen her?"

"Yes. You can understand why I was curious. I drove past her house, trying to catch a glimpse of her. I mean, the way I was figuring it at the time, she and I had to have *some* connection for her to be doing this to me. I thought if I found out what the connection was, I could talk with her, straighten all this out. But when I saw her come outside to put her trash bags at the curb, I didn't recognize her at all. I'm sure we've never had any previous contact."

"Did she see you when you were watching her that time?"

Brant looked disgusted. "I don't think so, and *that* time is the *only* time I've seen her, even though she's called the police several times claiming I've been harassing her, threatening her." Brant clenched his teeth and hissed through them in exasperation. "I seem to be getting the same reaction out of you that I got from the police."

Carver gazed out his office window, across Magellan to where a knot of teenage girls stood waiting for a bus. Beyond them, through the spaces between the buildings, he could see the blue-green Atlantic shimmering in the bright Florida sun. A tall, skinny teenage boy stood about five feet from the girls, who began giggling and jostling one another, and one of them playfully hit another with her purse, which was on a long strap. On the backswing she'd struck the boy. Carver was sure it had been on purpose. The girl turned around and apologized, and she and the thin boy moved away from the other girls and be-

| 4 |

gan to talk, tentatively exploring the fringes of one of life's great mysteries.

The tension between the sexes was usually what kept Carver busy, and here it was again, in the person of Joel Brant.

"What's this Marla Cloy telling the police about you other than that you're stalking her?" Carver asked.

"She's saying she's never seen me before, didn't even know who I was until the police told her my name after tracing my license plate number. She says I must be fixated on her. Some men are obsessive that way about certain women, Mr. Carver, but I'm not one of them." The finger touched the neck chain again. "Women's brains are wired differently; usually they aren't that way."

"But you think Marla Cloy is?"

"I don't know. I have no idea why she's doing this to me. That's why it's driving me nuts. She's ruining my reputation and might even get me jailed, and I don't have the slightest idea why. Do you realize how that feels?"

"I can imagine."

"I doubt it. I don't think anybody can know unless they're the target. After what she did last week, I was afraid it would somehow get into the papers. I've not only got my reputation to consider, but my business could be affected if any of this madness becomes public knowledge. I can tell you I don't shop at Newton's Market anymore, not after the way they stared at me at the checkout counter the last time I went in there."

"She did something last week at Newton's Market?"

"I stopped in there to pick up some groceries, then I drove home and was just finishing putting them away when the doorbell rang. It was the police. Marla Cloy had filed a complaint. She claimed I threatened her in Newton's parking lot with a knife when she was loading her groceries in the trunk of her car."

"The police arrest you?"

"No. They couldn't. There were no witnesses to this alleged crime. Marla Cloy told them I'd made sure to stay near a parked van where I'd be shielded from view, and I'd held the knife down low out of sight. She said I told her I'd been watching her and I was going to kill her and there was nothing she could do about it. She must have put on a real convincing act, the way the cops were looking at me, as if I was scum and they wanted to shoot me down right there."

"Maybe you read that into it."

"I don't think so, Mr. Carver. These days when a woman makes an accusation against a man, everyone believes her."

"Sometimes," Carver conceded.

"I've been notified her attorney's asked the court for a restraining order to keep me away from her under penalty of law. The court will probably comply, making me seem even more like a monster."

"Not many requests for restraining orders are refused," Carver said. "From the law's point of view, it's a better-safe-than-sorry way of operating."

"I'm not obsessed with Marla Cloy," Brant said with barely suppressed rage. "I know absolutely nothing about her and I don't want to harm her."

Carver knew what Brant did want, but he preferred to hear it from Brant. To some extent, Brant was right. Carver had listened to him and wasn't sure he believed him; sympathy automatically gravitated toward the woman.

But he'd made Carver curious.

"I can't get any help from the police," Brant said, "and if I probe around myself for the truth, it will only be interpreted as further harassment and will make things worse for me. So I came to you. I want you to look into this and find out who Marla Cloy is and why she's falsely accusing me." Pain and outrage flared again in his guileless blue eyes. "I want to know why someone would do something this vicious and ruinous to a complete stranger."

"Maybe you're not complete strangers."

"Then what are we to each other?"

Carver decided it was a question worth answering.

2

"I'VE GOT no answers," Beth Jackson said after Carver had told her about Brant's visit to his office.

They'd finished lunch in his beach cottage north of town, and now they sat in the shade on the plank porch, gazing out at the sea and drinking expensive gourmet coffee that smelled good to Carver but tasted like ordinary coffee.

Beth was wearing a white halter and yellow shorts and headband. The colors looked strikingly pale against her dark skin. Her long, bare legs were crossed and a white leather sandal dangled precariously from the big toe of her right foot. Carver's cane was resting against the arm of his chair, and his bad leg was propped up on the porch rail. Beyond the rail and the tan crescent of beach, the sea rolled and gulls screamed and circled gracefully above something dark and indefinable floating a long way from shore.

"I think I believe his story," Carver said.

"You would, being a man."

Carver didn't like her saying that. He wasn't a knee-jerk

male chauvinist. Not anymore. "It's not impossible that a woman would take advantage of the political climate and falsely accuse a man of stalking her."

"Why would she do that?"

"Could be a lot of motives."

"Brant said she doesn't even know him."

"No," Carver corrected, "he said *he* didn't know *her*."

"A difference without a distinction," Beth said. "He told you he thought they were strangers." She stared out at the ocean, the sun highlighting her prominent cheekbones, her dark features that hinted at nobility. Crow's-feet had formed faintly around the corners of her brown eyes. She looked like a high-fashion model put out of work by character lines.

Carver took a sip of coffee, savoring what the package said was its chocolate-cinnamon aroma. "Your reaction might be exactly what Marla Cloy is counting on. She wants to be seen as the typical helpless female victim being threatened and stalked by the typical compulsive male sexual psychopath."

"There are a lot of female victims and male psychopaths out there, Fred."

Carver couldn't deny that. "What would you do if a strange man was stalking you?" he asked.

She glanced over at him with a dark ferocity that let him know she understood the game he was playing. She didn't view herself as a victim and she didn't see why so many women cast themselves in that role. She'd said so and written it in *Burrow*, the local alternative-press newspaper that employed her. Carver was on dangerous ground, using her own words to snare her.

"I'd swiftly deball the bastard," she said calmly. "But then, maybe this Marla Cloy is an old-fashioned girl who doesn't like the sight of blood."

Carver thought he'd change the subject. "What are you working on?" he asked. She'd been sitting on the porch, hunched over her Toshiba laptop computer, when he'd parked beside the cottage.

"Story about how the Everglades is going all to hell ecologically, and the rest of Florida's going with it if we don't do something soon."

"Plenty of interest in that," Carver said.

"Gonna be one giant Disney World if people don't act."

"Good for tourism." Carver couldn't resist the jab.

"So long as the tourists don't mind bringing bottled water."

"Was the Everglades article Jeff Smith's idea?" Smith was Beth's editor at *Burrow*.

"Smith's been fired," she said. "Clive's doing most of the editing himself these days." Clive was Clive Jones, *Burrow*'s publisher and managing editor. "*Burrow* is downsizing, as Clive puts it." Beth tossed the remains of her coffee out over the porch rail. The sun caught it in the instant before it was claimed by gravity and transformed it into a glistening amber arc that hung in the air as if time were momentarily suspended. *Splash!* "That doesn't keep him from spending half the day riding around on his Yamaha motorcycle, though."

"He's the boss," Carver said. "That's life."

"Humph!" Beth said. "Life's what happens to you while you're making plans." She stood up slowly, a tall, tall woman against the blue ocean. "There's some chance I'm gonna be downsized, Fred."

"Hard to imagine."

Whatever the gulls had been circling had disappeared, and they'd flown in to shore to strut in the fringes of the foamy white wash of the surf.

"I could use what comes out of this Brant investigation," Beth said. "A story like that might make the difference in whether I keep drawing a steady paycheck or become a freelance."

"Every other time Jones has threatened to fire you, you've

dared him to go ahead and do it. Why are you so afraid of losing your job this time?"

"I think he might mean it this time."

Carver figured there had to be something more to it. Beth had been on and off Jones's hit list several times since she'd been at *Burrow*. It had never seemed to make a dent in her serenity. But he knew when not to press.

"What if it turns out that Brant's the one being victimized?" he asked.

She shrugged. "Then that's the way I write it. It's a good story either way it breaks."

"I admire your journalistic integrity," he said. "I'll keep you clued in."

She smiled, suddenly sweeter than the heady aroma of the chocolate-cinnamon coffee. "Do more than that. Make me part of the investigation, Fred." She really did want this story, no matter who was being victimized.

When he didn't answer immediately she bent low and kissed him on the forehead, then the lips. He felt the warm flick of her tongue, and the brush of her fingers on his shoulder.

"Maybe there is something you can do," he said, feeling like a victim.

3

AFTER LEAVING Beth, Carver drove to Del Moray police headquarters and asked to see Sergeant Greg Olson.

The desk sergeant relayed his request, but instead of Olson instructing that Carver come into his office, the graying, grossly overweight detective sergeant waddled into the booking area where Carver was waiting. He and Carver weren't exactly friends, but they trusted each other and had a mutual respect for professionalism. There was little enough of that going around these days.

Olson wasn't wearing a suit coat or tie. The top two buttons of his white shirt were unfastened and his sleeves were rolled above the elbows. He was sweating heavily. There were large crescents of dampness beneath his arms and his shirt took on a pinkish hue where the thin material was plastered to his flesh.

When he shook hands with Carver, his grip was strong and moist.

"You been exercising?" Carver asked.

"Naw. Damned air-conditioning's on the blink. It's not so

bad here, but you get back in the offices or squad room and it's a sauna. What can I do for you, Fred?"

"I need to know a few things about a woman who's lodged a sexual harassment complaint. Her name's—"

"Sorry," Olson interrupted, "I'm gonna have to refer you to Lieutenant McGregor."

The mention of McGregor's name made Carver's flesh creep. "Why's that? He have a personal interest in the case?"

Olson's chubby features creased in a sweaty smile. "He's got a personal interest in you. We got standing orders that whenever you come in here for any reason, you get referred to McGregor."

Carver wasn't really surprised. Lieutenant William McGregor hated him with a grand and nurturing passion and had warned him more than once that he'd like to nail him with a felony count that carried a prison sentence, even if the charge was false. Maybe especially if the charge was false. Like most of the people who'd had dealings with McGregor, Carver hated him right back. McGregor preferred it that way. In a gloating, candid moment, he'd once confessed to Carver that he wasn't really comfortable around people without the bond of mutual disgust. The sadistic, deliberately obnoxious lieutenant was the most corrupt human being Carver had ever met, in an occupation where you seldom consorted with angels.

"I suppose he misses you," Olson said, still smiling. A bead of perspiration dropped from his chin and left a tiny mark like a comma on the front of his white shirt.

"Like mean little boys miss flies when they need something to pull wings from," Carver said.

Olson exchanged glances with the desk sergeant, who was also smiling and sweating.

"He in his office?" Carver asked.

"Yeah," Olson said. "You know where it is."

"Better wait till I call back and tell him you're on your way," the desk sergeant said.

Carver stood and watched Olson sweat while the desk sergeant started to make the call. The desk sergeant suddenly began perspiring more profusely, maybe at the prospect of talking to McGregor. The uniforms all hated McGregor, their boss, and hate was impossible without fear.

"Lieutenant says you have permission to slink right in," the desk sergeant said, hanging up the phone. "His words, not mine."

"Buzz, buzz," Carver said. He set down the tip of his cane, turned his back on the two sweaty sergeants, and limped down the hall toward McGregor's office.

AFTER TAKING only a few steps, he understood why Olson was soaked with perspiration. The bowels of headquarters were sweltering. A rivulet of sweat trickled from beneath the hair behind Carver's ear and he felt its dampness as it worked its way beneath his collar. A shrill whine and chatter, like a powerful electric drill meeting resistance, cut through the hall. A muffled voice said ". . . mother-friggin' bastard!" as the drilling stopped, then was replaced by a loud, metallic hammering that came in irritating, intermittent bursts.

The first thing to hit Carver when he opened the door to McGregor's office was the stench. The lieutenant was one of those people who believed cheap deodorant was an adequate substitute for bathing. In the sultry heat of the office his perfumed, stale odor was almost unbearable.

McGregor was behind his desk, leaning far back in his swivel chair. For some reason he had his suit coat on, though his tie knot was loosened. His suit was brown and wrinkled and soiled, as usual. His severely parted, lank blond hair hung Hitler-style above one small, cruel blue eye. There was a shaving cut on a prognathous jaw that looked capable of crushing rock. He was a pale and elongated creature, well over six and a half feet tall and with the angular build and disjointed way of moving you often saw with very tall men. Despite his lankiness and concave chest, there was about him the suggestion of strength coiled and waiting.

"I thought the heat and that fucking drilling and hammering would be the worst things about this day," McGregor said, "until you showed up."

"I'd rather talk with anybody else," Carver said. "You're the one who left orders you wanted to see me."

"It's crazy," McGregor said, "but I just have to see you now and then. In the same way I have to glance at my own shit sometimes before I flush the toilet."

"Talking with you always makes the world seem cleaner and brighter," Carver said, as he moved nearer to the desk and leaned with both hands on the crook of his cane. He took shallow breaths through his mouth, trying to ignore the corrupt stench of McGregor. McGregor noticed and smiled. There was a wide space between his yellowed front teeth that he habitually probed with the tip of his tongue, making his smile remarkably evil.

The hammering and drilling began again. *Clang! Clang! Eeeeek!*

"You guys interrogating a suspect?" Carver asked.

"I'd like to interrogate the jerks working on that air conditioner," McGregor said. "They been banging away on it for two hours now and it's still hot as the inside of a pussy in here." He swiveled this way and that in his chair, stirring the fetid air and increasing the cloying odor in the tiny office. "So let's get to the reason you came," McGregor said. "I got things to do here or I wouldn't be staying in this sweatbox."

"A woman named Marla Cloy has filed harassment complaints against one Joel Brant."

"I'm familiar with that," McGregor said. "Del Moray's not so big a city it'd escape my notice. So what is it you need to know?"

"How many of her complaints do you have on file?"

"Couldn't tell you offhand. Three or four at least."

Carver knew that was as precise an answer as he was going to get from McGregor. "I understand she's filed for an order of protection to keep Brant away from her."

The pink tip of McGregor's tongue probed and squirmed between his teeth like a writhing worm. "You understand right. Judge'll probably grant her the order, too. I know him. He's one of those bleeding-heart, politically correct assholes all hung up on the Constitution."

"He's supposed to be hung up on the Constitution," Carver pointed out, "being a judge."

McGregor ignored that observation. "Why are you so interested, Carver? This Marla Cloy's just another dumb cunt some guy's declared open season on because of something she's done. What's the big deal?"

"You've met her?"

"Seen her when she came in and filed her second complaint. Ordinary looking bitch, says she's some kinda writer. Moved here recently from Orlando. Tell you the truth, she doesn't look worth all the trouble. I mean, why's this Brant even care about her? Why's he want to waste his time? You can tell by looking at her she's a loser that'll dig her own grave soon enough."

"I don't know Brant's motive," Carver said. "I'm not even sure he's actually harassing her. Are you sure?"

"Yeah, I guess so. I figure the guy's burning and wants to fuck or kill her or both. I seen it before. I also figure she's the type that did something stupid and's got it coming to her. Probably deep down she even wants it. Women are like that, you know. Most of them, anyway."

"I'm dazzled by your psychological insight."

"It's from when I worked the sex crime unit, taking statements from rape victims."

"Have you talked to Brant?"

"Not personally. Couple of uniforms who took Marla Cloy's calls talked to him. He denies he's out to get her. They all deny it. Hell, I'd deny it too."

"Maybe he's telling the truth."

"Hah! Maybe I am."

"What are you doing to protect her?"

"Nothing. If the restraining order comes through, we'll run a few extra patrols past her house at night. You know we don't have the manpower to stand guard over every scheming cunt that claims she's being stalked. What we do is, when the guy pesters her again, we take him into custody and the courts nail him to the wall."

"What if it's too late and he's already done whatever it is he's planning?"

"Well, that's how it usually works out. We get the call after it all happens, then we go there and clean up the mess."

"Seems kind of counterproductive."

"Yeah, but that's the kind of trouble women cause in this world. If they learned to dress and act with a little more good sense and respect for their husbands and boyfriends, they wouldn't all of a sudden find themselves in such deep shit they need the police. But I guess it's human nature, genetics or some such crap. In my job, you learn to be philosophical about these things or they drive you nuts. You know that."

Carver knew it, but he didn't have quite the same slant on the problem as McGregor. "You don't seem to have much concern for Marla Cloy."

"Oh, if we get the call in time, we'll save her fucking ass. I think that's concern enough."

The clang of hammer on steel became even louder, as did the ratchety scream of the drill. Carver was getting a headache, and his clothes were clinging to his perspiring flesh. It was truly miserable in the stifling office; he was glad McGregor was stuck there. "What do you know about Joel Brant?" he asked, noticing a bead of sweat dangling from the tip of McGregor's nose.

"The guy that wants to plant her?" The drop of sweat plummeted to his already stained tie to join coffee and gravy and maybe blood on the polyester. *Clang! Clang!* went the hammer. *Eeeeek!* screamed the drill. The workmen were persistent, probably suffering in the heat themselves and eager to finish the job. "From what I can recall, he builds houses or something. Doesn't have a record of violence, but that doesn't mean much in these cases." *Clang! Clang! Eeeeek!* "Guy's in his forties, probably got the hots for this Marla Cloy, then she did him dirty and now he wants to get even. Way the world works. Maybe if we knew what this cunt did to him, we'd think she deserved whatever it is he wants to do to her."

"You ever talk to him?"

"Not my department. Uniforms talked to him. Gave him the usual speech, I suppose. He hasn't done anything yet, so we can't charge him with a crime."

Clang! Clang! Eeeeek! "What about Marla Cloy? What if she does something to him?"

"That's his problem. If she snaps and picks up a gun or knife, or if he comes at her and she kills him in self-defense, then I get involved in a professional way."

"You think she's telling the truth about how Brant's stalking her? I mean, the details?"

Eeeeek! "Sure. They're usually telling the truth. Sometimes they deserve to have the holy hell scared outa them, sometimes not. It doesn't concern me until a crime's actually committed."

"Then?"

"Then I've got more paperwork." He picked up a few of the papers on his cluttered desk and let them fall back onto the felt pad, where a ballpoint pen lay. "Speaking of which, it's time for you to leave so I can get back to something worthwhile."

Carver's head was throbbing with pain and he found himself waiting anxiously for the next noisy assault on the faulty air conditioner. He didn't mind leaving. He used the back of his wrist to wipe sweat from his forehead. "Why don't you open the window?"

"Air conditioner works from time to time, and maybe you haven't noticed, but it's ninety-two degrees outside."

"You'd get a little breeze, maybe."

"The breeze I wanna feel is from you walking out the door, Carver."

"Me, too," Carver said, smiling. *Eeeeek!* He turned around and made for the door.

"Carver."

He paused and twisted his upper body over the cane so he could look at McGregor.

McGregor was standing up now, leaning forward with his knuckles on the desk and glowering at him. "I don't care if this Marla Cloy bitch is your client. Far as I'm concerned, she's just another citizen gets protected or stuffed in a body bag—whatever the job calls for."

Carver stood silently, letting McGregor assume Marla Cloy was his client.

"Even if that restraining order doesn't get granted," McGregor said, "I don't want you meddling in this and getting in the way of the police. You just peek through keyholes like usual and hang around your place on the beach and fuck that dark meat of yours. Be the best way for you."

Carver knew McGregor wouldn't let him leave without trying to infuriate him. It was a little game McGregor played with everyone. He fed on other people's rage and frustration, his own misery seeking company.

"It sure is hot in here," Carver said, keeping his voice calm even though sweat was stinging the corners of his eyes and his head was pounding. "You should try not to get overwrought. You could have a heart attack—if you had a heart."

And he went out the door into the equally hot hall, leaving McGregor seething and stinking behind him. *Clang! Clang! Eeeeek!*

He craved untainted air.

CARVER FOUND Marla Cloy's address easily enough in the phone directory. A freelance writer had to be listed and available for jobs from all comers. Then he picked up the phone and called his friend Lieutenant Alfonso Desoto at police headquarters in Orlando and asked him to get some information on Marla Cloy from when she lived in that city.

Desoto agreed to help, though he sounded reluctant. Carver understood. Desoto was basically paid to solve crimes, not prevent them. Which was also true of McGregor. That was how the system worked; there wasn't much emphasis on prevention. Perpetrators were caught and punished. Victims were finally finding much-needed help, in statutes and in support groups.

Everyone seemed to be covered except for intended victims.

4

THIS WAS one of those times when Carver loved the wind. It seemed to scatter troubles like leaves in its wake, though he knew that was only fancy. Trouble could hang on through a hurricane.

But he drove with the canvas top down on his ancient Oldsmobile convertible until he neared Marla Cloy's address on Jacaranda Lane. Then he pulled over to the curb and raised the top, but he left the windows down. The old car's air conditioner worked only slightly better than the one at police headquarters, and since it was now late afternoon some of the heat had gone out of the day. The breeze that swirled in the car when he began to drive again felt cool when he got up enough speed.

Jacaranda Lane was lined with scruffy-looking palm trees and untrimmed foliage, but there were no jacaranda blossoms in sight. The houses were small, relatively cheap, and not in very good repair. Most of them were stucco and some had faded red tile roofs. What residents were visible suggested the neighborhood was a mixture of whites, African-Americans, and Hispanics. Some of the houses had freshly painted shutters or well-tended lawns or flower beds, and one of them appeared to have a new porch roof. Though the area had declined, it was a long way from being a slum. It still had a chance.

Carver drove past the Cloy house to look it over before parking and settling in to wait for Marla Cloy to make an appearance. He kept the Olds's speed steady so as not to attract attention and took in the house with one long glance out the side window. It was small, like the rest of the houses in the block, cracked yellow stucco with a tiny concrete front porch shaded by a slanted roof. The grass needed mowing. There were several large terra-cotta pots nestled against the porch's black iron railing. The plants in them were all brown and dead. Some of the house's side windows had fringed green canvas awnings that drooped low to resemble half-closed eyelids. One of them was ripped and hanging crookedly. The house next door had a FOR RENT sign stuck in the front yard. Carver thought it was a good guess that many of the houses were rented, including Marla Cloy's.

There was no garage, but in the narrow gravel driveway that ran alongside the modest house, Carver saw a rusty maroon Toyota Corolla sedan, five or six years old, with a caved-in front fender. If Marla Cloy was a financially successful writer, she must be putting most of her earnings in CDs or mutual funds. She might also be home, since her car was there.

After circling the block of similar houses, Carver parked a discreet distance down from Marla's on the other side of the street. He was in the sparse shade of a palm tree, and because of the curve of the flat street would be barely visible from the house. At the same time, he could see the front porch and most of the small front yard from where he sat. The few folks he'd seen on the sidewalks hadn't paid much attention to him. It was that kind of neighborhood; everybody had plenty of trouble and didn't consciously look for more. And it was still too hot for many people to be walking around in the sun.

He leaned back on the warm vinyl upholstery and relaxed, his eyes half closed like Marla's awninged windows, slipping into the half-awake but hyperalert mode of the reptile on the hunt and the experienced cop on a stakeout.

IT WAS almost five o'clock before the house's front door opened and a medium-height, slender woman wearing black slacks and an orange and white striped T-shirt stepped onto the porch. She was carrying a large brown purse with its strap slung diagonally across her chest and over her shoulder, the way women do sometimes when they fear purse snatchers. From this distance she seemed a fairly attractive woman. Not at all the dreary number McGregor had described. But who knew what kind of female McGregor would find attractive? Something of another species, perhaps.

After rattling the doorknob to make sure the lock was set, she bounced nimbly down the three porch steps and disappeared as she walked around to her car.

Carver sat up straight and started the Olds's rumbling old V-8 engine. He was ready to follow when she backed out of her driveway and headed away from him down Jacaranda Lane toward Shell Avenue.

She didn't drive far. The maroon Toyota turned right into a McDonald's on Shell, jounced over a yellow speed bump, then stopped in a parking space near a Dumpster, facing a picket fence. Carver parked the Olds in a slot farther from the restaurant's entrance and watched Marla carefully lock her car before walking inside. He couldn't decide if she was acting like a woman whose life was in danger.

Since she had no idea who he was, Carver climbed out of

the Olds and limped with his cane across the heat-softened blacktop and into McDonald's.

It was bright and cool inside; he was glad Marla had come here. She'd just paid for her food and was carrying a tray toward the seating area. Carver ordered a Big Mac, fries, and diet Coke, then carried them to a booth where he could see Marla. There were about a dozen other customers scattered about the seating area: An old man, three teenage girls having a delicious confab, two guys in white coveralls loudly discussing the new Dodge pickup trucks, a harried-looking mother with three small children—the usual McDonald's crowd. Even the single woman sitting alone, glumly and methodically chewing her food then sipping soda through a straw, fit right in. Marla Cloy. She didn't look like a psychopath who'd try to ruin an innocent man's life.

In the harsh light of the low evening sun streaming through the window, Carver decided she was rather pretty, with delicate features and eyes that were probably dark blue rather than brown—it was difficult to tell from where he sat. Her medium-length black hair framed a round but not fleshy face with cheeks that were either rouged or naturally flushed to give her a healthy, hearty look, like a robust skier who'd just clomped inside from the cold. She moved her head as if sensing she was being stared at, and Carver looked away and concentrated on salting his fries.

When he chanced another glance at Marla she was twisted sideways in the booth and was drawing something from her large brown purse.

It was a paperback book. She opened it to a middle page that was bent at the upper corner, then became engrossed in it, eating slowly and automatically without looking at her food. Now and then, also with her eyes still trained on the book, she moved her head sideways to sip from the straw protruding from her drink. Carver stared hard and tried to catch the paperback's title. Marla's fingers covered most of it, but he could make out that the book was written by a novelist named Ruth Rendell.

He finished his supper while Marla was still eating and reading, then he went outside to wait for her.

Within ten minutes she emerged, carrying her purse with its strap slung diagonally across her body again, and walked to her car without glancing in Carver's direction. He wondered if she thought someone might try to snatch her purse between the restaurant door and the little Toyota. What might she have in there besides the paperback novel? Mace? A gun? This was Florida, land of sun, sand, and the occasional homicide. Not a few purses contained guns.

He followed her to a combination gas station—grocery store on Shell, where she filled the Toyota's tank with low-octane gas and bought a half-quart carton of milk. Then she drove the short distance back to her house on Jacaranda and parked in the driveway. She was disappearing inside and shutting the door behind her as Carver drove past.

He circled the block again and parked in his previous spot, but a few feet nearer the house this time so he could see the front and one of the side windows.

That didn't make much difference. Only faint movement was visible for a few seconds in the side window, then a pale hand as the shade was lowered. The front drapes were already closed.

A FEW minutes after seven-thirty, Marla came out of the house again and climbed into the Toyota. This time she was wearing a simple green dress with bare shoulders and had on black patent leather high heels.

Carver followed her to a lounge called Willet's Bullet on Tenth Street and watched her stride inside.

He sat in the heat and waited until it was almost dark before going in after her.

Willet's Bullet was crowded, which was no surprise to Carver, who for more than an hour had watched more people enter than leave. It was one of those bars that served finger food. Half the folks at the tables along the wall opposite the long bar were eating as well as drinking. An old man with stooped shoulders was acting as bartender while two women in black-and-white outfits were serving the tables. An all-female rock group with skull makeup, wearing black plastic trash bags cut to serve as dresses, was writhing around on a large video screen and moaning loudly and rhythmically about cancer and death and hell. Apparently girls didn't just want to have fun.

Carver saw Marla sitting alone at a small table in back, near the entrance to the rest rooms, staring at the video and sipping what looked like a glass of white wine. He sat at the bar where he could see her in the mirror and ordered a draft Budweiser.

"How long you walked with that cane?" the man next to him asked. His words were slightly slurred, and Carver figured he was only a little drunk. Just enough to be a pest, if he was talkative.

"Few years," Carver said, studying the man in the mirror. He was about sixty-five, with a wrinkled white shirt open at the collar and red suspenders. His hair was gray and bald on top like Carver's. But his face was pale and jowly and he had bags beneath his eyes. The much younger Carver was tan and the fringe of hair around his ears and down the back of his neck was tightly curled. His blue eyes were alert and slightly uptilted at the corners, giving him an oddly feline expression. His upper body, clad in a black pullover shirt, was lean and muscular from walking with the cane and swimming. He looked like a feral cat. The older man exchanged glances with him in the mirror, and Carver hoped he'd be sober enough to sense this wasn't a welcome conversation.

No chance.

"I used to walk with a cane," the man said. "Had this broken leg that just wouldn't heal. Doctors said it was something wrong with my bone. I mean all my bones. Like in the marrow. Never drank enough milk or ate enough bananas when I was a kid."

"That's too bad."

Carver was watching Marla in the mirror. She looked lonely there, a solitary drinker hypnotized by the glowing video.

"My name's Bernie," the man said.

Carver didn't answer. Hint, hint.

"How'd your leg get fucked up?" Bernie asked.

"I got shot."

"No shit? Vietnam?"

"Orlando."

"What are you, a cop?"

"Used to be. Till I got shot."

A tall man with slicked-back dark hair and tight Levi's had swiveled around off his bar stool and was approaching Marla. He had a sharp profile, pouty lips, and might have done OK as an Elvis impersonator. Marla continued to stare at the video and seemed oblivious of him, but Carver suspected she knew he was there.

"You stuck with that cane forever?" Bernie asked.

"Nothing's forever."

"My first marriage seemed like forever," Bernie said. "Time didn't start to move again till after my divorce sixteen years ago. Then it went in a hurry, and all of a sudden I was old. It's OK, though. I still enjoy sex and good food, though it's getting harder to tell the difference. I all of a sudden got six grandchildren, too. A guy with six grandchildren has to be very near death."

The man was standing close to Marla now, talking to her. She was looking right at him and smiling, but shaking her head no. He reached out as if to touch her and she turned away from him. The man shrugged and returned, grinning, to the two guys he'd been drinking with at the bar. It didn't appear that Marla had come to the bar for male companionship. Unless she was waiting for someone.

"Ever consider acupuncture?" Bernie asked. "That's what finally got me back on two sound legs. They stuck pins in my ears. I can run five miles now without breathing hard. You believe that?"

"Sure."

"Then you must have been one piss-poor cop."

Carver laughed. "I wouldn't believe you if I was still a cop."

Bernie sipped his drink. "How 'bout them Marlins?"

"They might win a pennant in ten years."

"You don't sound like a baseball fan."

"I am, though. That's the problem."

Bernie lowered his voice. "I notice you're more interested in that gal in the mirror than in what I'm saying."

Carver turned to face him, catching a whiff of alcohol fumes. Bernie was drinking bourbon on the rocks and there were three swizzle sticks on the napkin next to his half-full glass. "You know her?"

"Nope. Just seen her come in a few times."

"She ever in here looking for male company?"

"Nope. Willet's ain't what you'd call a meat market. Mostly working folks drop in here, just want to relax and be left alone."

"That how she is? A loner?"

"I think so. Now and then some guy tries to get next to her, but she always sends him away. Polite, though. Seems nice enough."

"Ever talk to her yourself?"

"Not me. She's too young for me. Anyway, I got this prostate condition, and what it does—"

"Maybe she likes alcohol too much," Carver suggested.

"Doubt it," Bernie said. "She usually nurses a drink or two along, then she leaves. I think she just wants to come in here and take time out from the world like the rest of us. She don't play the video games or nothing, and she don't seem interested in even talking to the other women in here. A person that drinks alone has got problems, usually. It ain't good. That poor girl's most likely got problems."

"Or is one," Carver said. He planted the tip of his cane on the tile floor and stood up. "Nice talking to you, Bernie."

"Don't run off. Hang around, friend, I'll buy you one."

"Thanks," Carver said, "but I gotta get home to the wife."

"Hey," Bernie said, "I know how that goes."

Carver laid a ten-dollar bill on the bar. "Next one's on me, Bernie."

"Next two," Bernie corrected, smiling broadly.

Carver made for the door.

He waited outside until Marla left alone, then he followed the Toyota back to the little house on Jacaranda Lane.

She stayed inside this time, and at 10:27 the lights winked out. He waited another twenty minutes before driving away down the winding street, enjoying the flow of air through the windows.

Her actions had all seemed innocent enough, he thought. An ordinary woman having an ordinary evening.

Almost as if she suspected someone other than Joel Brant might be watching her.

5

CARVER EASED the shower handle to cold and waited until his heart might stop before turning off the water. Then he swept the plastic curtain aside and, gripping the towel rack for support, stepped out of the tub and onto a thick, white terry-cloth bath mat. He'd had his therapeutic morning swim in the ocean and he could still feel sand he'd tracked in on the mat beneath his bare feet. With one hand on the washbasin he toweled himself dry, then he quickly shaved, rinsed his disposable razor, and replaced it in the medicine cabinet. He ran a comb through his thick fringe of wet hair then left the bathroom to get dressed.

He didn't use his cane when he had fixtures or furniture to hold on to for balance. It had been hooked over the bathroom doorknob. He used it now to cross to the cottage's screened-off sleeping area, smelling coffee. Beth must have gotten the Braun brewer going.

After sitting on the bed and working his way into underwear and gray slacks, he put on gray socks, black leather moccasins he didn't have to contort himself to lace, and a dark green pullover shirt with a collar and pockets. He didn't like shirts without pockets. He thought they should all be discounted as factory seconds.

Beth was perched on a stool, leaning with an elbow on the breakfast bar, when Carver limped into the cottage's main area. She was eating buttered toast and had a cup of coffee poured for him. While he was swimming, she'd showered and dressed. Her hair, straightened long enough ago to have regained much of its curl, was parted neatly on the side and combed back to fall almost to her shoulders. She was wearing a long, baggy white T-shirt with shoulder pads and lettering, too faded to read, on the chest. She had large, firm breasts for such a thin woman, and it was obvious she was braless beneath the shirt. On her feet were the same white leather sandals she had worn yesterday, and presumably she was wearing shorts that were concealed by the length of the shirt. Before her was her over-size coffee mug with newspaper-caption bloopers printed on it. JERK INJURES NECK, WINS AWARD was visible to Carver as he sat on the stool across from her, on the kitchen side of the butcher-block counter.

"Want toast?" Beth asked.

"Maybe later. Just coffee now."

She sipped. Her motion of lifting and tilting the mug rotated it to read RHODE ISLAND SECRETARY EXCITES FURNITURE EXPERTS. "So tell me about last night," she said.

"It was wonderful, as usual."

"Think back a few hours before that, Fred."

He related his evening following Marla Cloy, then he got up and poured another cup of coffee. It was ordinary coffee this morning, not the chocolate-cinnamon gourmet stuff. He was glad.

"How'd Marla Cloy strike you personally?" Beth asked.

"Not at all. Didn't lay a hand on me."

She stared at him. A warning to get serious.

Carver placed his cup on the breakfast bar before getting back on his stool. "She's not beautiful enough to storm beauty pageants, but she's attractive."

"Looks don't always play a part in it when a dangerous sexual psychopath develops a fixation on a woman. Was there anything unusual in her behavior?"

"Not unless you find going to McDonald's and reading a paperback novel unusual."

"What about her going to the bar?"

"Well, it's not the norm for a woman to sit alone and drink in a place like Willet's Bullet."

"But it's OK for a man to do it?"

"I didn't say it wasn't OK or never happened. But most women stay home to drink alone. If they're at a bar, they're usually with friends. Dare I say they're more convivial than us guys?"

"Maybe she's got a drinking problem."

"Bernie doesn't think so."

"Bernie?"

"An old guy who was nattering at me at the bar. He says she acts as if she just wants to step off the world, unwind, and be left alone for a while. Bernie's the sort who's had experience at that kind of thing; he'd know."

Beth buttered another piece of whole-wheat toast. She took a bite, chewed, and swallowed. "Want the other half of this?"

"Sure."

She slid the small plate with the half-piece of buttered toast to his side of the counter. "I did some checking, talked to Jeff Mehling." Mehling was the computer genius at *Burrow*. "Marla Cloy really is a freelance writer. She even sold a small piece to *Burrow* last year on the preservation of the manatee. I had Jeff fax me a copy. It's nothing original; there've been hundreds of articles during the past few years in Florida papers about trying to save the manatee. But it's competent. Filler for page six."

"Hmm. Professional jealousy showing?"

Beth gave him a look that would have made a lesser man scurry for shelter. "Not at all," she said. "I only wanted to establish for you that the woman's not faking it. She really is a freelance writer of professional caliber. She's genuine."

"She didn't act particularly afraid that Brant might be following her," Carver said.

"What do you want her to do, wear a bulletproof vest?"

"Maybe."

"Maybe she had one on. Or maybe she got her order of protection from the court." Beth had finished her toast. Now she picked up the slice she'd pledged to Carver and took a large bite out of it. Probably she was still thinking about that professional-jealousy remark. "You do realize," she said, "that what Marla Cloy has butted up against is typical male reaction. She says she's being threatened, and the police, and apparently you, think she's merely another hysterical woman."

"I'm not sure what she is. Neither is my client. That's why I'm trying hard to find out. I'm not some stereotype male Bubba who thinks that because a man has a grudge against a woman, she probably deserves it."

"But you do make the assumption Brant's story is fact."

"He *is* my client."

"So rather than see Marla Cloy as a victim, you see her as an aggressor."

"She might be."

Beth finished Carver's toast and licked butter off her finger. "Well, we could go round again, but I doubt if it would change anything. We're simply viewing this matter from two different perspectives."

"I'm trying to get at the truth," Carver said. "I don't have any preconceived notions."

She smiled. "Everybody has those, Fred. The truth nobody wants to face is that we all carry around our own ideas of the truth. We hardly ever know the real truth—or even if there is one. Life's an ambiguous experience, lover, so don't be too sure of anything."

"Found that out long ago," Carver said, gripping his cane and sliding off his stool.

"Keep finding it out," Beth advised. "Where are you going now?"

"I've got an appointment to meet with Brant at ten o'clock, to let him know what's going on."

"Doesn't sound as if you've accomplished much."

"If Marla happens to claim he harassed her last night," Carver said, "I'll know otherwise."

"There you go assuming her guilt again, even though she's the one being stalked."

"Maybe you're assuming her innocence because of what you two have in common."

"Our gender?"

"And you're both journalists. She wants to save the manatee, you want to save the Everglades."

"More than that," Beth said, "I want to save Marla Cloy."

BRANT WAS waiting in his car with the engine and air conditioner running when Carver turned off Magellan into the strip shopping center parking lot where his office was located. The car was a black Stealth sports car, sleek, powerful, and expensive. And possibly bought with his dead wife's life-insurance money.

Beth would suggest that, anyway.

By the time Carver had parked and climbed out of the Olds, Brant was out of the Stealth and leaning against the polished black door with his arms crossed. As Carver approached, he pushed away from the car, smiled, and walked toward him with his hand extended. "So detectives keep bankers' hours."

Carver shook his hand. "Not bankers' money, though."

He invited Brant inside, then unlocked the office door and stood aside for him to pass. The temperature outside was already in the mid-eighties, and the inside temperature was catching up fast. Carver moved the thermostat down enough for the air conditioner to start humming, then closed the drapes partway to block the morning sun from pouring in and warming the place. It didn't help much. The sun was sparking silver off the ocean visible between the buildings across the street, its rays entering through the window at a low angle. He leaned his cane against the wall and sat down behind the desk. "Hot this morning," he said.

"The tropics," Brant said, lowering himself into the small, padded chair in front of the desk. "Thank God for air-conditioning, or nobody would live here and I'd be out of business." He crossed his legs and laced his hands together in his lap, actually twiddling his thumbs nervously. He was wearing prefaded Levi's today, and a blue-checked short-sleeved shirt with a pen and some kind of slide rule sticking out of the breast pocket. Dressed for business at a construction site, Carver supposed, though he didn't think people used slide rules anymore, in the age of minicalculators that could compute what you needed to know in seconds and remind you when it was time for lunch. Brant had slept in one position too long and his hair stuck out in a clump on the right side of his head. It made him look boyish. And not at all the sort of lad who'd stalk and murder a woman.

Brant drew a pack of Camels from the same pocket the pen and slide rule were in and glanced at Carver questioningly. Carver nodded, and Brant got out his silver lighter and touched flame to the tip of a cigarette. Then, eyes narrowed to see through the resultant smoke, he looked at Carver inquisitively again.

"I followed her last night," Carver said.

And he told Brant about Marla Cloy's evening.

Brant snuffed out the butt of his cigarette in the sea-shell ashtray Carver had pulled from a desk drawer, then lit another immediately. The light streaming through the window invested the smoke he exhaled with a faint but colorful rainbow before the cool breeze from the vent caught it and dissipated it, not quite chasing away the heat and moisture that had permeated the office during the night and early morning. The tropics.

"She got her restraining order," Brant said.

"Was it in effect last night?"

"No. This morning. I'm not supposed to go anywhere near her or contact her in any manner."

"Should prove no inconvenience," Carver said. "I'd give you the same advice."

"But you must see how this is part of her strategy. The next time she accuses me of threatening her, I'm in deeper trouble. It's a more serious offense."

"I don't think the law will take action unless she has corroboration," Carver said.

"Hah! Don't kid yourself. When a woman cries wolf, there's an immediate hunting party."

"I was just hearing the opposite argument."

Brant let out more breath than was necessary to exhale smoke. He glanced around the office as if suspecting the walls were about to close in and crush him. "What am I gonna do, Mr. Carver?"

"It's Fred. And don't feel defeated. I'm going to find out more about Marla Cloy and discover why she's doing this to you."

Brant bowed his head and studied his cigarette, then looked up at Carver. "You *do* believe me, don't you, Fred?"

"I believe you." But Carver wasn't certain, the truth being the amorphous and slippery beast Beth had described. As soon

| 36 |

as he discovered Marla Cloy's motive, he'd know for sure that Brant was leveling with him.

Brant reached around for the wallet he carried in his hip pocket and got out a business card. He scribbled something on it with his ballpoint pen, then he stood up and laid the card on the corner of Carver's desk. "My cellular phone number is on there. I'm going to be out of the office and in the field most of the day, where we're grading for the extension of Brant Estates. Please call if you have anything at all to tell me."

"I will," Carver assured him. "And it would be a good idea for you to stay around people as much as possible, so they can verify your whereabouts in case Marla says you were some- place you weren't."

"That isn't easy to do, with my work," Brant said. "I spend a lot of time alone, either at the office or driving between con- struction sites. Anyway, the woman is devious. When she's ready to accuse me again, I'm sure she'll make certain it's for a time when I won't have an alibi."

"That won't be easy for her. And she'll probably wait a few days before making another accusation, knowing you're on your guard."

Brant snuffed out his second cigarette, began to light a third one, then changed his mind and replaced it in the pack. There was a rustling sound as he stuffed the crinkled, cellophane- wrapped pack back in his shirt pocket behind the slide rule or whatever it was. "Stay on this, Mr. Carver—Fred. Find out why she's doing this to me!"

Carver told him to try not to worry, he'd ferret out Marla's motive. He thought that right now he'd settle for discovering "if" rather than "why."

He knew "why" was a tough one.

Nobody knew much about motive, even if they thought they did.

6

CARVER PARKED the Olds in front of number 21 Cenit Street, picked up the brown vinyl folder containing a yellow legal pad from the seat beside him, then levered himself out of the car with his cane.

He'd bought the folder and legal pad ten minutes ago at a drugstore on Shell to use as a prop. As he stood alongside the car in the sun, he bent the folder back and forth a few times so it appeared well used, then tore out a sheet of lined yellow paper and folded it so it stuck out of the top of the folder, as if it had been hurriedly poked inside. Carver would be a busy insurance agent on his workaday rounds.

Cenit Street ran parallel to Jacaranda Lane, a block east. The backyards of houses on each street were separated by what looked like a long, curving ditch overgrown with weeds but was actually an electric and phone company easement. The backs of the houses on Cenit and Jacaranda faced one another.

As Carver crossed the street to number 21, the morning sun

felt heavy and warm on his shoulders. The houses on Cenit looked much like those in the next block on Jacaranda, small, in various stages of recent repair or decades of decay, most of them with the faded red-tile roofs that the builder, years ago, must have gotten at a discount and used as a selling point. A few of the houses made a pass at Spanish architecture, an arched window here, an exposed beam and some curlicued ironwork there. Not at all convincing.

Number 21 had a small porch like Marla Cloy's house. Around its foundation were rhododendron bushes and a lush and colorful flower bed. Peonies, hollyhocks, and violets were all seemingly planted in no particular order. When Carver got closer he could see bees circling above the blossoms. There were a lot of bees, but they ignored him and concentrated on their task, flying tight patterns then dipping to hover briefly at blossoms before rising and circling again. They had a job to do and so did Carver. It was a world of task and toil, all right.

He was pleased to see a name lettered on the black mailbox affixed to the cream-colored stucco next to the front door: Mildred Fain. The back of number 21 looked directly out on the back of 22 Jacaranda Lane. Mildred Fain might have logged a lot of collective hours glancing out her windows at the house behind her. If Carver got lucky and she was the nosy type, she might have seen quite a bit. She might know something that could give him insight into Marla Cloy and her motives. That was the idea, anyway.

He pushed the button near the mailbox and waited, in the shade but still warm. Out in the bright sunlight, the bees still circled and swooped. He could hear them in the quiet morning, a soft but discontented buzzing whenever the background rush of nearby traffic faded.

There was a creaking noise behind the door, then it opened and a small woman in a pin-striped blue and gray housecoat and fuzzy blue slippers peered out at Carver. She was in her late sixties and had wispy gray hair and sharp, wizened features. The sunken line of her thin lips and the jut of her jaw suggested she wore dentures but didn't have them in. She seemed wide awake, though; Carver didn't think he'd rousted her from bed.

"Mrs. Fain?"

The woman nodded, bright blue eyes fixed on him.

"My name's Frank Carter, with American Mutual Benefit." By using an alias close to his name he could always claim she'd misunderstood. "I'm making some routine inquiries about a neighbor of yours who's applied for a policy."

"Neighbor?" She said it as if surprised anyone lived nearby.

"That's right, a Miss . . ." Carver opened the kinked vinyl folder and peeked inside.". . . Cloy. Marla Cloy."

"Don't know her."

"She lives in the house directly behind you."

"Oh, yeah. Her. Well, I seen her. Talked to her a few times." No teeth were visible when she spoke, but she enunciated clearly. "Don't know much about her, though."

"Well, we only ask some very basic questions." Carver pulled a ballpoint pen from his shirt pocket and clicked out the point. "You say you've spoken to her. How many times?"

"Not more'n three or four. Once just to pass the time of day when we was both out in our backyards. 'Nother time about some stray dogs kept getting into people's trash around here. That's not much of a problem anymore, though. City animal control people came out and—"

"Do you recall if Marla Cloy smokes?"

Mildred Fain rubbed a small, arthritically gnarled hand over her jutting jaw. "No, can't say as I do. Why's that important?"

"Life expectancy. You'd be surprised what the actuarial tables demonstrate. If everybody read them, nobody would smoke."

"Well, I smoked like a smudge pot for forty-nine years, and I'm still here."

"Some of us are lucky," Carver said, "or have the right parents." He smiled. "You look like you come from good stock, Mrs. Fain."

She returned the smile. Still no teeth. "Dutch-Irish," she said.

"Oh-ho," Carver said, as if that meant something. "What about Miss Cloy's lifestyle?"

"Lifestyle?"

"Yes. For instance, does she seem to entertain a lot?"

"Hardly ever, near as I can tell. And my kitchen sink's got a window over it looks out on our backyards, so I can see her house. She seems a good woman that minds her own business."

"Good woman?"

"I never saw any wild goings-on, if you catch my meaning."

"Uh-huh." Another smile for Mrs. Fain. Carver was beginning to enjoy this. "No men coming and going at all hours?" He winked. "Nothing that would delight the devil and displease the Lord?" Too much? he wondered. Naw, this was Florida, the excess reach of the Bible Belt dangling south from the buckle to form a peninsula.

"Heavens, no! She keeps pretty much to herself. Works at home, I think. Said she was some kind of writer, is my recollection."

"That's what she gave as her occupation," Carver confirmed.

"Humpf! Can't be much money in that."

"Probably not. Is there any one man in particular you've seen visiting Marla Cloy?"

"Nope. You seem stuck on that. I told you, she didn't have men coming and going."

"That's right, you did. How long has she lived there? Just approximately?"

" 'Bout three months, maybe a little less, I'd say. Said she moved here from Orlando."

"Does she own?"

"Nope, that house is a rental. Had several people move in and out the last few years. Man who repaired computers lived in it before Marla Cloy. He got into some kinda trouble, I hear, had to move away in a hurry. Something to do with child molestation in Seattle followed him here because of his ex-wife's accusations. Bitter divorce. He abused her and the woman wanted to get even, though she did get the house and full custody of the two children, and all he got was the family car, his computer tools, and some personal possessions. Don't know much else about him, though. Got little time for gossip or keeping tabs on the neighbors."

"More people should think that way. Did anyone help Marla Cloy move in, or did she hire a mover?"

"Hired a mover, but there wasn't much big and heavy to move. Then she drove back and forth in that old car of hers, with loads of boxes and clothes on hangers. She don't have much that looked like good furniture or expensive clothes. But young people don't these days. Things are hard for them."

"Would you describe her as a woman of moderate habits? I mean, she doesn't drive crazily or drink to excess . . . that sort of thing."

"Seems to drive like everybody else. As to drink, that I wouldn't know about one way or the other. Never seen her take a drink when she was out in the yard or visible through her windows. Wouldn't mean much anyways. Drinking's no sin. Bit of alcohol every day's good for the nerves and heart."

Carver was beginning to suspect that Mildred Fain had a secret life. But then, everyone did. "You have a sensible slant on things, Mrs. Fain."

She grinned. "Never believed in life insurance, either."

Carver put on a serious expression. "Oh, Mrs. Fain, you're making a big mistake there."

"Mistake I'd be making, Mr. Carter, would be standing here letting you talk me into buying some. You seem like a pretty good salesman."

"I'm really more of a field agent than a salesman," Carver said.

"Well, then the company oughta be utilizing your real talents. Been nice talking to you." She started to close the door.

Carver thought for a second about sticking his foot between it and the doorjamb. But surely insurance agents didn't do that anymore, did they? Certainly not field agents who weren't salesmen.

He thanked Mildred Fain and let the door close all the way. A dead bolt clicked into place. A chain lock rattled faintly.

He was standing alone in the heat again, watching the bees intent on collecting nectar, the job for which they were by ability and instinct ideally suited.

Probably Mildred Fain was observing him through her window. On the way back to his car, he suddenly paused in the middle of the sun-washed street, as if jotting something in his notepad before he forgot it.

Faking it with conviction.

Utilizing his real talents.

7

MARLA WENT out for lunch that day. McDonald's again. Carver followed her, but this time instead of going inside he went up to the drive-through and got a Big Mac and a vanilla shake, then found a parking space where he could sit in his car and eat and keep an eye on her Toyota.

She must have read several chapters of the Rendell book while eating. It was over an hour before she came out and walked across the parking lot toward her car. She had her purse strap slung diagonally across her body in the same cautious manner. Today she had on a sleeveless gray SEA WORLD sweat-shirt, jeans, and white jogging shoes with what looked like red lightning streaks on the sides.

Her luck held. Nobody attacked her or tried to snatch her purse on the way to her car. She unlocked and opened the driver's side door, unhitched the purse from around her and tossed it over onto the passenger seat. She glanced around, but not in his direction, then got into the battered little maroon car. Carver started the Olds and followed her out onto Shell Avenue.

She stopped at the drugstore where he'd bought his note pad that morning and went inside. He didn't follow her. One of the disadvantages of a man with a cane was that he was especially memorable. Carver could risk being seen by Marla only so often before recollection might kick in.

She emerged from the drugstore within fifteen minutes carrying a paper bag. As she was juggling the bag and her purse and trying to open her car door, the bag dropped to the pavement and split open. A large plastic bottle of Pepsi-Cola rolled beneath the car.

Marla stood with her hands on her hips for a moment, then she stooped and picked up the other items that had been in the bag: A package of notebook or typing paper, a bag of potato chips, a box of tampons, and a new paperback book. She placed them inside the Toyota behind the seat, then bent low and groped beneath the car with her hand. It took her a while to find and get a grip on the errant bottle. When she had it, she stood up and held it out at arm's length to examine it, as if it were a fish she'd just caught. It wasn't a keeper. After locking her car, she carried the apparently leaking bottle back inside the drugstore.

A few minutes later she came back outside with another bottle wedged beneath her arm, got into her car, and drove away. Carver followed, thinking the protective way she carried her purse and was always locking and unlocking doors suggested that maybe she really was fearful of attack. Beth would no doubt interpret it that way.

After she'd driven home and gone inside, Carver parked on Jacaranda Lane, figuring he'd be there for a while.

But half an hour later Marla was back in her car and on the move again. She'd changed to a red blouse, black slacks, and high heels, and she had her hair pulled back and fixed with a bright red ribbon or barrette. She was carrying her purse and a small blue canvas carry-on or attaché case.

Carver followed her to the Holiday Inn on Magellan, about half a mile from his office. It was a newer luxury hotel that backed onto the sea. Marla parked near the entrance to the cocktail lounge and strode inside, still carrying the blue canvas case. Judging by the slow, abbreviated arc of her arm swing as she walked, it was fairly heavy.

With the Olds's windows cranked down, Carver could hear the surf rushing and slapping at the beach. A man and woman and three small children were strolling along the plank walkway toward the sand. The man and all three children were wearing swimming trunks. Only the woman wasn't dressed to go in the water. She was wearing shorts and carrying a blue-and-white plastic cooler and a wad of folded beach towels. She and the man had on dark sunglasses, and all three of the kids had globs of white sunblock on their foreheads and the tips of their noses so they looked like miniature clowns only partly made up. Family life. Carver had experienced it once, but it had come unraveled. Now his son was dead and his wife and daughter lived in St. Louis, half a continent away. Laura had remarried and now had another family, one that didn't include Carver. He'd once heard his daughter call Laura's new husband "Daddy." When moved by self-pity or masochism, he still probed that wound.

When the man and woman and kids had disappeared in the direction of the beach, he got out of the Olds and headed toward the lobby.

There were several people coming and going, or waiting for elevators. A black-and-gold metal sign on a stand was shaped like an arrow and pointed toward registration, out of sight around a corner. To the left were a tourism and ticket desk, car rental agency, and gift shop with a display of nondescript neckties in its window. The lobby was carpeted in green and had lots of artificial potted ferns and comfortable-looking beige chairs scattered about. Carver sank the tip of his cane in the soft carpet and walked around the corner, where he knew the cocktail lounge had an entrance off the lobby.

He didn't have to go inside. He found a thickly upholstered beige chair from which he could see into the lounge and sat down, leaning forward to pick up a golf magazine from a bulky dark-wood table with a glass top.

From where he sat he could see Marla Cloy seated alone in a small booth along the wall. She was staring straight ahead and holding a stemmed glass with both hands. White wine again. He was watching her almost in profile. Her face was one that became more attractive the longer he looked at it. The angle of her nose and the line of her jaw suggested a simple and pleasant serenity that had to be deceptive. He knew it concealed either willful duplicity or genuine fear.

He looked away from Marla when he noticed a small, skinny, slightly hunched woman in a brown skirt and blazer walk past him into the lounge. She left in her wake the faint scent of mothballs. He saw Marla look at her and smile. The woman picked up speed and scurried rather than walked directly to the booth and sat down opposite Marla, then placed her hands out of sight beneath the table as if she were ashamed of them.

A barmaid appeared and took the woman's order, then brought her a drink that looked exactly like Marla's. Both women sipped their wine simultaneously, pausing as they lifted their glasses to their lips, almost in a toast.

They talked for about half an hour, sometimes seriously, sometimes laughing at what might have been a shared joke. Next to Marla, the thin woman looked particularly drab in her brown suit and with her lifeless brown hair. Her coloring and ferretlike features brought to mind the word "mousy." Even from this distance Carver could see that she wore very little makeup and no fingernail polish. Her pale hands, animated when she talked, were quick and nervous.

Marla dragged the blue attaché case onto the table and unzipped it. When she opened it, Carver caught a glimpse of compartments in the lid that contained several yellow file folders. Marla drew a thick brown envelope from the case and laid it on the table in front of the mousy woman. It was a large envelope, almost square.

Marla got a pencil from the case and wrote something on the envelope, then she and Mousy put their heads close together and discussed whatever it was she'd written. Mousy borrowed Marla's pencil and added something of her own on the front of the envelope. Then she rested her arm over the envelope in a casual but possessive manner.

When the attaché case was zipped and placed back on the floor, the two women finished their drinks somewhat hurriedly. Then Mousy stood up, carrying the brown envelope. Marla remained seated and was fishing around in her purse for money to pay the check. Carver figured he'd have to make a decision soon. He already knew what it would be.

He laid the golf magazine back on the table, then gripped his cane and stood up. By the time Mousy came out of the lobby carrying the envelope, he was already in the Olds with the engine running. She walked around the corner of the building, and he had to drive fast along the row of parked cars to keep her in sight.

She climbed into a gray Volkswagen Rabbit, and when she left the parking lot and turned left onto Magellan, he was behind her.

THE MOUSY woman slowed her car on Fourteenth Street, in a neighborhood of small shops and old two-story apartment buildings, and parked it nose-in to a low stone wall in front of a building set well back from the street and shaded by mature sugar oaks. With the brown envelope tucked beneath her arm, she walked under a wrought-iron entrance arch that served as a trellis for bedraggled-looking roses. Carver watched her make her way around a pond with a statue of a leaping fish in its center, then enter the building through a large, heavy door with a decorative black iron ring for a knocker.

He got out of the car and saw "2-D" in faded black paint on the stone wall in front of the parked Rabbit. There were other such markings, obviously designating each of the parking slots to correspond with apartments. He stood for a moment listening to the Rabbit's little four-banger engine ticking as it cooled, then he traced the mousy woman's steps, passing through the rusty iron trellis of roses, noticing that the pond in the entrance courtyard was dry and contained a scattering of dirt and sun-browned dead weeds. Many of its square blue tiles were cracked or missing. The leaping fish had once been a sword-fish, he noticed, but now its sword was a mere jagged stub where it had been broken off, perhaps by vandals.

The building's foyer was small, also done in blue tile, but in better repair than the pond and fountain outside. There was a faint medicinal smell to it, or maybe the lingering scent of mothballs from the mousy woman's passage. Some of the tiles were cracked and some were replacements that were a brighter blue outlined in the pristine white of fresh grout. There was a bank of fancy brass mailboxes and buzzer buttons, old and slightly tarnished.

Carver saw that the building contained twelve apartments. The name above 2-D was W. Krull.

He thought about going upstairs and talking to W. Krull, trying to discover what was in the envelope Marla had given her, then decided against it. He doubted that she'd be cooper-ative or unsuspecting. Possibly it was his imagination, but there seemed to have been something vaguely furtive about the meeting in the Holiday Inn lounge and the exchange of the envelope. W. Krull might suspect he'd followed her from the hotel and be a good enough friend to tip off Marla.

Better to wait a while before approaching her.

Mildred Fain said he was a talented guy. He should be able to think up something more convincing than that insurance agent act.

8

CARVER HAD met with attorneys at four o'clock to give a deposition concerning a woman who'd hired him to find her missing teenage daughter, whom he'd found living with her forty-year-old uncle in Orlando. The girl had been fourteen, but she looked and acted like a twelve-year-old. After the daughter's return to her parents, statutory rape charges had been filed against the uncle. Carver's deposition would be instrumental in the ongoing plea bargaining process. Despite the prosecutor's tough talk, Carver figured the uncle's attorneys would whittle away the sentence so that the man would receive a short jail term and be placed on probation. Carver was thinking about the uncle's walking when he saw Beth's white LeBaron convertible pull into the lot and park in front of the office.

She entered the office smiling, wearing a gauzy tan blouse and a flowing darker brown skirt hemmed down around her ankles. Three-piece, square onyx earrings, loose-fitting gold and black bracelets, and a necklace of large black and green stones dangled and clicked and clacked as she walked.

She sat down in front of Carver's desk, her back rigid and not touching her chair, yet she seemed totally relaxed. Her hair was combed back to a bun and she wore a black headband. He thought she looked particularly regal today. She wore dark red lipstick and had her eyes skillfully made up so that they seemed faintly oriental. Her rigid posture caused her breasts to challenge the thin material of her blouse.

The air conditioner clicked on. Carver didn't blame it.

"I was in town for an appointment," she said, "so I thought I'd drop in."

"I'm glad."

"Give your deposition?" she asked.

He nodded. "I think the uncle's going to walk."

"Should he?"

"No. Where he'll walk is straight back to that kid, if it isn't prevented. She doesn't look old enough to trust with the toaster."

"Nothing you can do about it," Beth said. "It's up to the court. Maybe you should concentrate on what you *can* do something about."

"Marla Cloy?"

"Uh-hm. What have you learned?"

He told her about this morning's conversation with Mildred Fain. Then about Marla's meeting W. Krull at the Holiday Inn and handing over the envelope.

"Doesn't sound so suspicious to me," Beth said. "Maybe they met on business."

"I'm wondering what kind," Carver said.

"You'd like to catch her in a narcotics exchange, wouldn't you?"

"It would make things simpler. And it's not so illogical. After all, there's snow as well as sand in Florida."

Beth stared at him. "Maybe the meeting *was* for a payoff—a down payment, anyway—and Marla hired the woman to kill

Brant before he makes good on his threat and murders her."

"I thought of that. This woman wouldn't strike you as a hired killer."

"You know better than that, Fred."

He did.

"Are you going to talk to W. Krull?" Beth asked.

"Tomorrow."

"What lie are you planning to tell her? That pathetic insurance agent thing?"

"No," he said. "I'm going to tell her the truth, that I'm investigating the matter of Joel Brant threatening Marla Cloy."

"Going to say you're with the police?"

"Of course not," Carver said. "I'll let her decide that on her own."

Beth gazed out the window for a moment, then turned to face him with a somber, oddly pained expression he was seeing for the first time. It transformed her features so that at a glance he might almost have thought he was looking at another woman. She was always doing things like that, revealing new and unexpected facets of herself. Carver had the feeling her capacity to surprise him was infinite; she was a puzzle he would never quite solve. It bothered him when he couldn't get to the truth and meaning of things he cared about. It also kept him intrigued.

"I told you I had an appointment today," she said. "It was with a doctor."

There was something in her voice that scared him. He felt his heart accelerate. His mind whirled and searched for hints that she might be ill, symptoms he should have noticed. He knew he could be blind to such things.

"You're OK, aren't you?" he asked.

"I'm not sure. It depends."

"On what?"

"I'm not sure of that, either."

"You feel all right?"

"Yes and no."

"Damn it, Beth!"

He was shocked to see the flesh beneath her eyes dance. A look of wonder and fear crossed her face before she bowed her head and began to sob almost silently.

This was not her. Not her at all.

Using the desk and chair for support, he went to her and lowered himself to kneel on one leg beside her chair, his bad leg extended in front of him. He balanced himself with one hand on the chair while he held her with his free arm.

"Whatever it is," he said, "don't panic. These things are hardly ever as serious as they seem at first. We'll get second and third opinions, find a specialist."

She stopped sobbing, then she drew a deep breath and let it out slowly, using fresh oxygen to compose herself. She dabbed daintily at her eyes with a tissue, smearing her mascara. She sniffed, and wiped her nose.

"I've already got a specialist, Fred. An obstetrician."

9

CARVER SAT across from Beth at one of the small, round, white-enameled tables clustered around Poco's taco stand on Magellan, where he often ate lunch. They'd just left his office and he'd automatically driven her to Poco's, not remembering until they were already seated and he'd brought the food to the table that she didn't like to come here, as she hated the food. He was still in something of a daze from hearing her tell him she was pregnant.

A kind of instinct had taken over. He didn't want to talk to her about the pregnancy until he'd had time to assimilate the news and figure out how he felt about it. The wrong words spoken now could haunt them later.

He watched her looking at him calmly, her eyes still swollen with her tears. The white hulls of pleasure boats moored at the dock bobbed gently and in perfect unison behind her, as if in a subtle dance, the evening sun glancing off their brightwork.

"I'm still trying to digest the news," he said.

"It should be easier than digesting that taco," she told him, motioning with her head toward the greasy wrapper in front of him on the table.

"I got you a burrito," he said.

She glanced down at the contents of the small plastic tray he'd placed between them. "I think I'll just drink my soda, Fred. You know this isn't my favorite place. The food tastes like a bad day at cooking class."

"I forgot you didn't like it here," he explained, squeezing a plastic envelope and squirting hot sauce on his taco. Some of it splattered onto his shirt. *Oh, hell!* He wiped at the stain with a finger and made it worse.

"I'm not hungry anyway," she said. "Maybe it's because—"

"An irregular appetite is one of the symptoms," he interrupted.

She smiled. "I'm reassured I have an expert to consult." She touched a long, red fingernail to the side of her soda cup but didn't drink. She began pecking the fingernail against the cup, making a persistent tapping sound. "What are we going to do, Fred?"

"I don't know. Are you absolutely sure you're pregnant?"

"The doctor's sure. At least six weeks. I've missed two periods, and the uterus . . . well, never mind." She stopped tapping with her fingernail and laid her hand in her lap. "Believe it. I'm pregnant."

He didn't know what to say, so he poked at the taco in front of him as if it might have something to add to the conversation.

Beth touched the back of his hand very lightly. "Do you want me to have this baby?"

He continued staring at the taco. Suddenly he wasn't hungry either. An infant certainly didn't figure in his plans. And he was too old to be a father for the third time.

Still, somewhere in the core of his mind or soul, he was pleased by the news. He told himself it was a dangerous reaction, some reflexive thing that happened to help ensure survival of the species. Something out of the ooze. But he really *was* pleased.

"Fred?"

"My gut instinct is to say yes, have the baby." He tried to tilt the umbrella sprouting out of the center of the table so it blocked the low angle of the sun. Something was wrong with the aluminum mechanism and the umbrella kept rocking back to its previous position. He reached into his shirt pocket for his sunglasses and put them on, wondering if Beth would think he didn't want her to read his eyes. "There are problems, of course."

"Of course," she said.

"But as of this moment . . . yes." He fought a crazy impulse to leap up and whoop, as he had when Laura had told him about her first pregnancy.

"I'm not sure I'm going to go through with this, Fred."

He'd somehow known she was going to say it. The prospect of parenthood had been hanging off-kilter over them, like the umbrella. "Is it your decision alone?" he asked.

"I'm not sure. I'm not sure of anything right now. Goddamned hormones or something."

"You're not going to cry again, are you?"

"I make no promises." But she didn't look as if she was about to cry.

"We talking about an abortion?" he asked.

"Yes." She looked directly into his eyes, her own dark eyes still with a hint of the pain he'd glimpsed in his office.

He removed his sunglasses and wiped their lenses on his shirt, watching a bus bluster and bully its way through traffic on Magellan until it passed out of sight, leaving behind it a low, dark haze of diesel exhaust that dulled the gleam of sunlight on the lineup of less aggressive vehicles.

"How do you feel about abortion, Fred?"

"In this case, I don't know. It's different when it isn't in the abstract, when it's you."

"I always thought it was strictly the woman's call and that I'd opt out of a pregnancy," Beth said. "Maybe I still feel that way, but I gotta tell you, it's weighing on me. And I don't want to leave you out of it."

He put his sunglasses back on and smiled. "You want to share the guilt?" He hadn't meant to say it; he believed in a woman's fundamental right to control her own reproductive system.

"Dammit, don't start laying that kind of shit on me, Fred."

Quickly he said, "I'm sorry. I didn't mean . . . Jesus, I don't know!" He bit into his taco savagely and dribbled more sauce on his shirt. Quite a mess. He held the taco in one hand and used the other to pick up his napkin and wipe his shirt as clean as possible. "You're right," he said, dropping the taco, "these don't taste good. Not this evening, anyway."

"I've got to think hard on this, Fred. I don't know what I'm going to decide. What I have a right to do—or not do. It's a tough decision either way. I never did believe that bullshit about millions of women having abortions as a casual form of birth control. Now I know it's not true; nobody could take this lightly."

"A few people could," Carver said. "You're not one of them."

"Who I am is part of the problem, too."

"Meaning?"

"The child will be biracial. That carries its own troubles."

"It doesn't matter," he snapped, defending his offspring already.

"Not to you or me, obviously. But it matters to some people, and the child would suffer for it. I've seen people caught in that cold, empty zone between the races. And it ripples through generations. I've seen it cause agony and even death."

"I've seen it work out OK," Carver said.

"Yeah, some of the time it does."

"Some of the time's enough."

She half turned in her chair and stared at the boats looking white and antiseptically clean in the sunlight, and at the sea beyond them, gone from blue to deep green in the evening light. Night was on the way.

Then she stood up, very erect, still lean-waisted. "I've got to give this a lot of thought, Fred."

He shoved his chair back, scraping metal over concrete, and grabbed his cane. He didn't stand up, though. "Do you want me to be with you tonight?"

"I'd rather you weren't," she told him. "I need to think on it alone."

"I'll drive you back to your car."

"No, I'll walk along the beach awhile, then I'll take a cab. Do me good."

"You sure?"

She leaned down, careful not to bump her head on the umbrella, and kissed his cheek. "I'm sure."

He gathered up all the uneaten food and the wrappers and placed them on the plastic tray, preparing to leave.

"What are you going to do?" she asked.

He used his forefinger to push his sunglasses back up where they'd slid from the bridge of his nose. "If she's home, I'm going to talk to W. Krull." He stood up and carried the tray to a trash receptacle, dumped its contents, and sat it on top of a stack of identical trays around which several fat flies droned. "I've got to do something."

He watched Beth walk out of sight before he started the car and pulled out into traffic on Magellan.

As he drove, he thought about his son, Chipper, who'd been burned to death by a mentally disturbed killer five years ago.

The son who would forever be eight years old in Carver's mind, the age at which he'd died.

For the first time in years, he found tears tracking down his cheeks.

He thanked God he was wearing dark glasses.

10

AFTER HE parked on Fourteenth Street across from W. Krull's apartment, Carver peeled off his sunglasses and slid them into his shirt pocket. He'd stopped by the office to get his light gray sport jacket. He removed the jacket from its wire hanger, hooked over one of the convertible top's steel struts, and shrugged into it, fastening a button: instant officialdom, and the taco sauce stains on his shirt were concealed.

A young, blond woman and a tall Hispanic man were leaving the building as Carver limped with his cane around the dry pool with its maimed fish fountain. The man thought Carver was staring at the woman and shot him a glance that carried a mild warning. Carver wondered if they were married, or had children.

He made his way up a narrow flight of wooden stairs and found apartment 2-D halfway down a carpeted hall that smelled of mildew and had low-wattage bulbs in brass sconces every ten feet or so along the walls. At the far end of the hall was a small, square window that grudgingly let in light that fell in a rectangle on the carpet and ventured no farther. The doors lining the hall had been painted dark red years ago. The apartment numbers tacked to them were the plastic, reflective kind made for outside addresses.

Carver rapped lightly on the door with his cane, and a moment later locks clicked and bolts slid from their casings. A woman's voice called something he couldn't make out, then more locks were released. W. Krull seemed to share Marla Cloy's cautious nature.

The door opened about four inches and she peered out at him over a taut brass chain.

"I'm investigating the Marla Cloy harassment," he said.

She continued staring at him with her one visible bleary blue eye, like a mouse peeking fearfully from its hole. Carver the cat thought there was nothing friendly or approachable about the eye.

"Your name came up. I'd like to talk with you." He gave her his most reassuring smile and flipped open his wallet as if flashing police identification, holding the wallet well to the side so she'd have to strain to see around the vertical plane of the partly opened door.

"That isn't police ID," she said.

He couldn't lie about that one. Impersonating the police could be trouble. "No, it isn't. The court granted Ms. Cloy her request for a restraining order. There's only so much official manpower. Better than our taxes going up, I suppose."

"So you're employed by the court?"

He smiled again, tolerantly this time, as if used to the question. "We independent investigators have all sorts of clients," he said, walking the fine line. "I'll be glad to come back later, if this is a bad time." So nonthreatening and reasonable.

She stared at him for another half minute.

"Now and then time can turn out to be important," he told

her. "That's why I came by this evening instead of waiting till tomorrow."

"Just a second," she said at last.

The door closed, the chain rattled, and she opened the door to let him enter. She glanced at his cane, surprised and reassured. If she had to, she could outrun him, maybe even immobilize him first.

She was wearing a white blouse with a pale rose design, and navy blue slacks that hung loose on her gaunt, shapeless body. Her thin brown hair was just curly enough to be unmanageable and stuck out in wispy revolt behind her small, protruding ears. "What was your name again?" she asked.

"Carver. Fred Carver." He knew she'd probably read it when he'd flipped open his wallet. She would be testing him now. He wished he'd brought his insurance agent's notepad, now that he wasn't a cop. "I'll only take up a little of your time with a few questions."

They continued standing just inside the door. She didn't invite him to sit down. He limped a few feet farther into the room and leaned on his cane. The apartment was cluttered and dusty, with a threadbare oriental rug and meanly upholstered, spindly brown chairs and a sofa. Everything seemed to have been where it was for a long, long time, and there were few bright colors. It was a drab apartment for a drab woman. The place contained the same faint mothball scent he'd first noticed on W. Krull. On one wall was a dime-store print of Moses on the mount, clasping the stone engraved with the Commandments to his breast while sunlight and lightning played simultaneously among the clouds. Above the console television on the adjoining wall was a large crucifix, a pale Christ nailed to a dark plastic cross and gazing down at the TV with pain and pity. Next to the crucifix, also mounted on the wall, was a small glass display box containing a semiautomatic handgun. Florida in a nutshell, Carver thought.

"That's a Russian Tokarev 7.62-millimeter," W. Krull said, noticing him staring at the gun. "It was the official Russian sidearm during World War Two."

"Are you a collector?"

"Only in a small way."

"Then you like guns."

"I've learned to like them. It's become necessary."

He moved to the sofa and sat down without being asked, leaning his cane against the thinly padded arm. The sofa was even more uncomfortable than it looked, and he could feel its frame straining to support his weight.

"Exactly what is your relationship with Marla Cloy?" he asked.

"We're business associates and friends."

Carver's gaze fell on the neat stack of magazines on the table. *Shooter's World* lay on top. Its glossy cover showed an attractive woman dressed for a casual suburban barbecue blasting away with a shotgun at a clay pigeon. The subscription mailing label, conveniently upside down on the magazine's cover, was made out to Willa Krull.

"Do you shoot?" she asked.

Carver smiled. "No, the sort of work I do isn't as exciting as it seems in novels or the movies."

"I mean, for sport."

"Now and then at the police pistol range, to keep my eye." He tapped *Shooter's World* with his cane. "You seem to be quite a gun enthusiast."

"I bought my first gun and learned to shoot three years ago. You see, I'm a rape survivor, Mr. Carver. It won't happen to me again if I can help it."

"I don't blame you for taking precautions," Carver said. "And you went about things the right way, not just buying a gun, but learning how to use it."

"I've become proficient," she said. It sounded like a threat.

"How long have you known Marla Cloy?"

"About three months. After she moved here from Orlando, she answered my ad in the *Gazette-Dispatch*. I'm a proofreader and word-processor operator, and she writes on a typewriter or in longhand. Some of the periodicals she sells to have a policy of requesting the articles on disk. And she needed someone to proofread and prepare manuscripts for her larger assignments, to help her meet deadlines."

"Do you work out of your home?"

"Yes. I've turned the spare bedroom into my office."

"So your business relationship with Marla blossomed into friendship."

Willa seemed to become resigned to the fact that she was stuck with Carver for a while. She moved to a chair and sat down. "We got along well. Then, when that creep started to stalk Marla, we had a special empathy. As I said, I'm a recovering rape victim. I know the kind of terror she feels."

"Has she expressed her fear of this man to you?"

"Several times. I've tried to get her to buy a gun for self-defense and take up target shooting, but she doesn't want to. She will eventually, though. She's that afraid."

"Do you think her fear is genuine? I mean, we have to make sure in a case like this."

Willa's upper lip drew back over small, yellowed teeth, making her appear even more like a rodent. "Of course it's genuine! I've felt the kind of fear she's feeling now, and I can recognize it when I see it in someone else. My God, why *wouldn't* she be afraid? She's being stalked by a dangerous maniac."

"We're trying to do something about that," Carver said.

"But you can't do anything," Willa said. "I know how the system works—or *doesn't* work. The man hasn't broken any laws until he's killed her. Then it's too late."

"There's a law against stalking people."

She distorted her mouth in disdain. "It's a crime that's difficult to prove until the victim is dead."

"You have a point. I won't pretend it isn't a problem." Carver rested a hand on the crook of his cane. "Just for the record, do you regard Marla Cloy as stable and not the sort of person who might imagine things?"

"Of course she's stable! It's that Joel Brant sicko who isn't stable. She's not some kind of nut! This is just the kind of thing a woman can expect—Marla's the one being persecuted and here you are blaming *her* for what's going on. It's too bad you won't be able to arrest her for her own murder!"

"Take it easy, Willa. I agree with you. Nobody's trying to blame Marla Cloy for anything. It's just that I have to ask these questions, establish the facts. Maybe someday the law will be changed."

"Some of us can't wait."

"What sort of stuff does Marla Cloy write?"

"Whatever she can sell, I guess. Newspaper and magazine articles, short stories. A poem, once. She's been trying to sell a book, but that isn't easy. Marla says you can't sell a book without an agent, and you can't get an agent unless you've sold a book."

"Sounds like a lot of businesses," Carver said. "But Marla seems to be doing OK."

"She makes enough to pay the rent and buy groceries," Willa said. "Like most of us. It isn't easy for a woman alone."

"I guess not," Carver said. He shifted his weight over the cane and stood up.

"Guess is all you can do. There's no way a man could understand how it is being part of an oppressed minority."

"Aren't there more women than men in the country?" Carver asked.

Willa smiled, but not in a nice way at all. "You better hope we never all pull together."

Carver went over to the crucifix and gun display, trying to imagine Beth and Willa pulling on the same rope. He couldn't conjure it up.

The display case looked handmade but was neatly constructed and finished with thick coats of brushed-on varnish. The Tokarev was behind a small glass door and resting on pegs against a gray silk background. It was a blue-steel piece of work with a five-pointed star set into its grooved grip. It looked like too much gun for a woman as slight as Willa Krull.

"That one's only for display," she said, as if reading his mind. "It's not very valuable, but it's still something of a collector's item. I target shoot with a twenty-two revolver and have a small nine-millimeter for protection."

"You're a woman who means business, Willa."

"I don't want to hurt anyone. And I don't want to give the impression I'm the kind of simple-minded woman who automatically thinks all men are immoral, testosterone-driven beasts. My victimhood hasn't become my identity. But next time around, things will turn out differently. I'm absolutely determined about that."

"I understand," Carver told her.

"I no longer ask for understanding."

He thanked her for her time and trouble, then he moved toward the door. She didn't say goodbye when she showed him out. He didn't mind.

He sympathized with her, but she scared him.

11

EARLY THE next morning Carver drove over to Highway One, then south to the Bee Line Expressway and into Orlando.

Orlando police headquarters was a long, beige building with vertically pinched windows that gave it the look of a fortress. Desoto was in his office, listening to soft Latin music seeping from the Sony portable stereo on the windowsill behind his desk. He was dressed like a *GQ* model, as usual, in a cream-colored suit with a pale yellow chalk stripe, white shirt, yellow silk tie with a knot almost too small to see, and gold cuff links, watch, and rings. Desoto seemed to like jewelry more every year. Carver noticed that now he wore a diamond pinkie ring.

He was an impossibly handsome and collected man, with a classic Latin profile and sleek black hair that Carver had never seen mussed—a tough cop who looked as if he'd missed his calling as a gigolo, but not by much.

Desoto was seated behind his desk, talking on the phone. "Of course, Miss Belmontrosaigne," he was saying. "Of course, of course." He flashed his white, lady-killer smile, as if Miss

Belmont—whoever she was—could see him over the phone. Well, maybe the smile came through in his voice. "We're doing our best for you. That I personally guarantee. It's not only a duty, it's a pleasure. Yes, yes, yes . . ." he said soothingly.

He said goodbye as if he regretted having to break off the conversation, but they'd always have Paris.

"Who's Miss Belmontwhatever?" Carver asked.

"Woman whose shop over on Orange Avenue keeps getting held up. Three times in the past month. She called to complain that nothing's being done about it. We've got the place staked out, but it's best not to let her know that. She might behave suspiciously and tip whoever comes in. Which could put her in danger."

Desoto the chivalrous; he was the only cop Carver knew who might be described as gallant. He truly liked women. Not as conquests or ornaments, but as people. Miss Belmontwhatever was as likely to be a seventy-year-old woman as a young, nubile beauty.

"What about Marla Cloy?" Carver asked.

"Ah! Shut the door, *amigo*."

Carver did, blocking out the sounds of activity elsewhere in the building. The soft guitar music seemed louder. As Carver lowered himself into the chair angled toward the desk, Desoto reached back and delicately twisted a knob that gradually reduced the volume of the portable Sony.

"Why do you need to know about this Marla Cloy?" he asked.

Carver told him.

"The question is who to believe," Desoto said, when Carver was finished talking.

"Right now," Carver said, "I believe my client."

"Because he is your client?"

"That's not the entire reason, but it's a factor."

"And if you find out he's lying?"

"Then he's no longer my client."

"McGregor won't help you at all," Desoto said. "He's a human reptile and should be shot."

"That's why I called you," Carver said.

"Ah, to shoot him?"

"Maybe someday. He won't get involved in the Marla Cloy–Joel Brant problem until someone's dead. But I figured you could help, since she lived in Orlando until about three months ago."

Desoto leaned back and laced his fingers behind his head. The movement caused his jacket to gap, revealing an empty leather shoulder holster. Carver figured his gun was in a drawer. Desoto had all his suits altered to disguise the bulk of his gun, but he still resented the break in the line of his tailoring.

"To be stalked like a prey animal is a terrible thing for a woman," he said.

"If that's what's happening. Why would Brant come to me, if he was really stalking Marla Cloy?"

"Why would she lie about him stalking her?" Desoto asked.

"I don't know. To set him up, maybe."

"For what?"

"I'm not sure. Possibly she wants to kill him and claim self-defense."

"That would sound more logical if she had a motive."

"I'm trying to find one," Carver said. "Believe me, I want this to make sense."

"Yes, that's how you are. You need for your little patch of the world to be a just and understandable place."

"Call it a character flaw."

"More like an obsession. Do you know how they catch monkeys in Africa?"

Carver said that he didn't.

"They cut round holes in sheets of plywood just large enough for the monkeys to work their hands through to grab coconuts." Desoto accompanied this information with appropriate hand motions, scrunching his fingers together with a forward, twisting motion. "They can't remove their hands as long as they hold the coconuts, and the monkeys are too obsessed with the coconuts to release them."

"Catching monkeys in Africa, huh? That sounds like something you saw in one of those late-night old movies you watch."

"Well, maybe it was India. The point is, obsession can be dangerous. You're involved with people who might be out to kill each other, for all you know. Maybe you should let this one play out by itself, without your help."

Carver said, "What about Marla Cloy?"

Desoto turned his hands palms up in a gesture of hopelessness and did a thing with his eyebrows to show he'd at least tried to save Carver from himself. "She lived in an apartment in the 4400 block of Graystone Avenue until about three months ago, then moved to an apartment on Bailock where she stayed briefly before moving to Del Moray. She doesn't have a police record, and the neighbors described her as a quiet woman. Her only family's her mother and father. They live in Sleepy Hollow, a trailer court outside of town."

"What do you know about them?"

"Not much. He's a retired railroad worker. That's all I managed to learn. I figured it was the daughter you were interested in."

Carver nodded. "The name Joel Brant pop up at all?"

"No. But then it might not, when a policeman's asking questions." Desoto absently polished his pinkie ring on the arm of his jacket, four quick, short swishes to buff it to a brilliant-enough shine to send a pattern of light dancing over the papers on his desk. "There is one notable thing in her background, *amigo*. She moved from her apartment on Graystone because it was damaged when the building burned. Three of the tenants died. Arson squad said the fire might have been set deliberately, but they could never prove it. They also said it might have been the flame from a hot water heater igniting gasoline fumes from a nearby can where paintbrushes were being soaked to clean."

"Who'd be dumb enough to leave a can of gasoline near a hot water heater?"

"No one who'd admit it, apparently."

"Did you get the names of the tenants who died?"

"Of course." Desoto lifted a green file folder from his desk. "It's all here for you, my friend. If I were you, I think I'd nose around about the fire. Three deaths such a short time ago, and the prospect of death seems to be dogging Marla Cloy again. It was probably coincidence, an accident . . . but we don't believe in those things as much as some people, do we?"

"I'm not sure I believe in them at all," Carver said. He leaned on his cane and stood up.

Desoto handed him the file folder. "How's Beth?"

"Why?" Carver asked without thinking, realizing too late the brusqueness of his reply. But because of her background, her previous marriage to a drug dealer, Desoto had his reservations about Beth and hardly ever inquired about her.

Desoto appeared puzzled, then laughed. "I was only making conversation. You live with the woman, so I thought I'd ask about her. Is there a reason I shouldn't have?"

"No. And she's fine. I'll tell her you asked."

"Is she helping you on this Marla Cloy thing?"

"Yeah, she sees a story in it for *Burrow*."

"How does she figure it?"

"She thinks Marla Cloy is telling the truth about being stalked. Beth views her as another female victim of male oppression."

"Politically correct," Desoto observed, "and possibly correct all the way down the line. When you eliminate the improbable, whatever's left, however probable, must be the answer."

"From the same movie as the monkeys and coconuts, I'll bet."

"Yes, the same Amazon adventure. What it means is that what you're mixed up in could be precisely as it appears, a woman being stalked by a psycho with a deadly compulsion, and Beth's sized it up accurately."

"Maybe she'll change her mind," Carver said.

"Tell her to be careful. I mean, a fire and three dead people." Desoto languidly waved a hand, flashing a gold cuff link. "Who knows what might happen?"

Desoto had never before asked him to urge Beth to be careful. It struck Carver as odd that he'd worry so about Beth, a woman he accepted only grudgingly because she was Carver's lover. It was eerie. Desoto had instincts like sensitive radar, especially when women were involved. He seemed somehow to know something, to sense that Beth needed particular protection and care.

Strangely enough, that even more than the doctor's diagnosis brought home to Carver the unalterable and monumental fact of Beth's pregnancy.

"You all right, *amigo?*"

"Sure. Heat's been getting to me, is all."

Carver held up the file folder and thanked Desoto, then made for the door.

"You take care," Desoto said behind him in a concerned voice. "This kind of heat, you've got to baby yourself."

12

CARVER ORDERED a hamburger and a draft Budweiser for lunch in a restaurant on Robinson Street and sat in a booth by the window, examining the contents of the file Desoto had given him. It was cool in the restaurant, in pleasant contrast to the sunbaked street and sweltering traffic on the other side of the window. The exhaust fumes of passing cars rose in shimmers of refracted light, beautiful even as they slowly poisoned the air. A heavyset man in a sweat-stained blue T-shirt, wearing a bandana around his neck, trudged past outside and glanced in at Carver's beer mug with an expression of pure longing. Carver finished his hamburger, drained the contents of the mug, and ordered another beer.

When the second full and frosty mug was placed before him, he took a sip, then bent over the opened file with increased concentration.

Marla Cloy's present address was there, as well as her previous addresses in Orlando. The license number of her 1987 Toyota Corolla was listed. The extent of her criminality was that she'd pled guilty and paid a fine for a speeding ticket last year. Bonnie Parker she wasn't.

Her parents' address was in the file. Carver planned on talking to them. But first he'd check out Marla's address on Graystone, the apartment building that, according to the file, had suffered a serious fire several months ago that resulted in the deaths of three tenants. He lifted a page and found the names of the victims: Rita and David Kern, a married couple, and a woman named Gail Rogers.

The later address on Bailock might provide some information, though Marla had stayed there only a week before relocating to Del Moray. It was the Graystone address, and the fire, that Carver's gut told him might yield the most insight.

He closed the file folder, finished his beer, then left a ten- and a five-dollar bill on the table to cover lunch.

As he pushed open the restaurant's thick oak door, humid heat closed in and enveloped him like warm water. Remembering the way the guy in the blue shirt and bandana had gazed longingly at his cold beer, he limped reluctantly outside. All the way to where the Olds was parked, he could feel heat from the sidewalk radiating through the thin soles of his moccasins, softening the leather so that he was aware of even small objects and imperfections in the concrete.

THE GRAYSTONE AVENUE apartment building showed no sign of having been burned. It was a three-story, beige brick structure with three small, obviously nonfunctional, decorative dormers spaced evenly on its roof. The dormers' windows were mere framed wooden panels painted sky blue with white horizontal streaks, as if they were reflecting light. The building's real windows were flanked by narrow black shutters that were no more functional than the dormers. The door to the vestibule was tinted glass and topped by a fan-shaped transom with black spokes. A thick, jagged crack that obviously had been recently tuck-pointed ran like a lightning streak from just beneath one of the building's front windows down the foundation to disappear behind low-lying thick shrubbery. Carver thought it might be evidence of the fire; he'd seen brick walls wave, crack, and crumble in the intense heat of a major fire. It was an old building, but well kept, in a block of similar buildings not so well maintained. Most of the small front lawns needed mowing and were browned by the sun. Though the lawn in front of Marla's previous address had brown patches, it was mowed and trimmed, and there was an oleander tree in the front yard that had been neatly pruned.

Carver left the Olds unlocked, as he always did in questionable neighborhoods, so car thieves wouldn't slash the canvas top to gain access, which guaranteed a major expense if the vehicle was later recovered. He waited for a dusty black pickup truck to rattle and rumble its way down Graystone, then he crossed the street and passed through the dappled light beneath the oleander tree and approached the door with the fan-shaped transom.

The vestibule was mostly pink marble with a gray vein, crisscrossed with fine cracks that suggested antiquity. According to Desoto, Marla Cloy had lived in apartment 3-B. Carver checked the names above the mailboxes and saw that a D. Thatcher lived there now.

The building didn't have an elevator. Steel stairs, painted beige, that probably had replaced the original wood stairs, angled upward toward brilliant light streaming through a window on an upper-floor landing.

As he set his cane's tip and began climbing, Carver decided to leave D. Thatcher for last. It was the neighboring apartments that interested him most.

He was in excellent physical condition except for his permanently locked left knee. But the higher he climbed, the more stifling the building became. Ascending toward the pure, blinding light made going up the stairs seem like a near-death experience. He hoped it wasn't.

By the time he reached the third floor, he was slightly short of breath and perspiring.

After waiting a minute until he'd cooled down, he made his way to apartment 3-C, directly across the hall from Marla Cloy's old apartment.

He knocked, got no answer, and moved across the hall to 3-A. He could hear a radio or TV playing inside, so he rapped loudly with the crook of his cane.

The muffled music and voices inside were suddenly quiet, as if Carver had surprised transgressors at play.

The door opened, the smell of onions cooking emerged, and a stooped, gray-haired woman in her sixties cocked her head and stared inquisitively at Carver.

"I'm looking for Marla Cloy," he said. "I was told she lived at this address, but I'm not sure which apartment's hers."

"Her name downstairs on the mailboxes?" the woman asked.

"Couldn't find it."

"Then you probably got the wrong address. I couldn't help you much, anyways. Only lived here two months. But I never heard of any Norma Cloy."

"Marla," Carver corrected, and apologized for disturbing her.

He got similar results from the occupants of 3-D and 3-G. Apparently the building had a rapid tenant turnover rate. Not unusual in this kind of neighborhood.

When he knocked on the door to 3-B, Marla's old apartment, he heard movement inside almost immediately.

He'd expected D. Thatcher to be a woman, using her initial to disguise her gender for safety's sake. But the door was opened by a tall, blond man wearing pleated gray slacks and a tight blue pullover shirt that showed off his weightlifter's build.

He stood with his feet spread wide and his arms at his sides, hands turned palms backward, elbows crooked so they rode far out from his waist. It was the way people stood underwater.

When Carver asked him about Marla Cloy, he nodded. "Sure, I remember Marla. I used to talk to her now and then down in the laundry room. I wash stuff pretty often because I work out regularly. She was always down there doing a load, too. Must be one clean woman."

"She lived in this apartment, didn't she?"

"Right. There was a fire about three months ago. Burned hell outa this end of the building. She moved out, and when the place got fixed up, I gave up my old apartment on the second floor and moved in here. Another thirty a month in rent, but it's worth it. Everything's practically brand-new."

It occurred to Carver why the other third-floor tenants he'd talked to hadn't lived at the address very long. They'd all moved into newly renovated apartments after the fire. "Was anybody hurt?"

"Yeah. Three people died. It was a big fire, in the papers, on TV news. The apartments on this floor all had smoke damage, and a couple of 'em were totaled."

"What about this one?"

"Mostly smoke damage, but the kitchen was wiped out. The fire started in the basement and raced up the ductwork to the apartment right beneath this one. Then it spread through the rest of the place. Not much damage on the second floor other than to that apartment, but the flames came right up the ducts and between the walls and did a job on this floor. Firemen said that's not unusual."

"Who lived in the first-floor apartment directly above where the fire started?"

"Guy named Bill Swarthmore. People right across the hall, the Kerns, died in their sleep from smoke inhalation. Woman next to them, Gail Rogers, was found dead right inside her door. They say she suffocated, too."

"That's a shame. But Swarthmore survived?"

"Yeah. He was in Colorado skiing, or he probably would have died just like the others."

"Lucky break. Do they know how the fire started?"

"Not exactly. Last word I heard on it was somebody left some paintbrushes soaking in a can of thinner or gasoline, and it caught fire somehow."

"Do you know where I can find Marla Cloy now?" Carver asked, fishing.

"Nope. She kept pretty much to herself. Some kinda writer, is what she said she was. You know how *they* are. Good-looking gal, though, especially when she dressed up. I tried to date her a few times, but she always spun me right around. She was the smile-and-hello type, but didn't have any close friends I know of in the building. Well, wait a minute. She was friendly with Gail Rogers, I think, what with Gail living right across the hall. But that's not much help to you, I guess, Gail being dead."

"Did you know her at all?"

"Gail? Not really. Just to say hello to. I saw her and Marla walking together downtown once, so I'm sure they were friends."

"What kind of reputation did Gail Rogers have?"

"Reputation? Heck, I don't know. Never heard anything bad about her." Thatcher absently adjusted a shirtsleeve, creating ripples in the tight musculature of his arm. Carver figured he worked out a lot, and probably with a fanatic's dedication.

"Did you ever try to date her?"

Thatcher looked at him curiously, letting him know he was getting too personal. "Gail wasn't my type. Kinda plain. Seemed nice enough, though. Why do you ask?"

"If I can't find Marla Cloy any other way, I thought maybe Gail Rogers's friends or family might know where she is."

"Could be, but I don't know how you'd get in touch with them."

"During the brief contact you had with Marla, did you notice anything unusual in the way she behaved?"

"Can't say I did. She was standoffish, but not like she was a snob or anything like that. Distant, is all. She acted like a lady who'd maybe been hurt and was healing inside, in her mind."

"Hurt how?"

"That I couldn't tell you. I might even be wrong about it."

A woman's impatient voice called, "Don? Honey?" from somewhere inside the apartment. Thatcher scratched his flat stomach beneath his taut shirt and smiled at Carver. A conspiratorial, us-men-of-the-world kind of smile.

"I'm interrupting you," Carver said.

"Sorta."

He thanked Thatcher for talking with him, then gave him his card and asked him to call if he thought of anything else.

"Hey, you're a confidential investigator," Thatcher said, squinting at the card. "That's neat. A private eye."

"Shamus," Carver said with a smile. "But Marla's not in any kind of trouble."

"She inherit money or something?"

Why did they always ask that? "No," Carver said, "people who inherit money are usually easy to find."

"Don!" The voice was almost desperate.

Thatcher shrugged his massive shoulders and shook his head in apology for having to end the conversation.

Carver nodded wisely, letting him know he understood how women were with a handsome guy like Thatcher, and Thatcher closed the door—leaving Carver leaning on his cane and wondering about the woman who did her wash often and acted as if she'd been hurt.

13

TWO BLOCKS away from the Graystone apartment building, Carver found a drive-up public phone on the corner of a service station lot. He managed to maneuver the Olds close enough to reach the key pad through the open window without getting out of the car, then punched out the number of the beach cottage.

Beth was there, as he'd hoped, probably working on a *Burrow* assignment.

"How do you feel?" he asked, when she'd answered the phone.

"Pregnant."

"Still?"

"Why did you call, Fred?" She obviously wasn't amused by his pass at humor.

"I've just come from Marla Cloy's old apartment building in Orlando." He told her what he'd found out.

"She sounds like a more or less normal woman," Beth said.

"You wanted to be a part of the investigation. Can you keep

an eye on her while I check out things here in Orlando? I'm pushing my luck tailing her close every day; she's bound to notice I'm in the background too often for coincidence."

"Okay, I'll carry the ball for a while. It'll give her another car and another face to look at if she's peeking from the corner of her eye. Think she's home now?"

"Probably. She's like you: work, work, work."

" 'Cause of the bills, bills, bills."

"You sure you feel well enough to do this?"

"Of course I do. I'm okay. A little queasy in the morning, but after that I'm my usual self."

"Selves, now."

"Shut up, Fred."

He thought she was going to hang up, but she stayed on the line. He could hear her breathing as he stared out over the Olds's long hood at a row of greasy five-gallon oil drums. A brown and black dog, very fat, waddled out from behind the drums. Carver wondered if it was pregnant.

"Have you thought any more about the baby?" he asked.

"It's what I think about even when I'm thinking about something else," she said, evading what he was really asking.

"Are you positive you're focused enough to follow Marla Cloy without being noticed?"

"I'm positive, Fred." She sounded irritated now, almost to the point of attacking him. "It's not at all the way you think, when a woman's pregnant."

There was no way he could dispute that. Better stick to business. "Marla carries a paperback novel around with her and reads it from time to time. I don't think she's as involved in it as she'd like anyone watching to believe. And she's cautious by nature. Make sure you keep your distance from her in public places. And when you follow her in your car—"

Beth hung up.

Carver was left with the receiver pressed to his ear, listening to the distant sigh and static of the broken connection.

He had a few further instructions for her, but he decided against calling her back. Instead, he stretched out his arm and replaced the receiver in its cradle, then cranked up the car window and switched the air conditioner to its highest setting.

For a few minutes he sat with the car's engine idling, thinking about Beth's pregnancy. He couldn't deny he didn't want to be a father again. It didn't make sense at his age, in his circumstances. It would cause problems, turn his life upside down and sideways.

But at the same time, he couldn't deny he was tickled by the prospect.

Nothing's simple, he thought, and he yanked the transmission lever to drive.

THE APARTMENT Marla had moved to after Graystone was a notch down the economic scale. Bailock Avenue was in a rough part of town known for its drug-culture inhabitants and the accompanying crimes of burglary and assault. Kids growing up on Bailock were introduced to guns before getting acquainted with Dr. Seuss, and probably didn't understand why Sam I Am didn't simply pack a semiautomatic and force green eggs and ham on anyone he chose.

Driving along the avenue of tired brick-and-frame houses and ruined lives, Carver wondered if Marla Cloy was involved with drugs as user or dealer. It was a possibility everywhere these days, but especially in Florida, home of sun, fun, and gun, and drug smugglers' port of call.

Her temporary apartment after leaving Graystone wasn't really an apartment, but half of a small frame duplex. The building needed painting so badly it had been weathered to a dull gray with only traces of its once-white color showing in grainy streaks, as if an incompetent artist had attempted light breaking through an overcast sky.

Carver parked at the curb in front of the duplex, behind a ten-year-old rusty Plymouth that had once been a taxi. Then he climbed out of the Olds and made his way along a cracked and uneven sidewalk to the sagging porch.

The wooden porch floor was so spongy, he was careful not to lean with much weight on his cane; he feared its tip might penetrate a termite-infested plank.

Only half of the duplex was occupied. A middle-aged, dispirited-looking woman responded to his knock and opened the door to the occupied part, the half with curtains. She identified herself as Fern Neptune, the duplex's owner and manager. Her body odor was horrific and almost overmatched the bourbon fumes she breathed. She had poorly hennaed hair, mottled skin, and a bulbous and veiny nose that fairly or unfairly screamed of alcoholism.

She somehow managed to look haughty and told Carver up front she didn't have much time for him. She remembered Marla Cloy, of course, but had only rented the other half of the duplex to her for a week or so until she could move out of town. "Cheaper than a motel," Fern said smugly, and just as anonymously. Not getting to know the tenants was the best way for a landlord, she said. It prevented pain and problems in the long run.

No, Marla hadn't associated with the neighbors, Fern told him, but that wasn't unusual in this part of town. No, there were never any late-night goings-on or unusual sounds coming from the other side of the duplex. And no, Marla Cloy didn't entertain men or throw wild parties or play her stereo too loud—if she even owned a stereo.

"An unusually quiet and well-behaved woman," Carver commented.

"I don't know about *all* her behavior," Fern said. She smiled and exposed incredibly crooked and yellowed teeth. "What they say's true, you know, about still water running deep."

"It can be a breeding farm for mosquitoes, too," Carver said.

She glanced pointedly at her wristwatch, then faded back into the dimness of her duplex's interior and closed the door halfway, letting Carver know she was finished talking to him. He was afraid she was going to inform him that time had flown.

"Let me give you my card," he said. "Will you call me if you learn or think of anything else about Marla Cloy?"

"No," she said flatly, ignoring the card he'd extended to her. "I don't gossip about my tenants, past or present. Wouldn't be in the landlord business long if I did that."

"I guess you're right," he said, thinking it might be to his advantage in the future to stay on Fern's good side—insofar as she had one.

He could feel her staring at him as he carefully negotiated the tilted, uneven sidewalk to return to his car.

After starting the Olds, he jockeyed around the old Plymouth parked in front of it, then accelerated along Bailock. The stale odor Fern Neptune had exuded seemed to cling to his clothes.

He cranked down the driver's-side window and let warm but fresh air swirl into the car, barely noticing the black minivan that fell in behind him almost a block back, riding low and listing to the left to accommodate the great weight of the massive man behind the steering wheel.

14

SLEEPY HOLLOW, the trailer court where Wallace and Sybil Cloy, Marla's parents, lived, was almost twenty miles outside Orlando. Carver saw a sign featuring the cartoonlike silhouette of a headless horseman, slowed the car, and turned right onto Crane Drive.

Trailer courts in Florida were unlike those in other parts of the country. One difference was that their residents usually insisted on the term "mobile home" rather than "trailer." Carver, who had once lived in one himself and rather liked it, still thought of them as trailers even as he called them mobile homes.

Sleepy Hollow's streets were alphabetized and apparently all intersected Crane Drive. The lots were landscaped and relatively large, with established trees and shrubs. The trailers themselves were mostly double-wides, with artfully concealed wheels and an air of permanence about them.

The Cloy trailer was a block off Crane on L Street. It was a white double-wide with wooden latticework around the undercarriage, a porch with a blue-and-white striped metal awning over it, and a small backyard enclosed by a four-foot-high chain-link fence. Though there was no carport, there was a concrete driveway that ended abruptly near the north side of the trailer. A late-model blue Oldsmobile was parked in the driveway up close to the trailer. Beyond it Carver could see a black kettle-style barbecue smoker and two blue-webbed aluminum lawn chairs on the grass that began at the driveway's end. Next to one of the chairs was a Coors beer can in a coiled metal holder at the top of a rod stuck in the ground.

He parked the Olds behind its newer, smaller cousin, then got out and limped over the hard ground toward the porch with the awning roof. Tiny insects swarmed into the air each time the tip of his cane entered the grass.

The Cloys had heard him arrive. He was about to knock on the white metal door with his cane when the knob rotated and the door opened. A tall, thin woman in a salmon-colored, loose-fitting dress looked at him in a way that asked what he wanted. She was in her late fifties, with gray-streaked black hair and deeply etched lines around blue eyes that seemed to strain for focus. Her face conveyed a kind of amiable strength lent by classic bone structure. "You can tell she was once a beautiful woman," they would say about her someday when she was laid out for view in her casket. The beauty of her youth lay immortal just beneath the surface of time.

"Mrs. Sybil Cloy?" Carver asked.

She nodded, smiling, obviously wondering who he was.

"Detective Fred Carver," he said. "I'm here to ask a few questions in regard to your daughter Marla's complaints about Joel Brant." Let her assume he was with the police. Let them all assume it, as long as he didn't actually say it.

Sybil chewed on her lower lip and looked confused. "What kind of complaints?"

Carver was surprised Marla hadn't confided her fears to her family. But maybe they weren't close. "She says Brant is threatening her."

"About what?" Sybil asked.

"She doesn't know. He seems to be stalking her."

Sybil turned her head toward someone behind her. "It's a detective," she said, "saying some man is threatening Marla."

"Then she hasn't mentioned this to you?" Carver asked, making sure.

"Ask him in, why don't you?" a man's voice said inside the trailer.

"Of course," Sybil said, smiling like a hostess who'd made a *faux pas*. "Please come inside out of the heat." She looked uneasily beyond him as she spoke, as if something that lived in the heat posed a danger.

Carver climbed the two steps and entered the trailer. It was cool and bright inside, with dark blue carpeting and comfortable-looking early American furniture. Dividing walls were cleverly offset so there was no sensation of being inside two trailers attached together side by side. The interior was paneled in light oak to make it seem more spacious.

A short, bald man wearing blue denim cutoffs and an untucked flowered short-sleeved shirt sat a small table. He was older than the woman and had a moon face, a deeply cleft chin, and very dark eyes beneath bushy black eyebrows. There was a beer can in front of him, and a complex-looking jigsaw puzzle half assembled to display startled and wary deer in snowbound woods. A glass containing ice and a clear liquid sat on a coaster on the other side of the puzzle.

"I hope I'm not interrupting," Carver said, pointing toward the puzzle with his cane.

"It's only a hobby," the man at the table said. "I'm retired and got nothing else to do."

"I've come to enjoy puzzles, too," Sybil said. "Didn't at first, but Wally got me interested. Now we're both puzzle enthusiasts."

"I'm Wallace Cloy," the man at the table said. "Marla's father. He tugged at his ear, tucked in his chin, and stared at Carver. "Threatened, huh?"

"The man's been warned, and we think everything's under control," Carver said, "but it still bears some investigation."

Wallace absently touched a forefinger to the cleft in his chin, as if it were an old wound that was still sore. He had wide, square hands with very broad fingers. There was something menacing about him. "Marla never mentioned any of this to us. You say a *man* is bothering her?"

Carver said again that was the situation. "Does Marla talk with you often?"

"Not as often as we'd like," Sybil said.

Wallace glanced at her, but said to Carver, "Who is this guy?"

"Name's Joel Brant. He's a home builder over in Del Moray. Apparently he's developed some kind of fixation on Marla. It's not because of anything she's done."

"Oh, I'm sure," Wallace said.

"Some men have that compulsion and settle on a particular woman for their own reasons. Marla said she didn't even know who Brant was until he started harassing her. Have either of you ever heard of him?"

"I haven't," Sybil said.

"We wouldn't know Marla's friends," Wallace said.

He picked up a potato chip from a bowl Carver hadn't noticed on a counter within reach of the table, then bit into it almost savagely and began chewing noisily. When he'd bent over to reach the bowl, Carver could see behind him into the kitchen, where what looked like a complicated water filter with coiled white hoses was attached to the sink faucet. The Cloys seemed adequately protected from impurities.

"We're very proud of Marla," Sybil said. "We read all her work whenever it's published, and last year she gave us that photograph." She pointed behind Carver, and he turned around and saw an oak desk with a brass-framed color photo of Marla propped on it. It was a head shot, tilted so she appeared to be peeking around a corner while smiling. She was wearing makeup and had her hair styled in bangs. The Marla in the photo was wearing a demure white sweater and looked much younger and even prettier than the Marla that Carver knew. Prom queen material.

"Has Marla ever had any other problems with men harassing her?" he asked.

"She's been harassed some, but no more than any other pretty girl," Sybil said.

"She don't send out the kinda vibes that'd turn a man onto her like that." Wallace attacked another chip, then took a sip of beer to wash down the wreckage.

"Does she have any severe money problems that you know of?"

"What's that got to do with it?" Wallace asked.

"Probably nothing."

"We help her out now and then," Sybil said. "She doesn't ask often. She's trying to make her living in a very difficult business."

"Has she asked for financial help lately?"

"No. Not in over a year."

"Has a man phoned here for her recently?"

"Men don't phone here for her at all," Wallace said.

Sybil smiled. "Would you care for something to drink?" she asked Carver.

"No, thanks. I'm almost ready to get out of your lives and leave you alone."

"We don't mind," Sybil said, "if we can help Marla."

"Do you know a friend of Sybil's named Willa Krull?"

"Never heard of her."

Carver glanced over at Wallace, who was shaking his head no.

"Okay," Carver said. He thanked them for their time, smiling and easing toward the door. "This sure doesn't feel like the inside of a trail— of a mobile home."

"We don't think of it as a mobile home at all," Wallace said. "Except when there's a tornado warning."

Sybil opened the door for Carver. He caught a whiff of lilac perfume as he slid past her and made his way down the oddly angled steel steps with his cane.

She waited until he was all the way outside, then leaned forward out the door, as if she didn't want Wallace to overhear her. "If there's any way we can help you, help Marla, let us know."

"I will," Carver said. "And don't worry too much about this. It's not so serious that Marla even mentioned it to you."

"I worry about Marla. A mother worries."

"Most of them, anyway." Carver turned toward his car, watching a swarm of insects rise around his cane. "Good luck with the puzzle."

"Good luck with your own puzzle," Sybil told him.

15

WHEN CARVER entered the cottage, he saw the note tucked beneath the salt shaker on the breakfast bar, where he and Beth customarily left messages for each other.

She was staking out Marla Cloy's house and would return late that night.

The note also told him there was pressed turkey in the refrigerator. He found it, along with mayonnaise and lettuce, then built himself a sandwich on rye bread and ate it with a cold Budweiser. He hadn't realized how hungry he was. He made himself another sandwich, and while he ate it he finished a small bag of barbecue potato chips Beth had eaten most of, then sealed with a wooden clothespin. He wondered where she'd obtained such a domestic item. She looked like a beautiful tribal queen. He couldn't imagine her hanging wash.

After returning the turkey and mayonnaise to the refrigerator, he propped his sandwich plate in the dishwasher, then opened another beer. He carried the beer can and the cordless phone out onto the porch, sat down in a webbed lounge chair, and leaned his cane against the cottage wall.

He sat sipping beer and looking out at the ocean for a long time, watching a high bank of clouds move out to sea as gulls cried and wheeled in the dying light. Then he smoked a Swisher Sweet cigar, picked up the cordless phone, and called Vic Morgan.

"It's Carver," he said, when Morgan had answered the phone.

"You sure, Fred? You sound like you're talking from the bottom of a barrel."

"It's this cordless phone." Carver was often frustrated by technology that kept getting newer as he grew older. "I'm on a weak channel or something."

"Then change the channel."

"It does that automatically. I paid extra for that feature."

"Uh-huh."

"Can you hear me well enough?"

"Sure. As long as I just take your word for it that it's you."

"Given that it's me," Carver said, "I'd like to ask what you know about Joel Brant."

"The guy who's got the nutcase woman after him?"

Carver could tell where Morgan's sympathies lay. Like a lot of cops, he'd developed a negative view of women from his years on Vice. "Same Brant. He's my client now."

"I don't know anything about him personally," Morgan said. "But I had the strong sensation he was telling me the truth. And you know how it goes when a woman's accusing a man of anything these days. He's got a hell of a problem even if he's innocent. I thought you'd be the guy to get to the bottom of why this Cloy woman is out to get him."

"Assuming he's telling the truth."

"You think he's lying, Fred?" Morgan sounded surprised.

"I didn't at first, but now I'm not so sure."

"Hmm. That's odd. I've developed a feel for these things over the years, and I'd bet the ranch and all the livestock he's telling it straight. For some reason the Cloy broad is out to get him."

"What if she's the one telling the truth?"

"Then he kills her. That's the way the law works, Fred. Can't arrest a man for thinking about a crime—he's got to commit it."

"Kind of tough on the potential victim," Carver said.

"I'm not saying it isn't. I'm saying it's impossible to arrest somebody who hasn't done anything. And that's the way it has to be. Listen, Fred, I've seen plenty of stalkers, and this Brant isn't one of them. I'm convinced of it."

"You must be, or you wouldn't have sent him to me."

"That's something to remember," Morgan said. He sounded miffed that Carver would doubt his cop's instincts. "I might be retired, but some things don't change. When I hear a man's story, it counts for something if I feel in my gut he's telling the truth."

"It counts for plenty," Carver assured him. "Or I wouldn't have taken on Brant as a client."

After breaking the connection, he laid the phone on the floor beside his chair and lit another cigar, watching the smoke he exhaled roll under and off to the side. The breeze had shifted and was blowing in off the ocean, cooling the hot sand and rattling palm fronds to make them sound as if they were tapping out a complex code. The surf whispered like a conspirator on the beach, but neither it nor the palms had the answers Carver needed.

He sat there, smoking and thinking, until dark.

WHEN BETH arrived he was in bed asleep with the light on and the front page of the *Gazette-Dispatch* spread out over his chest. He awoke when he heard the crunch of her car's tires on the sandy soil and gravel as she parked outside the cottage.

He lay half in the world of sleep and listened to the door open and close, the thunking of her footsteps in the night-time silence as she crossed the plank floor. Water ran in the kitchen, then in the bathroom. When her footfalls got closer, he opened his eyes halfway and watched her undress. She made graceful motions out of the simple act of peeling off her clothes, almost like choreographed dance. Did she know he was watching?

Wearing only blue bikini panties, she approached him and gently removed the newspaper from his chest, then switched off the reading lamp. The room became dim in the moonlight that softened all objects. The window was open and the ocean breeze pushed in and played over Carver's bare chest and arms, suddenly and comfortably cool now that the newspaper had been removed. He could hear the night surf, and somehow it seemed like the sound of the gentle breeze.

The bed creaked and he felt the mattress shift as she lowered her long body down to lie beside him.

"You asleep, Fred?"

"No. I was watching you undress. You don't look pregnant."

"I don't feel it, either, right now. Makes it easier to be in denial." She extended a hand and stared at it. "I just quit shaking. As I turned onto the road to the cottage, a van came roaring out of nowhere and almost forced me into the ditch."

"The driver probably thought you were the police and panicked. Teenagers have been parking there to make out, since it's dark and secluded."

" 'Make out,' huh? You're dating yourself, Fred."

"Well, it's the age of safe sex."

"Couldn't prove it by me," she said, and leaned over and kissed his forehead, then dropped back onto her pillow. "I'm as pregnant as if it were nineteen-forty."

"Hubba, hubba," he said. "What kind of day did Marla Cloy have?"

"Normal, I'd say. She worked until late afternoon, then ran some errands in that little car of hers. In the evening she ate supper alone at a steakhouse—no steak, though, just a baked potato with a godawful assortment of goodies heaped over it till it had more calories than steak. After that she went home, came out half an hour later with a basket of clothes, and drove to a coin laundry. It was about nine o'clock when she went home and stayed there. I could see her through the window, folding and putting away clothes. Then she watched TV for a while and went to bed. Lights went out about ten-thirty. I hung around another half hour to make sure she was down for the night, then I left. Stopped for some doughnuts and slaw and drove back here."

"Doughnuts and slaw?"

"Sounded good. Was good."

"Marla still reading her Rendell novel?" he asked.

"Nope. She was absorbed in a different novel in the Laundromat. Something by Robert Parker." The mattress shifted again and she lay on her side in the shadows, facing him, propped on her elbow, her chin cupped in her hand. "The whole thing was *too* damned normal, Fred. I got a sort of sense about the woman."

"A sense?"

"There's something not genuine there."

"Maybe not. But I'm getting a different sense of Joel Brant, too. I thought Marla might be setting him up so she could kill him and plead self-defense. Now I'm not so sure. What if he's using me to help him set up an alibi for himself? Maybe he *is* the one doing the persecuting, just as Marla claims, and he's building a record of *her* having harassed *him*, so he can murder her and successfully plead self-defense."

Beth was quiet for a moment, then she said, "Damn it, Fred,

you almost sold me on the notion that Brant might be an innocent victim. After watching Marla Cloy, I think you were right—he could be the one being harassed. Now that I've moved to the position Marla might be playing a double game, you've moved to thinking Brant might be lying to you, using you to help set up his alibi."

"It's a possibility," Carver said, "and I don't like being used. One way or the other, I'm going to lay this thing bare and find out the truth."

Beth laughed, still grimly amused by their switched positions on Marla and Brant. "You've got too simplified and moralistic a view of the world, Fred. The real truth's sometimes too ambiguous for human understanding, and maybe that's the way it is here. If these two people don't want to level with each other or anyone else, it could be we'll simply never know the truth, despite your compulsion to dig and dig until everything's revealed. Who's doing what to whom, why they're doing it . . . there's more than one reason for most things. Brant and Marla might have lost sight of the truth themselves."

He didn't see how, but then there might be a lot he didn't know.

"Sometimes," Carver said, "the truth is gigantic and simple and so obvious we don't recognize it at first. Or there can be some of that denial you mentioned, if the truth's too terrible to bear. We all prefer to think we're on the side of the angels."

"Hmm. You been reading the Old Testament, Fred?"

"I talked to Vic Morgan on the phone today. He thinks Brant's on the level, but it's possible Morgan's judgment is skewed against Marla because she's a woman."

"Oh, you've been reading Naomi Wolf."

"Maybe Marla's toying with us," Carver said. "Poking her nose in a detective novel while you were tailing her."

"The irony wasn't lost on me. That's one reason I think she might be taking everybody for a ride on her delusion. Or maybe she's got a solid, old-fashioned motive for setting up Brant. Revenge, money, publicity. There could be a lucrative book contract in this for her if she claims she had to kill him in self-defense because the system failed her."

Carver hadn't considered that one. Another layer of possible meaning.

"She might not care if Brant's hired you," Beth said. "It could be presented as another example of male harassment. If Brant were dead, it would be your word against hers as to why you were hired. She might be using you, Fred, if Brant isn't."

Carver lay for a while with his hands behind his head, staring up at the dark ceiling, listening to the gentle rush of the surf.

"I don't like being used," he said again.

Beth moved close to him. He could feel the heat of her body as she leaned in and kissed his cheek. Her breath was warm. Her fingers brushed his chest, then trailed lower.

"That right?" she said.

"Wait a minute, I'll get a condom."

"Fred."

16

CARVER WAS on Jacaranda Lane at ten the next morning.

This time he parked the Olds directly in front of Marla Cloy's house. The maroon Toyota was parked in a patch of sunlight in the driveway, though there was no sign of life around the house. The drapes were closed and the green awnings drooped over blank windows. The lineup of dead plants on the small concrete porch hadn't been moved. The cracks in the faded yellow stucco oddly gave the house the look of permanence, as if it had obtained a patina of long-ago minor damage and wear as it settled in for centuries. Age-checked oil paintings had that look about them, as did ancient mausoleums.

It was warm but not yet brutally hot, and a slight breeze kicked up to pop the house's green awnings like sails and ruffle the palm trees that lined the sad avenue. A good morning to sleep in late with the windows open. Maybe that's what Marla Cloy was doing, escaping into sleep from her daytime nightmare.

Or maybe not escaping anything and not dreaming at all, sleeping the sleep of the not-so-innocent.

Carver thought it would be fine if he woke her. Then she might not be thinking clearly enough to maintain whatever facade she could be hiding behind. The cobwebs of sleep might reveal more than they concealed.

He'd decided it was time to confront Marla directly. If she really was persecuting Brant with false claims of harassment, knowing that he'd hired help might prevent her from continuing. At least make her think twice before doing anything bold.

And if Brant really was harassing her, and was using Carver in whatever scheme he was working, Carver might be able to find out why.

He limped up onto the porch and pressed the doorbell button with his cane. The button had been painted over, and he had doubts as to whether it still worked, but he heard faintly from inside the house what sounded like the old triple-note NBC signal chimes. It brought to mind hours spent listening to the twilight of radio drama when he was a boy, the tiny arched dial glowing feebly in the dark.

The drapes in the window to the left of the porch moved a few inches to one side, then back.

Then the door opened. Carver had passed inspection. Meaning he wasn't Brant.

Marla was wearing cutoff Levi's with a tucked-in white T-shirt with BEYOND BITCH lettered on it. She was barefoot, and Carver was fascinated by the perfection of her squarish feet with their pedicured bright red nails. For the first time in his life he wondered if he might be a latent foot fetishist. Her dark hair was slightly mussed and her eyes—so deep a blue they were almost purple—looked lazy and sleepy, and bruised because of their odd color, which seemed to reflect on the flesh around them. Beneath the bleached and stringy unhemmed cutoffs, her legs were shapely and tan, so free of blemish that sheathing them in nylon would be redundant. She smelled un-perfumed but clean, a fresh, soapy scent. Carver noticed that her hair behind her ears and around the back of her neck was wet. She might have just gotten out of the bathtub or shower. Maybe she bathed as often as she washed her clothes.

He told her who he was and that he was working for Joel Brant.

She didn't blink, but her eyes looked a little less drowsy. Close up, she was a lot more impressive. He thought he saw some of her mother's strength in her features, a beauty that hinted at character.

"He's not allowed to come near me, so he sent someone?" she asked, but she didn't seem afraid.

"No, Joel doesn't know I'm here. I decided on my own to talk to you and see if this thing can be settled."

A smile was slow to form but quick to disappear on her fresh-scrubbed features. "He wants money, right?"

"Not any more than the rest of us. His story is that he never heard of you until you began filing complaints about him with the police. He's puzzled, and he hired me to find out why you're harassing him."

A wasp was buzzing around the dead potted plants. The morning was beginning to heat up and get uncomfortable.

"May I come in?" Carver asked. He knew the sun wasn't doing his bald pate any good.

She stared appraisingly at him, at his stiff leg and his cane.

"I'm allergic to wasp stings," he lied.

She came to her decision about him and nodded, then stepped back to make extra room for him to pass, since he walked with a cane.

There didn't seem to be any air-conditioning running, but the house was still cool from last night. The living room was dim and full of overstuffed blue furniture clustered around an oval, woven rug that contained every known color and so went with any decor. On one wall was a crude bookcase fashioned from cinder blocks and unfinished pine boards. It held a small stereo and a lot of tattered paperback books. A wooden table stood near the window. On it were an old portable Smith-Corona electric typewriter, a stack of vegetarian magazines, a thick paperback combination dictionary and thesaurus, a bottle of liquid white-out, and two plastic in-out trays that contained typing paper and long sheets of yellow paper from a legal pad. The top sheet had writing in pencil on it. There was a lamp with a black shade on a back corner of the table, plugged into a long, frayed extension cord that ran across the floor beneath the window and disappeared behind the bookcase. A fire hazard.

"I see you're a writer," Carver said, lowering himself into the soft, sprung sofa.

"I'm sure you already knew that," Marla said. She walked over and opened the drapes so light flooded in over the worktable and made the room much brighter.

"I'd heard," he admitted. He pointed at the magazines with his cane, remembering her devouring a hamburger at McDonald's. "Are you a vegetarian?" he asked, giving her a chance to lie.

"No, I'm doing an article on it, though. Some people theorize that since humans are omnivorous by nature, being a vegetarian might hold hidden long-term health hazards."

"Oh? That's interesting. What do you think?"

She smiled. "I'm omnivorous."

She sat down in a bulging blue chair that matched the sofa and crossed her tan legs, pumped a perfect foot a few times. Deep inside him Carver felt a tugging sensation, as if something in him were attached to her toe by a string. He was undeniably attracted to this woman and wondered if in some complex way it had to do with Beth's pregnancy. Or maybe it was because she might be extremely dangerous. Beth had once pointed out to him that he was drawn to dangerous women. Well, he wasn't the only one with that failing; there were a lot of victims strewn along the landscape between Delilah and Lorena Bobbitt.

"Why are you doing this to Joel Brant?" Carver asked.

"I'm not. He's doing it to me."

"Why would he? He says he doesn't even know you."

"He knows me now. As to why he'd harass me, it's well known how some men become fixated on a woman. She doesn't have to be beautiful or behave in any particular manner. It all originates in the stalker, not in the object of his compulsion. She only has to strike some chord in his sick mind, and he chooses her for his victim."

"Most men aren't like that," Carver said. "Joel Brant doesn't strike me as an exception."

Again the smile, confident, superior. "I'm not surprised you don't believe me. You're a man. Only women really understand this kind of all-too-common oppression and victimization."

"I didn't say I disbelieved you."

"Yes, you did. Indirectly."

She might be right; he couldn't recall. "I came here to listen to your story," he said. "That means I must have harbored some tiny doubt about Joel's."

"My story is that I turned around one day and Brant was there, and I was in the crosshairs, where I've been ever since. He's stalking me. It's a familiar story, but too often the woman being stalked isn't believed until she's proved her point by dying."

"You're an enigma," Carver said.

"Maybe I am. Men can't stand an enigma. They have to try to figure it out, to master it so they can discard it and move on."

He was getting tired of her talking like a 1970s militant feminist, but he didn't tell her so. "It sounds as if you've had some bad experiences."

"Some. They made me realistic, but they didn't make me paranoid or delusionary. I'm not imagining Joel Brant is a threat to me. He showed me a knife and said he was going to kill me."

"He denies that."

"Can he say where he was at the time it happened?"

"Yes. He was at the grocery store the same time you were, but that could be because you made it a point to be there at the same time he was."

"Uh-huh. As I said, I'm not surprised you don't believe me."

Being a man, Carver thought. "It's not a gender thing," he said.

"Sure it isn't."

Trying not to show his irritation, he decided he could never convince her that he wasn't a misogynist. "Are you writing about this?"

"This what?"

"You and Joel Brant."

She laughed bitterly. "Sure, I'm persecuting an innocent stranger so I can do an article."

"A book, maybe."

"I'm afraid not, Mr. Carver. But I'm not at all shocked that you'd think so. Did you ever consider that Joel Brant might be writing a book? You don't have to be a pro to be published."

Carver smiled. "You've got me." He tapped soundlessly on the woven rug with the tip of his cane. From the rear of the house he could hear a soft humming now, probably a window air conditioner. "Do you feel safer now that a restraining order's been issued?"

"Safer," she said, "but not safe."

"If Brant were really stalking you, why would he hire me?"

"That's a question he might want asked in court some day." She stood up and crossed her arms beneath her breasts. "I was just about to settle down and try to do some work."

Carver leaned his weight over his cane and fought his way up out of the deep, deep sofa.

"Something bothers me," he said. "You don't seem frightened."

She moved a step closer to him and her face got hard. Her dark eyes sparked with pinpoints of light as she moved into the sun pouring through the window. "I'm frightened, all right," she said, "but I'm also determined. I won't be brutalized or die a helpless victim who didn't fight back. I intend to defend myself if I must."

Carver remembered Willa Krull telling him she was trying to talk Marla into buying a gun. "Defend yourself how?"

"Any way I can."

"Do you own a gun?"

"Does Joel Brant?"

"I don't know. He didn't say."

"Neither did I."

Carver made his way to the door, walking slower than he had to with the cane. She walked ahead of him and held the door open.

Heat moved in as he moved out. Marla didn't flinch or move her body an inch as he edged past her onto the porch.

He turned to face her. "Believe it or not, I agree with you about how women are at a disadvantage in something like this," he said. "I'm only trying to get a sense of what's really going on."

"Thanks for you sympathy." She said it with a faint curl of her upper lip. "I'm going to do whatever I can to make sure you won't be expressing it at my funeral."

He looked directly into her deep blue eyes and found nothing he could read. She stared back at him with no sign of discomfort, only calm determination. He didn't hear the door close behind him until he was almost to the street.

When he'd started the engine and switched on the air conditioner, he sat for a while in the car before driving away. It was unsettling to him that he felt himself drawn to Marla Cloy even though she was no less a dilemma and a danger than when he'd rung her doorbell.

And something else was unsettling. He had the feeling that despite her brittle and wary talk, she might be attracted to him.

Of course, he could be dead wrong about that. He'd been wrong that way before. Male ego, Marla would probably say.

Beth would probably say the same.

He drove.

17

AFTER LEAVING Marla, Carver drove to Brant's address, which turned out to be in Warwick Village, a luxury condominium complex on the east side of town, not on the ocean but with an ocean view if you were on a high floor.

Half a dozen identical white brick buildings made up Warwick Village. They had powder blue shutters and decorative black iron balconies. A network of pale concrete sidewalks connected the buildings, all emanating from a fancy white gazebo as if it were the hub of a wheel. Flowers were planted around the gazebo, and it had a rooster weather vane on its roof. The rooster's head was tossed back and its beak was spread wide as if it were crowing. Someone had painted an oblong eye on it that looked like the eye of a human.

On a cedar board near the gazebo was a directory of Warwick Village, under a sheet of Plexiglas to protect it from the weather. There was also a small sign directing prospective buyers to Red Feather Realty, the agency that apparently handled all Warwick Village listings.

A man wearing plaid slacks, a white shirt, and a white cap emerged from one of the buildings, walking a short-legged, grayish dog of indeterminate breed. The dog was in a bigger hurry than the man and kept the leash tight while all four legs churned on the grass just off the sidewalk. It was sniffing around, searching almost in a panic for the precise spot to relieve itself, the way dogs did when they'd been indoors too long and had finally found hope for relief.

Carver made his way casually over to the gazebo so the dog walker couldn't avoid passing him.

It was easy enough to act interested in the place and strike up a conversation with the man, who told him that the condo was five years old and had been built by Brant Development. He didn't know Brant personally, but he knew which of the white brick buildings he lived in, and that Brant was on the condominium board. "That means a lot," the man said, "that the condo builder thinks enough of the place to live in one of the units." The little dog wasn't interested in any of this. It was yanking around on its leash, acting desperate and staring intently at Carver's cane. Carver thought it was time to end the conversation.

He drove to Red Feather Realty, whose main office was in a small strip shopping center not unlike the one where Carver's office was located, and pretended to be a prospective buyer of a Warwick Village condo.

The agent handling Warwick Village, a middle-aged and ferocious woman named Hilda who wore an obvious wig, said she knew Joel Brant and used the fact that the builder himself lived in one of the units as a selling point. "Very important," she said. Apparently she'd talked to the man with the desperate little dog. Brant had moved in nearly six months ago, after his wife died in an auto accident, Hilda said. He was a nice man.

Could be, Carver thought.

Hilda loaded him up with glossy and colorful brochures

about Warwick Village and gave him her card, took his. She reminded him that membership in the Warwick Village Racquet Club was built into the monthly maintenance fee, then asked Carver when he wanted to tour the display units.

He wasn't positive he was ready to move, he admitted, but he assured her that if that was his decision, Warwick Village would be the first place he'd look.

Out in the heat, he made sure no one was looking out the window of the realty company, then dropped the sales brochures into a curbside trash receptacle. He got in the Olds, feeling the heat pulsing down on the top of his head through the canvas top, and started the engine. He switched on the air conditioner before maneuvering around the black minivan parked in front of him and pulling out into the stream of traffic.

In his office, Carver called Brant's cellular phone and reached the developer at Brant Estates. They were pouring concrete for a side street and foundation slabs today, Brant told him, so he'd be at the site for a while. Carver told him about his conversation with Marla.

"Did she strike you as crazy?" Brant asked.

"No. But that doesn't mean she isn't. Have the newspapers or any of the local publications ever done a piece on Brant Development? Or on any of your projects?"

Brant thought for a moment while Carver listened to a loud grinding sound in the background, probably a cement mixer gearing up to pour.

"Other than paid advertising, there've been a few articles in the paper. Once a feature on a beachside condo development."

"Warwick Village?"

"No," Brant said, "one farther down the coast." More of the grinding sound of the mixer, an engine being revved up. "Were you at my condo looking for me?"

"Earlier," Carver said. A half truth. "Do you remember the author of the piece on the other condo project?"

"No, but I think the byline on the feature article was a woman's."

"How long ago?"

"I'd say about four years. In the *Gazette-Dispatch*. I've got copies somewhere back at the office."

"Could it have been written by Marla Cloy?"

"Doesn't ring a bell, but I suppose it's possible. I'll look."

"Let me know what you find," Carver said.

He hung up, then lifted the receiver again. Ordinarily he would have called Beth. Instead, he punched out the number of Lloyd Van Meter in Miami.

Carver didn't remember much about Laura's pregnancies. Anyway, Laura wasn't Beth. He wasn't sure how much he should call on Beth to do. Not that she wouldn't do it; she was tough and, as she'd said herself, in denial sometimes about her condition. But threats had been made. Or a double game was being played by Marla, which could be even more dangerous. He had to remember that with Beth he might be putting two lives in danger.

Van Meter, who was perhaps the most successful private investigator in Florida, had offices in Miami, Tampa, and Orlando. His headquarters was in Miami, but he wasn't there. His secretary told Carver she'd have Van Meter call him from his car phone.

Carver thanked her and replaced the receiver, wondering when he was going to have to buy a cellular phone so he could chat while he drove. He would have to become part of this fast-developing mobile technology or be run over by it. He didn't want to become road kill on the information superhighway.

He did paperwork until Van Meter called him just before noon.

"Been a long time," Van Meter said. He must have had a terrific car phone; he sounded as if he were leaning over Carver's right shoulder. Carver could picture the obese Van Meter with his flowing white beard, half reclined behind the steering wheel of his big Cadillac, his thick arm draped limp-wristed over the top of the wheel. He didn't know quite how to dress Van Meter in his vision; Van Meter always surprised. He was a flagrant violator of every rule of style and color. He usually looked as if he'd gotten dressed in a kaleidoscope.

"I need some help here in Del Moray," Carver said.

"That's the only reason you ever call, because you need help. What kind of pickle are you in this time?"

"I need someone followed, and I can't do it myself."

"Why not?"

"I'm following somebody else."

"What about Beth? She busy too?"

"She's pr—— Yeah, she's busy, doing a piece for *Burrow* about the Everglades drying up."

"Good for her. The wetlands are disappearing faster than Disney World is growing. And we need one more'n the other."

"I didn't know you were a conservationist."

"I'm not. I like alligators."

"As shoes, you mean. What about my request?"

"Well, I got a good man in Orlando can drive over and take up the task. You know Charley Spotto?"

Carver did. Spotto was a brash little man with a huge mustache, gimlet eyes, and the heart of a terrier. "Sure. He'll do fine."

From the corner of his eye Carver noticed a black minivan make a right turn into the parking lot.

"Give me the name and address of whoever you want watched," Van Meter said. "Spotto will be on him like a second skin he doesn't know he has."

Carver gave him Brant's name, then his home and office addresses, as well as a physical description.

"This guy dangerous?" Van Meter asked.

"I don't know. That's one thing I'm trying to find out."

"Okay, Spotto should be there by late afternoon."

"Usual rate for this, Lloyd?"

"Of course. I didn't think you were asking for a favor. You're too proud."

Carver hung up, thinking that sometimes Van Meter sounded a lot like Beth.

He resumed trying to clear his desk of paperwork, then he suddenly realized he'd skipped lunch and was hungry. Quickly he placed everything in a semblance of order beneath a paperweight that had been a gift from his daughter, Ann. It was one of those glass globes with miniature buildings in it and imitation snowflakes that swirled around when it was shaken. Carver had moved it enough to cause flurries. He sat thinking about Ann in St. Louis, where some winters a lot of snow fell, and long, gray stretches of cold kept it from melting.

The snowfall in the globe held him hypnotized until it ended.

He was reaching for his cane to stand up and go out into the searing Florida heat when the door opened and the biggest man Carver had ever seen ducked his head to enter the office.

18

HE WAS even taller than McGregor, and wide, without a hint of excess flesh anywhere. He wore filth-encrusted jeans and a dirty, wool-lined distressed leather vest without a shirt. At the end of each muscle-corded long arm was a huge hand with hairy-knuckled fingers like sausages. On his feet were immense white sneakers, loosely laced and with their tongues hanging out as if they were exhausted just from transporting him around all day. As he stepped farther into the office, Carver saw that he wasn't wearing socks.

"Help you?" Carver asked.

The man laughed, almost a giggle. The shrill sound, so incongruous coming from such a mountain, made the flesh on the nape of Carver's neck crawl.

Carver stood up, not quite leaning on his cane, keeping his weight balanced and his grip tight so he could lash out with force with the hard walnut if the man meant him harm.

The man did mean him harm. His wide face, guileless as a child's and marked with blackheads and a smudge of grease on the bridge of his nose, broke into what appeared to be a mindless smile. His eyes were so pale they could hardly be called blue or gray; they were almost one with the whites so that Carver couldn't even be sure they were trained on him. He moved toward Carver with confidence and a surprising liquid grace. When he drew back a gigantic fist, Carver shifted his weight and swung the cane hard, using both hands.

The fist opened in a flash and caught the cane. It was snatched from Carver's grip as if he'd been fishing and hooked a shark. The man snapped the cane in half and tossed it in a corner, then effortlessly kicked the desk aside so he'd have more room. Carver had been leaning with his thigh against the desk and would have fallen, only one of the giant hands grabbed the front of his shirt and supported him. He punched the man's stomach, and pain lamed his right hand and wrist as he made contact with a large silver belt buckle.

He felt himself being dragged across the office, then he was slammed against a wall, lifted, and held there with his back pressed to the plaster and the mammoth fist still clenching his shirt front. He heard material rip and he eased down a bit inside the shirt, then he was held fast. He tried to knee the man in the groin with his good leg, but his knee made contact with a tree trunk of a thigh and bounced off.

That seemed to irritate the big man. With his free hand he began slapping the left side of Carver's head, holding him in such a way that with each blow his head would bounce off the wall and into the next slap of the meaty palm. It was making a *bam-pocka-bam-pocka-bam-pocka!* sound, like a speed bag being rhythmically pummeled in a gym. Pain exploded in Carver's head and he felt bile rise in his throat.

Then the dizzying pain and motion stopped abruptly and he felt himself slide down the wall until his feet were on the floor. The fist balled around his shirt still held him tight, and he was staring at the man's hairy chest, smelling stale perspiration and maybe gasoline.

"Stop going around asking your questions," the man said. It was a rumbling voice not at all like his high-pitched giggle.

To emphasize his demand, he shook Carver like a lifeless doll. Carver couldn't summon the strength to resist the whip-like motion. His head began bouncing against the wall again, causing an increasing pain that made him nauseated.

"You understand my meaning?"

"Who are you?" Carver managed to gasp.

Bam-pocka-bam-pocka-bam! The room whirled and jerked crazily and Carver could barely see it through his tears as his head bounced between palm and wall again.

He was on the floor then, with no recollection of having fallen. His head pulsated with pain and his stomach heaved. There was a terrible stench that it took his addled brain a few seconds to recognize—feet! He saw one of the boat-size, odorous white sneakers draw back. It kicked him almost lazily yet with such force that he felt his breath shoot from his lungs.

"Stop going around asking questions," the man growled again. "Do you get my meaning this time?"

"Got it," Carver moaned. There was a hitch in his voice because he couldn't catch his breath. He hoped he'd spoken clearly enough to be understood.

"Agreed?" the voice thundered above him.

"Agreed," Carver confirmed.

Nausea overcame him and bile tasted like copper at the base of his tongue. He turned his head toward the wall, trying not to vomit.

"You bastards," the giant said calmly, "you learn hard, but you learn."

Carver was braced for another kick at any moment. Then he realized he could no longer smell the man's huge feet.

He turned his head, craned his neck, and saw that he was alone in a room that was tilting and swaying. He let himself lie flat on his back, breathing more freely now, taking in oxygen and waiting for his stomach to settle and his head to stop aching. There was a stitch of pain in his right side where he'd been kicked, as if he'd run too far and become winded.

What appeared to be a small brown spider was on the ceiling, and he found himself staring at it, mesmerized, trying to determine if it was actually moving or if its subtle change of position was only in his mind. Then he wondered if it was even a spider. The eyes could play tricks.

His stomach calmed down to a knot of pain and the nausea became steady but controllable. His head began to ache more.

He rolled over and started to crawl toward the closet, where a spare cane was hooked over the clothes rod, but every time he moved, dizzyness swept over him and he had to stop.

The phone had fallen to the floor with the rest of whatever was on the desk when the big man had shoved it aside to get at Carver. The receiver had miraculously stayed on the hook. Or maybe the giant had for some reason replaced it. Carver rolled onto his back, then his side, and could reach the phone.

He punched out the number of the cottage, getting it right on the third try. His arm and hand told him the receiver was pressed to his ear, but he couldn't feel it as the phone on the other end of the connection rang, rang, rang.

Finally, Beth's voice.

Carver managed to mumble something into the phone that even he couldn't understand. He was alarmed to find he couldn't recall what he'd attempted to say. A plea for help. He knew that. Jesus, his mind was mush and he couldn't think!

He rolled onto his back again, still clinging to the receiver and hoping he wasn't pulling the cord from the phone jack.

A spider, he decided with satisfaction, staring straight up at the small brown dot that undoubtedly had moved a few feet from where he'd noticed it on the ceiling earlier. The question of its authenticity was answered.

It was definitely a spider.

"Fred?"

He made an effort and dragged his mind down from the ceiling. "At the office," he said.

"Fred!" Alarm in her voice now.

"C'mon in here. Need some help."

"What's happened?"

"Big guy . . . slammed my head . . . warned me . . ."

And suddenly he wondered if the man had been demanding he stop asking questions about Marla? Or about Brant?

That was the question Carver needed answered. Not the one about the spider.

"Beth?"

"I'm getting you an ambulance, Fred."

"No, just you . . ."

". . . ambulance," he heard her say again as the room dimmed, then became dark.

He should never have called her. She was always bitching at him for never wanting to see a doctor, as if a pill . . .

The floor pressing against his back spun and dropped faster and faster through the darkness, a wild carnival ride from long ago.

His pain, and his question, followed him into unconsciousness.

19

CARVER FLOATED up from sleep slowly, listening to women's voices far away. Light seemed to sift beneath his closed eyelids, and he couldn't understand what the women were saying. Soft voices, distant murmurs.

He moved his head only slightly, but it exploded in pain.

"Lie still," one of the women was saying, nearer to him now. Was hers the hand on his shoulder? When he tried to move again, a sharp pain grabbed at his side and his headache flared.

"Lie still, Fred."

He opened his eyes and saw Beth standing over him. Above her head was a white metal smoke alarm, and a stainless steel pipe with a green curtain slung from it by plastic hooks. A faint medicinal scent struck him and he knew he was in a hospital room.

"The nurse has gone to get an ice pack for your head," Beth told him.

"It doesn't hurt if I lie very still," Carver said.

Beth smiled. "Good." There were tears in her eyes. "Lie still, then."

Most of the room's illumination came from indirect lighting around the perimeter of the ceiling. Vertical blinds on the window were angled so that only cracks of light penetrated and he couldn't see outside. "Where am I?"

"You're in Good Samaritan Hospital, Fred. After you called me, you were found in your office unconscious."

"So you brought me here?"

She shook her head no. "Ambulance. To Emergency. By the time I got here they were well on their way to having you diagnosed."

"And?"

"Concussion, and a cracked rib."

"How bad?"

"Rib not bad, concussion not good."

"Huge guy came into the office—"

"I know, Fred. You were babbling yesterday when you were half conscious."

Oh-oh. "Yesterday?"

"Right. It's"—she glanced at her watch—"two-fifteen now. That's in the A.M., Fred. You remember anything else about the big guy, now you're awake?"

"That's an odd question," Carver said, "considering I was half conscious when you heard me tell it the first time and wouldn't remember what I said."

She grinned. "Testing you, Fred. Your gray matter's still working OK."

He told her the story as he recalled it. He didn't remember calling her on the phone but he took her word for it, hoping it wasn't another of her tests.

A stout, redheaded nurse came in with an ice pack and laid it gently on Carver's forehead.

"Better?" she asked.

"I don't need it," Carver said.

The nurse removed the ice pack and set it on the green plastic tray on the table by the bed. Also on the tray were a green plastic water pitcher sweating with condensation and a small green plastic glass. Next to the tray was a box of white tissues, one erupting from it like a freeze-frame explosion.

"It's right here if you change your mind," the nurse said. She came around the bed and pinned the cord with the call button to the sheet where he could reach it easily. "I'll be nearby if you need me." Whenever she moved, her rubber-soled shoes yipped softly on the slick floor.

Another woman entered the room, dressed not in white like the nurse but wearing a surgical gown the same green as the water pitcher and glass. She was a dark-haired, attractive woman about forty, average height but slender, with shrewd, assessing eyes, gaunt cheeks, and lips that pouted crookedly as if she were thinking so hard she was making a face. The name tag on her gown said she was Dr. Woosman.

"How do you feel?" Dr. Woosman asked.

"OK if I don't move," Carver said.

"That's to be expected." She stared at him as if he were a cut of meat she was considering serving guests. "We'll keep you here and monitor you for a while, Mr. Carver."

"I want to leave in the morning."

Dr. Woosman looked at Beth. Beth shrugged.

"It's possible," Dr. Woosman said. "We'll see." She shuffled some papers and looked at something on the clipboard she was carrying. "Your lowest right rib has a hairline fracture, so you'll have to wear a support for a while. For the concussion, you need to rest, be observed, and take what I prescribe for you to alleviate pain. Don't try to do anything the least bit violent. No exertion. No swimming or any other kind of exercise."

"I'll keep him still," Beth said. The redheaded nurse, thinking no one was looking at her, grinned.

"Your head will let you know if you try to overdo. But don't push it." Dr. Woosman turned to face Beth. "Check his eyes from time to time. If they become dilated or one pupil is slightly smaller than the other, get him back in here." She trained her shrewd brown eyes again on Carver. "The cuts on your head are only superficial," she said, "and there are no skull fractures. The damage was done by the violent motion, the series of instantaneous reversals of direction when your head was struck or bounced off the wall. Each time, when your head stopped, your brain didn't. It was bouncing back and forth off the inside of your cranium with considerable impact. That resulted in concussions. They're to be taken seriously."

"Feels serious," Carver said.

"What happened to your rib?"

"I was kicked."

"You didn't mention that yesterday."

"Didn't seem I was kicked hard enough for anything to break, but then I wasn't thinking too clearly."

"It's a wonder you were thinking at all." She lifted the ice pack from the tray, as if about to place it on his forehead as the nurse had done. He shook his head no. *Ouch!* She put the ice pack back on the tray. "I'll look in on you again," she told him. "Tough guy, all right," she said to Beth. Then she and the red-headed nurse left the room. He could hear the nurse's shoes yipping a long way down the hall.

"You two have been talking about me," he said to Beth.

"Uh-huh. Quite a lot, actually."

Carver saw her eyes dart toward the door, and he braced for pain and slowly moved his head so he could look in that direction. The wide oak door was swinging open slowly.

It stopped when it was open about two feet, and McGregor poked his head around it. When he saw Carver, he smiled. Not the kind of smile to cheer an invalid.

"I wanted to make sure I had the right room," he said.

"Didn't want to walk in on a nurse doing it with a doctor. That kinda thing goes on all the time in hospitals, you know. It's all those empty beds. And the drugs." He came all the way into the room. His brown suit was wrinkled, the coat unbuttoned to reveal a stained white shirt and the edge of his leather shoulder-holster strap. He glanced at Beth but didn't otherwise acknowledge her presence.

"You two have met," Carver said.

"Sure," McGregor said. "Roberto Gomez's widow."

Carver saw Beth stiffen. She didn't like to talk about her marriage to the late drug czar. It was a life she'd escaped with Carver's help and would rather not revisit even in conversation. There were memories there she shared with no one. Not even Carver.

"So you got the shit beat out of you," McGregor said. "There is some justice."

"Did the hospital call and report I was here?" Carver asked.

McGregor nodded. "Violent crime and all that. Ordinarily I would've waited a while and sent a man over. Then, when I realized it was you got beat up, I thought I'd handle it myself. Especially since I was the one warned you to stay out of that business with Marla Cloy." McGregor walked closer to the bed, picked up the ice pack, and pressed it to his forehead experimentally.

"Why don't you swallow that?" Carver said. "I'd feel better."

McGregor dropped the ice pack and smiled. The pink serpent of his tongue peeked out from the space between his yellow front teeth. Carver could feel the hostility emanating from Beth. McGregor didn't seem to notice it, but Carver knew he was basking in it.

"Some people have mentioned you'd been around asking questions," McGregor said.

"What people?"

"Woman named Willa Krull, for one. Says she thought you were a cop."

"I didn't tell her that," Carver said. "She must have drawn her own conclusion."

"Oh, no doubt," McGregor said. "I made sure that was how it happened and you took care to cover your ass. If I ever nail you for impersonating a police officer it'll be to the cross, and you'll fucking die and rot up there."

"Why did Willa Krull call the police?"

"She was checking on you. Didn't think you smelled right. Then we got another call, this one from Marla Cloy herself." McGregor's tongue flicked again and his smile widened. "A dickhead like you is full of surprises. Here I was thinking you were working for her, and it turns out she never heard of you till you came around pestering her."

"Well, that's a conclusion you jumped to on your own. You and Willa Krull will do that kind of thing."

"Turns out you're actually working for Joel Brant. Working for the guy that's stalking her! That's fucking great! What are you doing, helping him set the Cloy bitch up for the kill?"

"I'm doing that like you're working to prevent her from being killed."

"Preventing ain't my job. After they bleed and shit their last is when I move in."

"A crime was committed against Fred Carver," Beth pointed out. "Isn't that what you're here to investigate?"

McGregor glared at her. "Sure, officially." He got out a notepad and pencil from an inside pocket of his wrinkled suit coat. "I'll try to be objective here, do my job. Did you get a look at this guy I already regard as a friend?"

"Too good a look. He was big, taller than you, and maybe two-eighty. Muscular. Wore a leather vest, no shirt, dirty jeans, white sneakers, no socks. Had grease smudges on him like he might have been working on a car or some other kind of machinery. Pale blue eyes, filthy, smelled bad, looked as if he wasn't too bright. If you had a big brother, this guy might be him."

"I like him more and more."

"He might have been driving a black minivan."

"Why 'might'?"

"I remember catching a glimpse of one pulling into the parking lot a few minutes before he came in. Didn't think anything of it at the time."

"A black minivan almost ran me off the road near the cottage," Beth reminded Carver.

McGregor gave her a look to let her know she was on hold, then turned his attention back to Carver. "Did you get the license-plate number?" he asked.

"Being unconscious when it drove away, I didn't see the plates," Carver said.

"What about you, Mrs. Gomez? You saw this phantom van too. You catch the plate number?"

Beth shook her head no, staring angrily at McGregor. "Do you have any idea who the assailant is?"

"No."

"Are you going to find out?"

"Of course! I'm the law. But I have to warn you not to be optimistic. I mean, the description could fit almost anyone."

"You're really some kind of cop."

McGregor grinned and absently scratched his left armpit.

"He tries to get people mad at him," Carver explained to Beth. "He feeds on it."

"He's gonna goddamn choke on it," Beth said softly.

McGregor loved it. He threw back his head and laughed, stretching his mouth open wide. A thousand fillings were visible.

"This guy who beat you up," McGregor said, when he was finally finished laughing, "was he white, Hispanic, or Afro-fucking-hyphenated-American?"

"I told you he had blue eyes and brown hair. He was white."

McGregor bent lower so he could look directly into Beth's eyes. "Well, you never know, the way the races are mingling these days." He snapped his notepad closed and tucked it inside his suit coat, then straightened up and poked his pencil into his shirt pocket.

"You truly are disgusting," Beth said.

This time McGregor ignored her. He ran a hand through his lank, greasy hair, then turned to face Carver directly, pointing a long forefinger at him. There was a lot of dirt under the nail.

"Listen, dickhead," he said, "you stop fucking around with this Marla Cloy thing. Final warning."

"It's no concern of yours until she's been killed," Carver reminded him.

"I'm making *you* my concern. You step an inch outa line and you'll regret it forever. If Marla Cloy gets killed, I'll see that you and Brant take the fall. They say once you try black you'll never go back, and you ignore my warning and I'll see you're put away and you never get back to Mrs. Gomez here."

Then he spun on his heel and strode from the room.

Beth was fuming, pacing pantherlike with her fists clenched. "That asshole!"

McGregor poked his head back around the half-closed door. He was grinning wickedly, his tongue flicking like a serpent's between his yellow teeth.

Then he was gone and the door closed.

"That man is some ugly piece of work!" Beth said.

"He'd be complimented if he heard you say so," Carver said. "I told you, he feeds on other people's rage. It's his way of establishing human contact."

Beth was incredulous. "You telling me I should feel sorry for him because he's lonely?"

"No, no," Carver said. "Once people get to know him better they really hate him. Nobody feels sorry for him."

"He should be shot," Beth said. "He definitely should be shot."

Carver said, "Hand me that ice pack."

|20|

USING THE spare cane Beth had brought from the office, Carver had left the hospital at nine that morning. Dr. Woosman had been busy in surgery, so there hadn't been much of an argument.

But within fifteen minutes after they'd reached the cottage and Carver was lying on the sofa with the drapes closed, he heard Beth call Dr. Woosman and discuss the situation with her. He couldn't understand any of her words, only her mood and speech rhythms. Beth spoke for ten minutes in that intimate, conspiratorial tone that women could achieve within a short time after meeting one another, and that men achieved only after years of tentative trust—unless they were used-car salesmen.

When she was off the phone, Carver called Desoto and told him about the attack in his office.

"So you're all right?" Desoto asked when Carver was finished. Concern was evident in his voice.

"I will be soon enough."

"I don't think you can expect much help from McGregor," Desoto said.

"That's why I called you. The giant who did a job on me is a bad memory for anyone who's seen him." Carver shifted position slightly and the elastic support around his ribs reminded him it was there. "Have any idea who he might be?"

"No, *amigo,* but I'll see if I can find out. Crime in Florida these days has a high turnover rate. High mortality rate, too. They come and go. Sometimes I wish they wore numbers outside of prison. You said the big man told you to stop asking questions about Marla Cloy?"

"Not exactly. That's part of the problem. I've done some snooping around about Joel Brant, too. I don't know if the big man was warning me about Marla or about Joel."

"You might consider not asking any more questions about *either* of them. No," Desoto corrected himself quickly, as if he'd given it second thought and changed his mind, "that won't happen. You're probably even more obsessive now. If they had twins, you'd start asking about them, too."

"I feel more concussive than obsessive," Carver said.

"All the more reason you should lie low and rest."

"Will you let me know as soon as you find out anything on my oversized friend?"

"Of course. Is Beth watching over you now?"

"Afraid so. Like a nurse from the CIA."

"Good. You need somebody. Do as she says, *amigo.* Take your medicine like a big boy and try not to make an ugly face."

Even as he spoke, Beth walked in from the kitchen area with a glass of water and the vial of pills Dr. Woosman had prescribed and no doubt reminded her about over the phone.

"I don't have much choice," Carver said, and hung up.

"If the subject of your conversation's what I think it is," Beth said, "you've got no choice at all."

She watched while he swallowed the pill and downed the entire glass of water, then she switched on a lamp and leaned over him. "Now, let's take a look at those eyes, see if the pupils are the same size or if one's round and one's square."

He looked directly at her without blinking and thought about crossing his eyes to alarm her, then decided he'd better not if he didn't want more medical input from Dr. Woosman.

AT ONE O'CLOCK, after Carver had felt well enough to sit up and managed to eat a light lunch, the phone rang.

Beth snatched up the extension before he had time to answer.

"Somebody named Spotto," she called from where she was working with her computer at the breakfast counter. "He wants to see you."

Before she could protest, Carver lifted the receiver of the phone by the sofa and gave Charley Spotto directions to the cottage.

SPOTTO HAD called from near Carver's office and reached the cottage before two o'clock. He was a small, wiry man who, every time Carver had seen him, wore a natty blue pinstripe suit, white shirt, and shamelessly polyester red tie, like a cut-rate politician without the influence to rate much graft. He had thinning black hair combed straight back, a narrow face, and an incredibly crooked nose that gave the impression he was peeking from the corner of his eye. He also had a permanent case of nerves; this or that part of him was always twitching as if hooked up to electricity.

Carver stood and introduced him to Beth, who made polite noises then ostensibly busied herself in another part of the cottage, though she stayed within earshot. Spotto gave Carver a slanted look, as if to ask if it was okay to talk in front of Beth, and Carver nodded.

He offered Spotto a beer but the offer was declined. Aware of Beth's baleful gaze, Carver sat down very carefully in the chair by the sofa. Spotto remained standing and went into an unconscious little shuffle, like a dance step that kept him in one place.

"I've been busy," Spotto said.

Carver couldn't imagine him not busy.

Spotto began making weaving motions in the air with his hands. He laid out some preliminary information on Brant, most of which Carver already knew. Then he got down to what Carver was more interested in, his impression of Brant. "Your guy Joel Brant seems to be pretty much the way he represented himself to you. He's a successful home builder in central Florida, here in Del Moray and a few years ago in Winter Park.

"His reputation with employees and acquaintances seems solid. His social life's not much. He goes out to lunch or dinner with business people now and then, sits in on poker games with a group of old friends at least once a week. Plays a little golf. Seems like a straight arrow workaholic. No history of violence except a fight one time over a poker game, and apparently he got the worst of it."

"Any stories on him concerning women?" Carver asked.

Spotto did some more air-weaving with his nervous fingers. "Guy's a widower, all right. His wife, Portia, was killed just over six months ago on A1A when a drunk driver hit their car head on. She died instantly. Brant's still grieving, according to a few people I talked with. Couple of folks said he blames himself for the accident. Didn't say why. Maybe the Brants had an argument before they got in the car, and he figures he provoked it and it might have caused the accident. Maybe he blames himself for drinking enough to affect his driving so he couldn't swerve the car out of the way, then only suffering minor injuries and not dying along with his wife. Maybe he blames himself, period, for whatever might in any way have been his fault. Grief works like that, leaves some people with a load of guilt no matter what."

"Wait a minute. You mean Joel Brant was driving?"

"Right. Portia was the passenger. The guy driving the car that hit them was blind drunk."

"Was he killed too?"

"Only injured. The cars hit off-center, passenger side to passenger side. There were no passengers in the drunk's car."

"If Brant was driving, I can understand why he might be suffering guilt pangs."

"Sure," Spotto said. "He does have a fairly steady female friend. A real estate agent named Gloria Bream. But I couldn't tell you whether it's romance or business."

"Did the name Marla Cloy come up?"

"Only a few times. Some people in the construction business are aware the Cloy woman's claiming Brant's been harassing her. The people who mentioned it—a lumber salesman and a plumbing contractor—don't know whether to believe it. Brant's a solid type, so he's getting the benefit of the doubt. From his male friends, at least."

Carver's gaze went from Spotto's active hands to his face. "Did you talk to any women who think there's something to Marla Cloy's accusations?"

"Nope," Spotto said, "I'm just assuming. You know how it is, women usually believe another woman when she accuses a man of something like harassment. They sympathize with one another."

"Apparently Gloria Bream doesn't think Brant's a threat to her."

"Apparently," Spotto agreed. "Or it could be she's mighty kinky and doesn't care." He drew a folded sheet of lined notepaper from his pocket. "Here's a list of people I talked to, and a few I haven't seen yet that were mentioned along the way. You want me to do some more on this?"

"I don't think so," Carver said, accepting the list. He'd found out what he needed: On the surface, Brant seemed much as advertised. The list of names would serve as a starting point for him to learn more. As with Marla, there seemed to be nothing in Brant's past that suggested the deviousness or instability that might lead to plotting a stranger's murder.

"Brant's busy with some houses being built on the west side of town," Spotto said. "Brant Estates. One of those cookie-cutter subdivisions. I can keep tabs on him for a while if you want."

"It wouldn't be worth the bother," Carver said. "If he is up to something, he'd be doing the normal act at this point."

"His background *is* pretty much normal," Spotto said. "Doesn't mean he's not putting on an act now, of course. But I'm sure he didn't know I was watching him and making in-quiries."

"If he hears that someone was asking around about him," Carver said, "he'll probably assume it was the police."

Spotto cocked his head to the side and peered around his nose. "How'd you get those cuts on your head?"

Carver told him about the attack in the office.

"A guy like you describe," Spotto said, "he oughta be easy to identify."

"Desoto's doing some digging for me. McGregor says he never heard of such an animal."

"McGregor says, huh? That doesn't mean much. The guy sounds like he might be McGregor's illegitimate offspring."

Beth laughed, reminding Carver that she was in the cot-tage. Both men looked over to where she was leaning with her elbows on the breakfast counter, now obviously absorbed in their conversation.

"Beth and McGregor don't get along," Carver explained.

"McGregor and the human race don't get along," Spotto said.

"They're not at the same point on the evolutionary scale," Beth said.

Spotto laughed. "I will take that beer." He walked over toward the kitchen area, and Beth got a cold Budweiser from the refrigerator and popped the tab. Spotto refused a glass. "I've never heard of the big man you described, either. And apparently he's unknown to Desoto. So McGregor was probably telling you the truth this time. Which means the guy who played handball with your head is probably new to the area, probably new to Florida. Want me to ask around about him?"

"Yeah," Carver said, watching Spotto draw on his beer, "that could be productive."

Spotto gave a nervous little chuckle. "Don't go looking for revenge till your head heals."

"He's got a cracked rib, too," Beth said. "If you find the giant geek who beat him up, do him a favor and don't let him know."

Spotto looked at Carver, looked at Beth. "I'd probably be doing you both a favor staying quiet. But I gotta be honest, Beth, I'm working for Carver, and I take my job serious, so I'm honor-bound."

"Honor?"

"Something like that."

Beth shrugged her elegant shoulders, as if resigned but not surprised. "Men," she said. "Fucking testosterone."

Spotto laughed. "You got a valid point, I guess. But estrogen can be problematic too."

He finished his beer, then said goodbye, leaving Carver wondering if morality could be reduced to chemistry.

21

CARVER SLEPT most of the afternoon on the sofa, awakened only occasionally by Beth so she could assess his condition and feed him a pill. Did all women love to dispense medicine?

He came fully awake a few minutes past eleven o'clock, in bed without recalling how he'd gotten there. Beth was sleeping beside him, resting on her back, her long body covered by the thin white sheet, which made her look ethereal. Carver had worked his way out from beneath the sheet and lay naked on top of it. The room was dimly lit by moonlight, and the only sounds were the rushing of the surf and the whisper of Beth's deep breathing, seeming to become one sound. It was warm in the room, with very little breeze sifting through the screened window. It occurred to Carver that he no longer had a headache.

He moved his hands and brushed his ribs with his fingertips. The elastic support was gone, as Dr. Woosman had instructed for nighttime. Beth had been playing nurse again. He rolled partly onto his side, causing a twinge of pain in the damaged rib, and felt along the wall and floor for his cane. He couldn't find it. Looking around, moving tentatively for fear of hurting his side or igniting a headache, he didn't see the cane. Maybe he'd misplaced it.

Or maybe Beth had deliberately moved it out of his reach to discourage him from getting out of bed.

The possibility irritated Carver so that he came wide awake. He was especially sensitive to being deprived of the cane, of his mobility. It evoked a helpless feeling out of proportion to reality. Years ago a woman had told him that since being shot and made lame, his cane had become a phallic symbol for him and he felt deprived of his virility without it. He never had figured out if she was right.

Though he felt a persistent weariness throughout his body, and a precarious balance on the edge of pain, he knew it was pointless to try going back to sleep. He slowly struggled to a sitting position without disturbing Beth, then he stood up, bending over and using the mattress for support.

He hobbled to the TV near the foot of the bed and got the remote from on top of it, switched it on with the volume off, then worked his way back into bed. The rib felt OK. The headache stayed dormant. He aimed the remote at the TV and ran up the channels until Jay Leno appeared. Then, very gradually, he increased the volume to the point where he could barely understand what was being said but Beth wouldn't be disturbed.

Beth muttered in her sleep and rolled onto her side, facing away from him. Quickly he lowered the volume another notch and her breathing evened out into the measured rhythm of deep sleep.

He couldn't make out what was being said on TV now, but he didn't really care. Leno was interviewing a tiny, pixielike brunette actress who looked vaguely familiar and waved her arms around a lot as she talked. Every few minutes Leno would say something and they'd both laugh uncontrollably. That would cause the pixie's nose to crinkle in a way that was undeniably precious, and she would lean forward in her chair and squeeze her clenched fists between her knees as if she had to go to the bathroom.

She was cute, all right. Carver wondered if in twenty years she would be a character actress. It didn't seem possible.

Leno pointed to the camera, said something to the pixie, and the picture faded to a local commercial, a customized van dealer in Del Moray standing in front of a gizmoed-up Ford Aerostar and grinning and talking and throwing phony money into the air simultaneously.

Real money went like that sometimes, Carver thought.

Ignoring the incomprehensible low-volume chatter emitted by the TV, he stared at the van, picturing it dusty black with tinted windows, and decided it was probably the model van he'd seen pull into the lot outside his office a few minutes before the giant with mechanic's fingernails had entered and beaten him.

The odds were, he decided, that his attacker had been trying to warn him away from asking questions concerning Marla Cloy. Of course, there was no way to be sure. But another run-in with the man wouldn't be wise so soon after the first, so Carver decided to play the odds and follow Joel Brant tomorrow rather than Marla. He wasn't too obstinate to give himself time to heal.

The commercial was over and the camera caught the pixie-like actress with a serious expression. Damned if she didn't look like a pocket-size Ava Gardner. Then she realized she was on camera and grinned, crinkling her nose. She moved over a seat as Leno stood, applauding vigorously, and Eric Clapton strolled into the picture, tall and lanky and smiling and waving to the audience.

Carver thought Clapton was great, and he decided that if he played his guitar and sang it might be worth risking waking Beth by raising the TV's volume.

But within minutes after Clapton had sat down and self-consciously scratched his scraggly beard with a forefinger, Carver was asleep.

H E   W A S awake before six the next morning and thought he'd be able to get away from the cottage without rousing Beth, but when he came out of the bathroom after showering and shaving, there she was in her terry-cloth robe, seated at the breakfast counter. She was drinking a cup of the coffee Carver had made in the Braun brewer.

"Where you going, Fred?"

"I plan on making it an easy day," he said. "Maybe follow Brant around and see what kind of mischief he gets into." He gripped his cane and made his way into the sleeping area.

By the time he'd dressed and returned to the kitchen, she was munching soda crackers and had poured a second cup of coffee for him. It was the second time in the last few days he'd seen her eating dry crackers.

"Maybe I should go with you," she said.

"How can you eat crackers for breakfast?" he asked.

"So I'm *not* going," she said, keying off his mood. She didn't say anything about the crackers; she was still in some kind of denial and not willing to talk about how pregnancy had strangely altered her diet.

"How about using *Burrow*'s resources to see what you can find out about Brant Development?" he asked.

"Sure. That oughta keep me out of your hair for a while."

He smiled, passing his hand over his bald pate.

"How do you feel?" she asked.

"Almost normal if I don't do any deep breathing. Want to

help me with this brace?" He held up the elastic support that had been draped over a stool.

She came around the counter and he raised his pullover shirt while she fastened the brace around his lower ribs. He felt a little pain now, and he wondered if she'd deliberately cinched the support too tight so she could make her point that he should rest another day. They'd fallen into fighting petty subterranean duels.

"Want some breakfast?" she asked.

He tucked in his shirt. "No. I'll get something to eat at a drive-through. People in construction start work early, so I want to be outside Brant's condo before seven."

"He's a boss," Beth said. "They don't start at any seven o'clock."

"They do if they own the company and they're successful."

He downed half the coffee she'd poured for him. Now that his rib support was in place, he made his way back into the sleeping area.

As quietly as possible, he got his Colt .38 semiautomatic from where it was taped to the back of his top dresser drawer. He used the leather belt holster and concealed the gun beneath his shirt.

Beth seemed not to notice that his shirt was again untucked when he returned to the main room. Pregnancy might have taken the edge off her alertness.

"OK if I take your car today?" he asked. "Brant might recognize mine."

She got down off her stool and walked to where her purse sat on a table near the door. After fishing out her key ring, she detached one of the keys and came to him, kissed him lightly on the lips, then handed him the key. Her kiss tasted like coffee. He held his body slightly away from her so she wouldn't feel the gun.

"Don't forget these," she said, and with her other hand gave him the vial of pills Dr. Woosman had prescribed.

He brushed his lips against her forehead, which was surprisingly cool. "Thanks. I'll take one if I need it."

She returned to her stool at the breakfast counter, and he headed toward the door.

"Fred."

He turned.

"Don't wait any longer than you have to, if you've gotta use that gun."

He nodded and left her drinking coffee and munching dry crackers and thinking God knew what.

22

BETH'S LeBaron convertible wasn't as fast as the Olds, but it also wasn't as noticeable; there were a zillion like it in Florida, most of them rentals driven by tourists living the fun-and-sun fantasies pictured in color travel brochures. Life was a series of illusions large and small, and some of them could be bought.

Carver had topped off the gas tank and now was parked near Brant's condo. He had the car's top up and the windows closed and the air conditioner humming away. It was cool in the LeBaron; it had a more efficient air conditioner than the Olds, maybe because it hadn't labored through so many merciless summers. And the Olds was rusty enough to let some of the cold air escape.

At 7:30 Brant drove from between the white-brick mock guard kiosks marking the entrance to Warwick Village. He was behind the wheel of a LeBaron convertible, not the sleek black Stealth. His convertible was red, however, and he drove with the top down. Carver hadn't figured him for a two-car kind of guy, but then maybe the Stealth was in the shop and he was driving a loaner. It was difficult to identify a rental car in Florida. The leasing agencies operated under new restraints, since some of the local criminals had decided to view tourists as game animals.

Carver depressed the accelerator and stayed well back of the red LeBaron. Another LeBaron convertible turned from a side street and rode between them. If they all lowered their tops and had beauty queens as passengers, they could have a parade. Brant was wearing a white shirt and had his sport jacket or suit coat folded and draped over the back of the passenger seat, so he was easy to track even in heavy traffic. Carver, wearing the horn-rimmed dark glasses that he fancied made him look a little like Jack Nicholson only with less hair, didn't think he'd be at all conspicuous in Brant's rearview mirror if he kept his distance.

The red LeBaron led him west of town to Brant Estates. He parked on the highway shoulder and watched the sleek red car glide along recently poured concrete streets to where three display houses were lined facing north. They were ranch houses with pale gray or blue siding, powder blue roofs, and two-car garages. The house in the middle had a low white picket fence around the front yard, and its garage had been converted into a sales office. Carver watched as Brant parked in front of that house, climbed out of the red convertible, and walked into the office with his coat slung over his shoulder.

He didn't emerge from the office for almost an hour. Carver sat watching cement trucks rumble one by one to where slab foundations were being poured at the far end of the subdivision. Several workmen were standing around, leaning on shovel handles and staring as if hypnotized by the mixers. Each time one of the mixers released its gravelly soup to pour down its steel funnel, they would get to work frenziedly shoveling, evenly distributing the wet concrete. A bulldozer was grading not far from where the concrete work was being done, raising copious clouds of dust that hung almost motionless to blemish the china blue sky. Beyond where the bulldozer was relentlessly moving earth, about a dozen houses seemed to have been completed. There were a dozen more in various stages of construction, spaced out around the new streets. Carver remembered Charley Spotto referring to them as cookie-cutter houses. Spotto was right. Though they were attractively designed, there was a numbing sameness about them.

A man in jeans, a blue pullover shirt, and a red hard hat came out of the office and strode toward where the foundations were being poured. He was tan and muscular and walked with a swagger, and he appeared to be wearing cowboy boots. He only went a short distance before climbing into a brown pickup truck with a tall antenna mounted on its rear bumper. A rubber ball had been run through with the antenna and rode halfway up it to keep it from whipping around with too much range and bashing into the truck roof.

As the man sat in the pickup, a large red truck pulling a flatbed trailer stacked with lumber snaked its way along the flat, curved street. It headed toward another far section of the subdivision, and the brown pickup followed, its antenna with the rubber ball doing a mad dance behind it as if trying to keep up.

Brant emerged from the office. He was wearing a red hard hat like the other man's. He got in the LeBaron and drove toward where the lumber truck had stopped. The trailer bed tilted back on hydraulic lifts, and most of the lumber, bound in a mass with steel bands, slid smoothly from the flatbed onto the ground as the truck jerked and pulled away, its front wheels lifting momentarily then bouncing back down. The stack of lumber made a sharp, reverberating report like an echoing rifle shot as the boards slapped against the hard ground and one another. Another cloud of dust rose and hung in the air.

Brant parked behind the brown pickup and got out, and he

and the other man in a hard hat stood talking to the truck driver, who had leaped nimbly from the trailer as soon as the lumber was deposited on the ground.

Brant slapped the truck driver on the shoulder, a bill of lading was signed, and the lumber truck drove the pattern of streets to turn around. It roared and clattered past Carver again on its way out of Brant Estates.

Work continued as Brant and the other man—whom Carver assumed was the foreman—wandered around checking on the job and coordinating events. Carver was learning something about home building, but little else. Brant seemed a plain vanilla guy, all right, just as Spotto had described.

Carver was getting bored, and he could only hang around so long before drawing attention, even if he was parked off the highway, well away from construction activity. If it weren't for the cane, he could raise the car's hood and pretend engine trouble for a while without looking suspicious. But even from a distance, a limping bald man with a cane might catch Brant's eye and prompt recognition and curiosity. For a moment Carver himself even questioned what he was doing here. Private investigators didn't generally spy on their clients.

Wondering if he'd gone hormonal in some sort of symbiosis with Beth, he put the LeBaron in drive and waited for a break in traffic before pulling out onto the highway.

What would be next for him, dry crackers for breakfast? Some world. A father. Again. He still hadn't sorted that one out.

The LeBaron's tires sang on the warm concrete as he drove toward the Del Moray public library.

IN THE library's cool green reference room, Carver sat hunched at one of half a dozen microfilm viewers and scanned back issues of the *Del Moray Gazette-Dispatch*.

Portia Brant's accident had been front-page news. According to witnesses, the Brant Mercedes might have been speeding when a car coming from the opposite direction crossed the dividing line and collided head-on with it. The photograph indicated that the cars had struck a glancing blow. Both drivers survived, as Spotto had said. Portia Brant, the passenger in Joel Brant's Mercedes, hadn't been wearing her seat belt and was decapitated.

The driver of the other car was a retired postal worker from New York named Sam Chavez. Thanks to his seat belt and air bag, he'd sustained only facial lacerations and a broken leg. His blood alcohol level was well beyond the point where he was legally drunk. Joel Brant's alcohol level was just low enough to keep him from being legally drunk. He'd suffered only minor abrasions and contusions and hadn't been hospitalized.

Carver concentrated on the viewer and followed the story from "Wife of Local Builder Killed in Head-on Collision" to "Portia Brant, A1A Accident Victim, Is Buried." Portia's photographs showed a beautiful dark-haired woman with kind eyes, a neck like a ballerina's, and a knockout smile. There was a shot of mourners at her funeral. Joel Brant was visible standing among a knot of men wearing what looked like identical dark suits. Portia's obituary mentioned no surviving family members other than her husband, and stated that she'd been president of the Del Moray Garden Club and had been active in local charities.

Carver stared at her photograph, at her smile and elegant neck. His mind flinched at imagining her beheaded by a slab of windshield glass or sharp-edged flying wreckage, and he wondered how much of the accident Brant remembered, how much of it troubled his dreams.

They had been driving home from an AIDS benefit ball at one of the big hotels when the accident occurred. Both had been drinking. The autopsy revealed that Portia's blood alcohol content had been slightly higher than her husband's.

Carver figured out how to work the viewer to make a copy of the image on the screen and fed it a quarter. Portia Brant's photograph duplicated well. He made three more copies, then switched off the microfilm viewer and removed the reel.

Portia's face haunted him. The death of a woman like that, the way she'd died, how might it have affected her husband beyond normal grief? If Joel Brant was psychologically askew after such an experience, who could blame him?

As long as it didn't result in the stalking and killing of an innocent woman.

Feeling slightly queasy, Carver stood up and walked from the library, nodding to a stern-faced librarian on the way out.

Outside in the heat and sun, the nausea stayed with him. What now? Sympathetic morning sickness?

Pushing such nonsense from his mind, he decided his stomach was probably upset from the constant sideways motion of the microfilm being run through the viewer. Something like seasickness. He would skip lunch and drive directly back to the Brant Estates construction site and see if Joel Brant was still there.

THE RED convertible was gone from where it had been parked, and Brant was nowhere in sight. The cement mixers had gone, too. Carpenters were swarming over the studwork of a house near the recently poured foundations, and farther down the same street roofers were hard at work. Their hammering was a discordant symphony only slightly softened by distance.

Carver's stomach was okay now, but his damaged rib was aching. He decided to drive to his office and find something to do that wasn't strenuous or stressful. Maybe he'd even down one of the pills Beth had stuck in his hand as he was leaving the cottage that morning.

Half a mile down the highway he passed a low, flat-roofed structure with a sign proclaiming it to be the Egret Lounge. Despite the early hour, a row of vehicles was nosed tightly against the front of the building. They reminded Carver of suckling pigs lined against the side of their reclining mother.

One of them was the brown pickup truck driven by Brant's foreman.

Carver braked the LeBaron and pulled onto the gravel shoulder, made a slow but tire-squealing U-turn, and parked two spaces down from the truck.

What he might learn in the Egret Lounge he wasn't sure, but there was at least one person inside who knew Joel Brant.

23

THE EGRET LOUNGE was cool and dim inside. The mini-blinds along the front windows were sharply slanted so that bars of light traversed the low ceiling. A paddle fan, the kind that mounts flush with the ceiling to allow more headroom, was slowly revolving. It wasn't needed to make the place cooler, but it seemed to be doing a pretty good job of keeping the tobacco smoke circulating. The Egret hadn't yet caught up with the nonsmoking movement.

As Carver's eyes adjusted to the dimness, he saw a long bar fronting about a dozen round tables with blue-and-white checked tablecloths on them. Each table had a napkin holder and a cluster of condiment bottles in its center, along with a large glass ashtray. Except for the bar itself, the Egret looked more like a restaurant than a lounge, though a lunch menu mounted behind the bar featured nothing other than hamburgers, cheeseburgers, and fried potatoes and onions.

The place smelled like fried beef and onions as well as cigarette smoke. Carver's stomach, which had calmed down, gave a slight twitch. Country and western was also in the air, a Randy Travis soundalike singing in a deep, deep voice about God and the flag and an old hound and the wife and kids and something about a '75 Ford. Carver couldn't make sense of it, but it was sad.

About a dozen customers were scattered about the Egret, four of them slouched on stools in the habitual drinker's posture of relaxed despondency at the bar. Brant's foreman was sitting alone at a table, staring at a full mug of beer in front of him. It must have just been drawn, because it had a thick, foamy head. The foreman looked as pensive as the melancholy lost souls at the bar. Maybe because of the music.

Carver approached the table, and the foreman looked up at him. Without his hard hat he had a head of bushy red hair that curled wherever it wanted. Unruly red eyebrows, too. His face was sunburned so that his nose was peeling; he had the kind of skin that would never tan. He squinted blue eyes at Carver, as if trying to recognize him.

"Howdy," Carver said, also maybe because of the music. "You're the foreman over at Brant Estates, aren't you?"

The man nodded.

Carver used the crook of his cane to pull back a chair. "Fred Carver," he said, extending his hand. "I noticed you over where they were building this morning."

"Wade Schultz." Schultz's grip was strong, dry, and callused.

"I'd offer to buy you a drink," Carver said, "only that one looks fresh."

"It is," Schultz said. He seemed neither friendly nor unfriendly, and not particularly curious.

"I was thinking about buying at Brant Estates, and when I saw your truck parked outside, I thought it might be wise to drop in and talk with you. My theory is, talk to the foreman if you really want to find out how sturdy a house is built. What do you say?"

"About what?"

"Those houses good and sound?"

"I'd say so. We're a company that doesn't scrimp on materials, and I can guarantee you the building codes are followed right to the letter."

"The houses are only half of it," Carver said. "The company itself, Brant Development, is it as sound as the houses? A guarantee's no good if the company goes out of business."

"Company's sound. Brant's been building houses in Florida for a while now, and we don't get many complaints."

"What about those you do get?"

"We jump on them and fix what's broke," Schultz said promptly.

"How about the guy that owns the company? Joe Brant, is it?"

"It's Joel. Joel Brant." Schultz toyed with the handle of his beer mug. Muscles and tendons danced in his bulging forearm.

Carver leaned in closer to Schultz, speaking confidentially. "This won't get back to your boss, but . . . well, is he a reasonably honest man?"

Schultz smiled. "He's my boss. What am I gonna do, tell you the truth if he's a crook?"

"I don't know. Are you?"

"He's honest enough," Schultz said.

"Just enough?"

Schultz took a pull of his beer and wiped a foam mustache away with the back of his hand. "You buy in Brant Estates, Mr. Carver, and you won't be sorry. Those houses are a solid product and they're priced right. And the honest to God truth is, Joel Brant's as straight as any builder you can buy from."

Carver smiled. "Sounds good to me. So he's an honest businessman. And you tell me he's solvent, or at least his company is. But what about his personal life? I mean, I knew a fella bought into a subdivision and the builder ran away with one of the saleswomen. Place went all to hell in no time while they were winning limbo contests in Hawaii. This Brant married?"

"Not anymore. His wife died a while back in a car accident." Another pull of beer. "He isn't going to run away with anyone, Mr. Carver. He's not the irresponsible type."

"Wife died? That's a shame. He a young man?"

"Fortyish." Schultz tilted back his head and drank his mug of beer down past the halfway point.

"I'd like to think that's young," Carver said. "It can hit a man hard, losing his wife so suddenly. Make him somebody other than himself for a while, if you know what I mean."

"Some men."

"Is Brant one of them?"

"Listen, I been on an extended lunch hour, waiting on some lumber deliveries." Schultz glanced at his watch. "They oughta be there by now." He stood up. "Been nice meeting you, Mr. Carver. I hope to be building your house one of these days."

"It's possible," Carver said.

He watched as Schultz swaggered from the Egret, opening the door and disappearing from dimness in a blast of sunlight that made it appear he was walking into a stoked furnace. The door swung back quickly, cutting short the rude interruption of the outside world.

When Carver turned back around in his chair, a woman was sitting at the table.

She was in her early forties, with gray hair cut short as if for summer and surf, even though it wasn't flattering. Her face, pretty with a kind of cheerful eagerness about it, was browned and seamed, as if she'd spent a lifetime in the Florida sun. She was wearing a light gray blazer with shoulder pads, but it was obvious that her shoulders were plenty broad without help from the pads. The neckline of her blouse beneath the blazer was low enough to reveal a lot of freckles and the very beginning of cleavage. Her hands were feminine but strong-looking. In the dimness and haze of tobacco smoke, she was strikingly tan and healthy looking, like an Olympic swimmer in the autumn of life.

She raised a cigarette from beneath the level of the table and took a long drag, shattering her Olympian image. Turning her head slightly to the side and exhaling, she smiled and said, "I overheard you talking to Wade about Brant Estates."

"I'm thinking of buying there," Carver explained. Lie, lie, lie.

"I work there. My name's Nancy Quartermain."

Great. Someone else who might talk with Brant and mention the man with the cane who'd inquired about a house. "Oh? Are you a salesperson?"

"No, the bookkeeper. I just wanted to make sure Wade didn't . . . well, scare you off. He's a good foreman, but he's not the best at dealing with potential customers."

"That's OK," Carver said, "it's not his job."

A waitress came over and Carver asked Nancy Quartermain if he could buy her a drink. She asked for a diet Coke with a lemon wedge, and Carver ordered a draft beer like the one Schultz had been drinking. Two men in work clothes came in and joined the lineup at the bar. "Fish sandwich, Lorraine," Carver heard one of them say to the waitress, even though it wasn't listed on the menu.

"From time to time," Nancy said, "Wade and Joel Brant get into violent arguments. It happened this afternoon."

"Really? Over what?"

"It doesn't make any difference. All of their arguments are over work matters. You know, financing, or completion dates, that kind of thing. They always blow over fast. Like storms out of the Gulf. But I wanted to make sure Wade didn't say anything derogatory about Joel Brant. He's a fine builder, a fine man."

"You know him well?"

She took a final drag on her cigarette, then snuffed it out in the glass ashtray as she exhaled a faint trace of smoke. "Just as a boss who's only in the office occasionally." She stared at Carver. "No romantic interest whatsoever, if that's what your question meant."

It hadn't meant that, and he was surprised she would think it had. Was she protesting too vigorously?

"Schultz told me Brant was involved with a woman named Gloria Bream," Carver lied again. It had been Charley Spotto who'd ferreted out that piece of information.

"That's none of my business. Or Wade's." The waitress came with their drinks, and Nancy was silent until she'd gone. "I can tell you this, though. Mr. Brant's wife was killed in an auto accident about six months ago. Mr. Brant was driving when their car was hit by a drunk driver. He sort of blames himself, though he shouldn't. The other driver was soused to the gills. Say, did Wade tell you about this?"

"No."

She shrugged her athlete's shoulders and sighed into her diet Coke. "Well, Mr. Brant shouldn't torture himself. But you know how it is, he was driving, so I guess it's hard for him not to feel he was in some way responsible."

"That's a shame," Carver said. "Maybe the Bream woman will be good for him."

"Maybe they'll be good for each other, but they've probably got a lot to work through. From what I hear, Mr. Brant has terrible dreams about his wife's death."

"What kind of dreams?"

"Just horrible dreams. His wife—Portia was her name—well, her head was cut off in the accident and he was trapped in the wreckage with her for a long time. I mean, to have to live with that kind of memory. What do you think that does to a man?"

"I'm not sure. Nothing very pleasant."

"I'd think it would have more of an effect on Mr. Brant than he's shown."

"Everyone's different," Carver said.

"Yeah. Makes horse races, I guess. Come to think of it, there have been some stories about Mr. Brant being accused by some weird woman of pestering her."

"Pestering her how?"

"I don't know. They're only rumors anyway, I'm sure. A successful businessman like Mr. Brant, young and handsome in the bargain, and single now, he's bound to attract the attention of kooks. I thought maybe Wade Schultz had mentioned it to you." She picked up the lemon wedge that had been stuck on the rim of her glass and that she'd removed and placed on a napkin. Holding her hand to shield him from any wayward spurts of juice, she squeezed the wedge over her glass, then with an odd reluctance dropped it into what was left of her Coke, as if committing a body to the sea.

It struck Carver that maybe Nancy Quartermain didn't believe for a second that he was really a prospective home buyer. She'd seen him trying to pump Wade Schultz for information and become curious.

"How long have you been with Brant Development?" he asked.

Something in her eyes over the rim of her raised glass told him she knew that he knew. There was a slight smile on her lips as she lowered the glass. She'd play the game. "About three years. Usually I'm in the main office in town, but when we reach a certain stage of a project, I spend some of my time at the site."

"You like working for Brant?"

"Yes, quite a lot."

"Do you like Wade Schultz?" He leaned toward her. Soul-to-soul time. Two posers leveling. "I mean, really?"

She pursed her lips, thinking about it. "I don't like him much, I guess. He's arrogant."

"What about Gloria Bream? You like her?"

"She seems fine, what I've seen of her. She doesn't work for Brant Development, but she comes into the office now and then to see Mr. Brant, and sometimes on business."

"Business?"

"She's a sales agent for Red Feather Reality. They have the listings on some of the Brant properties. And they drive red company convertibles as a promotional gimmick. That was probably Gloria's car Mr. Brant was driving today." Her eyes were thoughtful as she sipped her Coke, buying time to formulate what she was about to say. "What's this actually about? Are you really a prospective home buyer?"

"Sure. We all have to live somewhere."

"Uh-huh." She grinned at him. "I won't mention it, you know, if you confide in me."

"There's nothing to confide about," Carver said.

"You wouldn't be with the police, would you?"

"Nope. If I were, would you be honest and tell me Brant might be the type to harass a woman?"

"Nope," she said, in the same tone he'd used.

Carver finished his beer. "I guess one 'nope' deserves another." He figured his conversation with Schultz, and possibly with Nancy Quartermain, would get back to Brant, so he might as well own up to the truth partway. "I'm not with the police, Nancy, but I am looking into the woman's complaint. So your opinion of Joel Brant is important to me."

"Well, I told you all I know about him," she said, wary now.

He could see that he'd lost her. She didn't want to say too much and have word get back to her boss.

He stood up. She noticed his cane for the first time, her eyes flicking up and down. No change of expression, though.

"We can keep this conversation just between us if you want," he told her.

"Sure," she said, "even if there's nothing to be confidential about."

"The truth is, we can't be certain of that until later," Carver admitted.

He thanked her for talking to him, then he moved toward the door to follow Wade Schultz out into the heat and glare of harsh reality.

After leaving the Egret Lounge, he drove past Brant Estates again. The red convertible was parked exactly where it had been this morning, in front of the middle display house. Brant had probably gone to lunch while Carver was at the library researching Portia's death.

Off in the distance, the brown pickup was parked behind a blue work van with aluminum ladders stacked on a rack on its roof, and Schultz was standing alongside a man in white overalls in the front yard of a framed-in house.

Instead of hanging around watching more construction, Carver drove to his office.

THERE WERE two messages on his machine. One was from a woman he'd never heard of who said she'd call back. The other was McGregor, telling him to return his call sooner than soon.

The machine indicated that McGregor had called at 2:02, just ten minutes ago. Carver sat down behind his desk, phoned police headquarters, and asked for the despicable lieutenant's extension.

"Listen, dickface," McGregor said, even before Carver had finished identifying himself, "your client's been at it again.

Marla Cloy phoned and said Joel Brant threatened her, pretended to shoot her with his finger."

"What time was this?" Carver asked.

"She said it happened about twelve-thirty this afternoon."

Terrific. That was when Carver was in the library and, as it turned out, should have been watching Brant.

"Any witnesses to this threat?" he asked McGregor.

"No. It happened on the parking lot of a McDonald's near the Cloy cunt's house. He drove up close to her and mimed bang, bang with his finger and thumb and scared the living shit out of her."

"Does Brant deny it?"

"Who knows? We're looking for him now."

"If there were no witnesses, and he denies it, you can't nail him for violating the restraining order."

"What are you, his goddamn attorney now?"

"No, it was just an observation."

"Well, observe this: I'm telling you to control your client, and I mean it."

"You've got it backward," Carver said. "I work for him. And like you pointed out, I'm not his attorney."

"Maybe you got something there. And maybe Brant oughta trade you in for one, after what happened today."

"You mean, what Marla Cloy *says* happened."

"Don't be such an asshole and make something so simple seem so complicated. Brant's got a thing for Marla Cloy. Can't help himself. Like bears with honey. Happens all the time. This guy's paying you, so you're making something else out of it."

"Maybe you're right," Carver admitted. "Thanks for telling me about the complaint."

He should have known better than to thank McGregor. That sort of thing infuriated the lieutenant.

"I'm not doing you a fucking favor, Carver. I'm warning you. This Brant jerkoff is your client, and if he keeps harassing

Marla Cloy and eventually winds up killing her, I see you as his accomplice."

"You're out of your mind."

"I'm not, but sometimes juries are. Once you're indicted and your ass is hauled into court, there's at least a chance you'll be convicted. Keep fucking with me, and I'll see you've gotta take that chance. And you look exactly like the kind of prick who's guilty until proven innocent."

"What about the big guy who did a job on my head? Have you made any progress finding out who he is? After all, you're a public servant and he beat up a taxpayer."

"*You* say he beat you up, just like Marla Cloy says Brant is threatening her." McGregor laughed and slammed down the receiver.

Carver slowly hung up the phone and thought about what McGregor had said. Maybe he was right and it was all really very simple. Brant was a closet psychosexual harasser, or even killer, who'd set his sights on Marla Cloy. Misogynists who raped and murdered looked and acted like other men. They were expert at leading outwardly normal lives that concealed their compulsions; sometimes the only clue was their model citizenship.

But something in his gut told Carver that McGregor was wrong about this one being simple. Even if Brant really was stalking Marla Cloy, it was complicated.

And Beth was wrong, too.

Despite her assumption that not everything in human affairs was understandable, he'd somehow work through the maze of deception and find out the truth. Discovering the truth was what he was about; he wouldn't—he couldn't—stop trying.

His headache was threatening to flare up. He gulped down one of Dr. Woosman's pills without water. Then he picked up the phone again and called Joel Brant's cellular number.

24

"I WANTED to talk to you," Brant said in an angry voice. "The police were just here to see me."

"Where's here?" Carver asked.

"Brant Estates. The subdivision I'm building. I was turning from the subdivision main drive onto the highway, on my way to see you, when you called."

"I heard that—"

"Wait!" Brant interrupted. "Cellular phones can be eavesdropped on by anyone with a scanner. It sounds paranoid, but the way things have been going lately . . ."

"Do you want to come the rest of the way to my office and talk?"

Brant said that he did, then hung up.

FIFTEEN MINUTES later Brant entered the office looking more worried than mad. He was again handsome in his chinos and sport jacket, his white shirt and paisley tie, a boyish operator on the way up. But there were faint circles beneath his innocent blue eyes, and a weariness showed on him like a thin layer of dust.

"She accused me again, Carver," he said, not bothering to sit down. It was "Carver" again, not "Fred."

Carver leaned far back in his swivel chair until he was on the very edge of teetering, keeping his balance with his fingertips on the desk. "I know. I've talked to the police."

"She said I threatened her in the lot of a McDonald's restaurant, a place I've never even been to. That I leered at her and pretended I was shooting her with my finger." Brant's expression suggested a bug had just flown into his mouth. "Hell, I'm not sure I even know how to leer. The police came to Brant Estates and talked to me where my employees and the subcontractors could see what was happening. Some of the buyers, too." He brushed back his wavy dark hair with his hand in a quick, nervous gesture. "This is no damned good for my reputation, Carver, or for business. In my case, they're one and the same."

"How did the police treat you?"

"Like a criminal. As if I'd already killed Marla Cloy, who I admit I'm feeling more and more like killing."

"But they didn't take you in."

"Only because they can't come up with a witness at McDonald's who saw either me or Marla Cloy there. Which is easy for me to understand, having been somewhere else at the time of the supposed attack."

"Where were you?" Carver asked.

"Eating lunch at Belle's Cafeteria in downtown Del Moray."

Carver knew the place, a large and impersonal restaurant without any sort of table service. It did a booming lunch business; it was doubtful anyone would recall Brant as one of hundreds in a cafeteria line. "Were you alone?" he asked.

"Of course," Brant said. "If I hadn't been alone, she wouldn't have accused me. She knows nobody there will remember me. And she knows nobody at McDonald's will be able to swear that neither of us *wasn't* there! She must be watching me, following me, making sure I can't supply an alibi for the times she accuses me. And I tell you, it's convincing the police I'm really stalking her." He dragged a pack of Camels from his pocket. "I gotta light up. You mind?"

"Go ahead." Carver watched him go through the ritual of flame to tobacco to smoke to a measure of calm that was bought with addiction.

Brant held the smoldering cigarette up and stared at it as if it had saved his life.

"Do you own a gun?" Carver asked, taking his hands away from the desk and dropping forward in his chair.

"The police asked me that. The answer is no. But I'm considering getting one."

"Wouldn't be wise."

"Maybe not. But who knows what Marla Cloy has in mind? She might be setting me up so she can kill me and make it look like self-defense. If one of us has to die, Carver, it's going to be her!"

More talk of guns and killing. Only talk, Carver hoped. "You're getting into dangerous territory, thinking like that."

"No, no—I'm goddamned *in* dangerous territory already, because I was pushed there." He drew on the cigarette again; a lifeline burning like a fuse.

Convincing, Carver thought. If Brant was actually stalking Marla Cloy, he was doing a great job of enlisting Carver as a witness to his innocence and persecution. A victim of an evil woman's wiles, unable to stem the tide of political correctness and approaching catastrophe. Usually it was the woman pinned helpless by official apathy while the crushing sphere of unfair destiny rolled toward her. But it was possible to put a reverse spin on the thing: *What do you mean, no one would help her? No one would help me!*

"The police gave me a stern warning. They're within an inch of arresting me. Charging me with violating the restraining order. What do you think I should do, Carver?"

Carver smiled. "Hire a private investigator."

Brant stared at him for a long time, then released a long breath and slumped down in the chair by the desk. He killed his half-smoked cigarette in the sea-shell ashtray on the desk corner.

"Yeah, I'm sorry," he said resignedly, staring at the floor. "I guess there are limits to what can be done when a crazy woman is out to get somebody."

"There are limits to what the crazy woman can do, too," Carver said. "She can't manufacture witnesses any easier than you can."

"But she can establish a record of circumstantial evidence. There's no way for me to establish a record of *not* harassing her."

Carver said, "Gloria Bream."

Brant looked at him, frowning. "What? How do you know about Gloria?"

"The information turned up when I was asking questions. You and this Gloria Bream are supposed to be close. I suggest you make it a point to spend a lot of time with her. When you're with someone else and can prove it, you can't be harassing Marla Cloy."

Brant stared at the floor again. He had his hands cupped over his knees and was squeezing hard. "My wife hasn't been dead long enough, Carver."

"I understand, but maybe you shouldn't be alone at night."

A helpless, shadowy smile crossed Brant's face. "I'm not alone, in a way. It's true I'm involved with Gloria, but I can't get Portia out of my thoughts. I wake up sometimes at night thinking she's lying beside me. *Knowing* it." He stared at Carver in a kind of beseeching agony. "I mean, I can hear her breathing there in the dark."

"Ghosts," Carver said. "We all have ghosts. Sometimes in a crowd I think I hear my son calling me. For an instant the fact of his death isn't real, and I turn around and expect to see him. Then I remember, and it falls on me like a wall."

"I'm sorry," Brant said. "How long has he been dead?"

"Almost five years."

Brant shook his head slowly from side to side. "And it hasn't stopped for you yet."

"Maybe it never will," Carver said. "I've learned to accommodate it."

Brant released his grip on his kneecaps and stood up. "I suppose that's the best we can hope for."

"Think about Gloria Bream. About my advice."

"Sure." Brant moved toward the door. "Incidentally," he said, "I checked and I'm sure Marla Cloy never wrote anything about Brant Development."

"I've checked way beyond that," Carver said, "and I haven't found any connection at all between you and Marla."

"Because there isn't any."

"I'll keep searching."

"Sure," Brant said again. "I can tell that about you, but I'm getting more and more afraid it isn't going to help." He bowed his head and closed his eyes for a few seconds, almost as if offering up a silent prayer, appealing to a power infinitely higher than Carver. Then he went out, leaving behind him a haze of smoke in the sunlight near the ceiling, and the acrid smell of the snuffed-out cigarette.

Carver stared for a long time at the closed door. Right now Brant seemed innocent. And even if he was the real stalker, he'd stay away from Marla for a while after the McDonald's incident.

Carver decided to take up the watch on Marla again, beginning that evening. In the meantime, he wanted to see Beth. Wanted very much to see her. He understood why at times they lay desperately locked together so far into the night.

It wasn't always love and lust.

Each of them had ghosts to hold at bay.

25

"I'VE BEEN to the library," Beth said when Carver had parked the car and limped toward the cottage. She was sitting in the shade on the porch, her Toshiba computer glowing in her lap. Carver didn't blame it.

"So have I," he said, taking the porch steps and lowering himself into the webbed lounger next to her aluminum-framed chair. "In the middle of the afternoon."

"I went there not long after you left here this morning," she said. "Had to go out for crackers anyway."

He didn't know if she was kidding, so he kept quiet.

"We should have coordinated our efforts," she said. "I expect you were there for the same reason I was."

"Reference room?"

"Right. To check the *Gazette-Dispatch* back issues on the Brant accident."

He nodded.

"Duplication of effort," she said.

"We screwed up, all right," Carver said, squinting out at the sun glancing off the calm sea. "One of us should have been on Marla or Brant. She claimed Brant threatened her again. This time at a McDonald's near her house, at the same time I was looking at microfilm."

"Any witnesses?"

"Of course not. It probably didn't happen."

"You're coming around to my way of thinking, Fred. Marla Cloy might not be a typical harassed female, though I confess I can't quite figure out her game."

Carver didn't remind her that that originally had been his approach to the case, the reason Joel Brant had hired him. Then he'd drifted away from that theory; maybe Brant was using him and in a clever double game really *was* a threat to Marla. It might be either way. And now . . . he didn't know.

It was complicated and confusing, just as Beth predicted it would be. He didn't remind her of that, either. It was best not to push a pregnant woman who'd driven miles for crackers.

"The accident must have been terrible for Brant," she said. "The decapitation, the fact that he was driving and had alcohol in his bloodstream. It might have been enough to unhinge him mentally. Make him unpredictable."

Carver stared at her. "Good Lord, are we switching positions on this again?"

"I never had a firm position," she said.

"Oh? I thought yours was the feminist position."

"You don't understand. You're as much a feminist as I am, Fred."

That surprised him.

"You're a humanist," she explained. "That's somebody who believes in a life directed toward the well-being of other people. You might not know it, but that's why you run around like a combination bloodhound and pit bull, searching out truths that will provide the gift of justice."

"I thought it was my fee," he said.

"One reason, anyway. A humanist is automatically a feminist. A feminist isn't automatically a humanist, but should be." She switched off her computer and closed its lid, then carefully set it down on the plank floor beside her chair. "There's something else I don't have a firm position on."

He knew what she was going to say, and dreaded hearing it. Time was nudging them into a corner, forcing a decision before it was too late. You delayed in some things and you belonged to fate.

"I went into Del Moray for another reason," she said. "I made an appointment for next week at an abortion clinic."

A coldness moved through him. "I thought you said you were undecided."

"I am. But you can't just walk in and have the procedure the same day. The only other clinic in Del Moray closed last year after threats and demonstrations by pro-lifers. Somebody threw a Molotov cocktail through a window. It didn't ignite, but it injured one of the patients. The doctors there called it quits, so there's a long waiting list of patients."

"Jesus!" Carver said.

"They say He has something to do with it. How do you feel about this, lover?"

He was numb. "I'm not sure. I can't deny you're the one carrying the baby, so it's your decision."

"I know that. But I don't want to make it without you."

He looked over at her and smiled. "Should I force you to carry a child to term? Is that really an option for me?"

"No," she admitted. "I just want you to know I don't take it lightly. The people demonstrating in front of the clinics . . . I see their point, Fred. At least the ones who are nonviolent. Don't agree with it, but I sure see it."

"You're saying this is a close call."

"Yes. And I'm sure it is for most women. Remember my telling you about the breech birth the last time I was pregnant? About Roberto's son strangling on the umbilical cord?"

"I remember."

"I was secretly glad, Fred. I didn't want to bring a child into that world of drugs and cheap money and violence. The illicit drug business itself seduces and destroys people like a narcotic. Money's addictive. Money's a drug. In the recovery room afterward, I told the doctor I was glad the child died."

"Did you tell Roberto?"

"No. He wanted a son. Afterward, when he learned what I'd said, he wanted to kill me. Others intervened, and I went away for a long time. Eventually he swore he forgave me, but I don't think he ever really did."

"He didn't kill you," Carver said. "That's as much forgiveness as you could expect from Roberto Gomez."

"I don't often talk about those years. There's no point to it. But I remember my guilt and fear. I don't want to decide alone."

"I don't know if I can help you," Carver said.

"Maybe you can't. But I wanted you to know ahead of time I might abort. At least I've told you that. We're in it together."

Carver watched a sailboat far out in the sunny haze. "I don't know what to do," he said helplessly.

"Now you know how I feel, though," she said. "I wanted you to understand."

He reached over and held her hand, watching sunlight glimmer and move like inexorable time over the ocean. The waves foamed higher and higher on the beach as the tide slowly rose, reminding of things gestating, always. Life was as persistent as death.

The cordless phone chirped alongside her chair and her hand jumped beneath his. She answered the phone, then gave it to Carver.

Desoto.

"A few pieces of news, *amigo*."

"Good or bad?"

"It's not that simple. What do you think this is, Disney World? The big man who beat up on you is a giant will-o'-the wisp, which in itself is odd. But he might be Achilles Jones, out of Georgia. Not much is known about him even by the Georgia law, other than that he rides a big Harley motorcycle and is rumored to have killed people. They say he has some sort of mental deficiency, the IQ of a child. People hire him for things like beating up other people, and he no doubt gets his money in other ways, but he has no police record. No one seems to know where he came from. One day he was just there. Georgia State Patrol heard about him, even pursued him once after he beat a truck driver almost to death in a motel restaurant. That's one of the places they got his name and description, and an idea he wasn't quite right in the head. He's right in the body, though. The driver he beat up used to be an NFL lineman. So Jones is genuinely tough even in his weight class. Nature compensates, I guess."

"Was he registered at the motel?" Carver asked.

"Yes. As Achilles Jones of Atlanta. They never heard of him there, though. Handwriting like a child's, and he spelled it 'Atlantis.' The address he put down doesn't exist. He's probably a thug-for-hire without roots. There are freelancers like that, though usually not so conspicuous. We're checking to see if anyone like him was sprung from a mental institution."

"I doubt if they rode Harleys in Atlantis. If there really was an Atlantis. If there really is an Achilles Jones."

"Slow progress, I admit."

"Hardly progress at all. We know nothing about the giant in my office except who he might be pretending to be."

"It's more than we knew before."

"Hardly qualifies as news, though," Carver said. "What's your other scoop?"

"A body was found a few hours ago in a rental car in a parking lot downtown. Little guy dressed like a Wall Street banker down on his luck. At first the lot attendant thought he was sleeping, then he saw that his head was turned the wrong way so he was staring backward. His neck was broken."

Carver felt his breath turn icy in his chest. "Charley Spotto," he said.

"That's right. Did you know him?"

Carver told him he did know Spotto, and told him how.

"You're a strong swimmer, *amigo*," Desoto said, "but you're in shark-infested waters."

"Achilles Jones is the shark that killed Spotto," Carver said.

"Maybe. He's number one on our list right now. I'm afraid it's not a very long list. We need to keep each other informed on this matter."

"Don't worry about that from this end," Carver said. "I'm the one with the most to lose."

After hanging up, he told Beth what Desoto had said, saving news of Spotto's death until last.

She looked at him with a kind of deep sadness in her dark eyes. He wondered if she was weighing his world as she had Roberto Gomez's.

Then she stood up. "I'm going inside and get a beer, Fred. You want one?"

He told her yes. She hardly ever drank beer.

The screen door slammed behind her and he stared out at the ocean. Life and death.

26

IN BETH'S car again, Carver parked on Jacaranda Lane.

Less than an hour later, Marla emerged from her house. She was wearing dark slacks and a lacy white blouse that criss-crossed in some way in front and was tied at the small of her back. Her oversize purse was slung securely across her body by its thick strap and she was carrying a plaid tote bag.

She passed out of sight for a moment while she went to her car in the driveway. Carver could see the rear of the little Toyota. Its exhaust pipe vibrated and sent out a brief puff of oily black smoke as the engine was started.

Feeling rather foolish, he slouched down out of sight as the Toyota began to move. Marla would be looking over her shoulder as she backed the car from her driveway, increasing the odds that she might see him. And though she would probably drive toward busy and accessible Shell Avenue, there was the possibility she'd point the Toyota in Carver's direction and pass him where he sat parked by one of the frazzled-looking palm trees that lined the block like tired sentries.

His bad leg didn't want to fit beneath the dashboard, so he had to edge over at an awkward angle and bend his neck uncomfortably. Looking up at palm fronds silhouetted jaggedly against the cloudless sky, he listened to the sound of the Toyota's clattering engine.

When he was sure it was moving away from him, he sat up straight, started the LeBaron, and followed as he rubbed the back of his neck.

Marla turned right on Shell and drove past the McDonald's where she claimed she'd last been threatened by Joel Brant. A few blocks down Shell, she stopped at the Good Times Liquor Emporium, went inside after locking her car securely, and soon came out carrying what could only be a brown-bagged bottle.

Carver had brought along his Minolta 35-millimeter camera with a 200-millimeter zoom lens. If Marla claimed to have been elsewhere at the time he was following her, he wanted a photographic record to prove she was lying. The photos, along with his statement and statements from the liquor store clerk and from wherever else she might stop, should accomplish that. He hurriedly focused the lens and got two quick shots of her with the liquor store in the background as she was walking toward her car. Then he did his unseemly scooting low in the seat again, his stiff leg angled beneath the dashboard and his neck and the left side of his head crammed against the door, as she backed out of her parking slot in front of the liquor store. He was getting too old for these kinds of contortions, and he found himself wondering briefly what he'd do when and if he no longer practiced his arcane trade.

He didn't think Marla would take the bottle home, and he was right. A few seconds later he was following her again through the brisk traffic on Shell, in the same direction she'd been driving.

Within ten minutes, he knew where she was going.

He watched the Toyota's brake lights flare as she parked on Fourteenth Street across from Willa Krull's apartment.

He eased the LeBaron to the curb half a block away, where he had a clear view but wouldn't be noticeable.

Carrying the plaid tote, possibly now containing the brown bag, Marla crossed the street and walked beneath the rusty iron trellis of bedraggled roses. She was halfway around the dry pond and fountain with its defaced swordfish statuary when Willa Krull came out of the building to meet her. Willa had on white shorts, revealing spindly legs, and a pink T-shirt yanked tight at the waist and knotted elaborately on her thin right hip.

The two women stood alongside the ruined pond talking for a few minutes, still-life figures in the genteel decay of the front courtyard. Then Marla reached into the plaid tote bag and handed Willa a large envelope like the one she'd given her in the hotel lounge the first time Carver had seen them together. Another article to be copyedited and word processed?

Marla reached into the bag again and lifted out what appeared to be a wine bottle. She gave it to Willa, and both women laughed and chatted a while longer. Carver used the camera to get a shot of them, then backed up the lens to include more of the building to establish locale.

He thought they'd part there by the dysfunctional fountain and that would be that, but a few minutes later Marla followed Willa into the building.

He could see the windows of Willa's apartment from where he was parked, but the lowering evening sun reflected off them in a golden glare that made it impossible to see inside.

More waiting. It was what his line of work was mostly about.

He switched on the radio and listened to an all-talk station while he sat watching the apartment building. A listener called in and claimed that the evidence indicated the same person was behind the J.F.K. and Robert Kennedy and Martin Luther

King assassinations, and that person was Charles Manson. It was something Carver had never considered.

In the soft light of dusk, Willa Krull and Marla came out of the building together. Marla no longer had the wine bottle or plaid tote bag, or else they were stuffed down inside her big purse. She and Willa stood talking again almost where they had stood before. Willa raised a hand slowly, tentatively touching her mousy brown hair above her ear, as if reassuring herself of an elaborate and delicate bouffant that had the fragility of meringue.

Marla said something to her that made her smile and duck her head. She turned and started to move away, but Marla reached out and touched her shoulder, stopping her and drawing her back without any discernible physical effort. Then she kissed her swiftly but firmly on the mouth.

Willa pulled away again, twisting her body with unexpected grace and dexterity, but she was laughing. Marla said something else to her, then turned and walked beneath the rose trellis and toward the street and her car. She paused once, looked back, and waved to Willa.

Willa stood motionless with her hands at her sides, watching Marla as she crossed Fourteenth Street, climbed into the little Toyota, then drove away.

Carver stayed where he was. He couldn't follow Marla without driving past Willa and risking being recognized by her.

He waited a few minutes after Marla's car had disappeared. Willa still hadn't moved.

Finally he started the LeBaron and backed it into a driveway, then emerged to aim the gleaming white hood in the opposite direction, away from the apartment building.

As he drove away he caught a glimpse of Willa in the outside mirror, still standing motionless by the dry fountain in the amorphous shadows of dusk.

27

"I DON'T see what it changes," Beth said beside him in bed that night. They were both lying on their backs, contemplating the day's events as the warm breeze from the window played over them.

"Marla's apparently a lesbian," Carver said.

"Maybe they're only good friends and were being affectionate."

"No, it wasn't that kind of kiss."

"That bothers you?"

"It surprises me."

Carver stared into the darkness. He'd never been able to bring himself to be judgmental about people's sexual orientations. As long as everything was consensual and no children or animals were involved, it was all right with him. If any of it was evil and harmful to society, as the fervently devout proclaimed, it was probably a lesser evil than a society that policed its bedrooms.

"Why's it surprise you, Fred?"

"I'm not sure. I think because if Marla is being stalked by Brant, I'd assumed it evolved out of some form of sexual attraction. Something she must have done, some kind of behavior that maybe even she wasn't aware of that turned him on to her. That seems less likely if she isn't interested in men."

He heard Beth give a low chuckle. "You mean if he's after her to kill her, it's partly her fault?"

"No, I wasn't talking about blame. It's just that sexual attraction is a two-way current." He knew what Beth was thinking, knew he was only getting more and more entangled in his inadequate male rhetoric. But damn it, he didn't mean to blame the victim, didn't want to sound like the male chauvinist pig Beth had recently told him he wasn't. It was just that if a woman was attractive to men, it was sometimes because she was attracted *to* men. It was a subtle but powerful electricity that arced between people. He was only talking about odds, but it was impossible sometimes not to be misunderstood.

Beth said, "Oink."

"Meant for me, I suppose," Carver said glumly.

She touched his bare arm, leaving her hand there. "OK, I'm being too rough on you, Fred. I told you before, you're actually a feminist, and I meant it. Though you do have lapses. But even if Marla's sexual orientation might somehow change Brant's motive—or Marla's, considering she might have been trying to lure him into a trap because of some sort of black-widow complex—it still doesn't get us any closer to knowing who's the genuine stalker. For that matter, Marla might be bisexual. And have you thought about Gloria Bream?"

"Thought what about her? You mean her sexual orientation?"

"No. I guess I'm not really sure what I mean."

The effects of pregnancy, Carver figured. "The other woman, Willa Krull, told me she was a rape survivor."

"Which sort of illustrates my point about Joel and Marla,"

|175|

Beth said. "I doubt if the rapist asked Willa about her sexual preference before attacking her."

"Rape isn't easy for any woman, but might it leave more of a mental scar in a lesbian or bisexual?"

Beth thought about it for a few seconds. "I don't know. It's an interesting question. Here's another one. Rape's an especially serious physical assault. Would it have left more of a scar in you if the person who beat you up in your office had been a woman?"

"Yes," Carver said. It hadn't required a lot of thought.

"Men," Beth said. "They're wired different from women."

He scooted sideways on the mattress and kissed her cheek. "Thank God for that."

With his lips still against her flesh, he felt her smile.

"Finally, Fred, we agree."

IT HAD rained in the early morning hours, and the sun broke through hot and brilliant enough to cause steam to rise from the damp ground. After a breakfast of scrambled eggs, bacon, and coffee, Carver drove into Del Moray with the film containing the shots of Marla, dropping it off where he could get it developed and printed by noon.

Marla apparently hadn't told McGregor she was bi or lesbian, though in a case like hers it might be considered pertinent. Carver decided he wouldn't mention it to McGregor, either. McGregor seldom passed up opportunities for prejudice and persecution. In fact, he valued them like unexpected trinkets found on the beach.

At 11:30 Carver picked up the prints and sat in his car outside the lab to study them. He'd gotten a good, clear shot of Marla outside the liquor store. Foliage concealed her face in one of the shots taken when she was standing with Willa in front of the apartment building on Fourteenth Street, but the second shot showed both women's faces. Marla's expression was amused, her lips twisted in a half-smile as she spoke, while Willa seemed to be listening with an intentness that bordered on the religious.

Carver ate lunch at Poco's taco stand on Magellan, then smoked a cigar and read the paper until almost two o'clock, when he thought some of the bars on Victor Street might be open. There weren't that many gay or lesbian hangouts in Del Moray, only the three or four on Victor, and one that was more upscale on the east side of town. It shouldn't take long to check them out and perhaps discover more about Marla.

He was driving toward Victor when he noticed a motorcycle in his rearview mirror. No sooner had he seen it than it turned right onto a cross street. It had been a block behind him, yet there was something about cycle and rider that had held his gaze and caused a spur of fear and rage to dig into his stomach.

Probably nerves, he decided, but he realized with regret that he'd left the Colt beneath his underwear in his dresser drawer.

M O S T of the bars on Victor did their main business in the evenings, and only two of them were open. The first one had a lunch trade and was still serving. Neither the bartender nor the waitress recognized Marla or Willa when Carver showed them the photographs.

Halfway down the block he entered the other open bar, which had a red-and-blue neon sign out front that identified it as Spunky's. It was decorated in a way that reminded Carver of a funeral parlor with a dance floor. There were a few plush velvet chairs at round marble tables, and there were two small sofas as centers for a cluster of small wing chairs and coffee tables. The bar was polished walnut. Leaded-glass doors sheltered the shelves of bottles behind it. Near the back of Spunky's was a slightly raised stage containing a large amplifier, a microphone, and a set of drums. The sign behind the stage advertised a group called the Bobbitts. Two women dressed in business clothes were seated at one of the marble tables, discussing papers spread before them. Another woman sat on a stool at the bar, drinking coffee. The bartender was an attractive woman wearing no makeup and with her sleek black hair pulled back and woven in a braid that reached to her waist. With the addition of Carver, an unknowing customer walking in might think it was a straight bar.

Then he noticed two restroom doors close together along the back wall. One was labeled GODDESSES. So was the other.

The braided bartender looked at him and smiled a barkeep's amiable greeting.

Carver ordered a Budweiser. No one seemed to wonder or care if he knew that men weren't the usual run of customer in Spunky's.

The bartender, who was quite beautiful close up and was possibly a Native American, set his beer mug on a coaster. She was wearing a black vest over a white blouse. There was a red AIDS ribbon pinned in a brilliant little V on the vest.

Carver reached into his sport-coat pocket and withdrew the photos of Marla alone in front of the liquor store and with Willa outside the apartment. He placed them on the bar so they were right side up to the bartender.

"Do you recognize either of these women?" he asked.

Her gaze traveled to his cane, hooked over the edge of the bar, then to his face. "Are you police?"

"No."

"We don't usually give out information about our customers."

"Then these two are your customers?"

She grinned with strong white teeth. "You're not very slick," she said.

"You should see me when I'm trying to be."

She laughed and said, "Is this where I ask you for money in exchange for information?"

"Only if your information's for sale."

"Why do you want to know about these two?" She waved a hand above the photographs as if she were a conjurer trying to make the two-dimensional subjects spring to life.

"I'm trying to locate them to tell them they've won the lottery."

"I'm not very slick, either," she said, pulling the old Carver leg. "I don't sell information about people who come in here. But on the other hand, I wouldn't want to see anybody miss out on millions in lottery money. Dream of a lifetime." She tapped a clear-lacquered fingernail on the photograph of Marla. "The other woman I don't recognize, but that one's been in here several times."

"Lately?"

"Now you mention it, no. I haven't seen her for about a month."

"What do you remember about her?"

"Not much. She sits and drinks, mostly turns away any advances by other customers."

"That's what somebody told me about her in a straight bar."

"I said 'mostly.' She's gotten friendly and left with someone at least once that I can recall. A woman I hadn't seen before. But they might have gone out mall crawling, for all I know. People come here mostly to drink, socialize, and listen to good music. It isn't like some of the other places on Victor."

Carver had an idea and unfolded the copy of Portia Brant's newspaper photo and spread it out on the bar. "What about her?"

"Never seen her."

"You sure?"

"I'd remember. I'm sure."

"Did the woman you recognized frequent any of the other bars on the block?"

"Probably. But I've been in most of them and don't remember seeing her anyplace other than here. I do recall seeing her over in that chair sitting with her eyes closed, her body swaying slightly with the music. Whenever somebody asked her to dance, though, she always refused. Maybe she's a little bit prissy, or maybe that's her act. You might try Lip Gloss, over on the east side. It's upscale and expensive, but she's been well dressed when she's been in here. I can picture her in Lip Gloss."

"Would you describe her as a lipstick lesbian?"

The bartender grinned. "My, my, aren't you informed? Yes, I'd say she fits the label." The grin got wider and whiter. "The connection you make between Lip Gloss and the expression 'lipstick lesbian' isn't quite accurate, though."

The woman drinking coffee a few bar stools away looked over at Carver. She was grinning, too. Carver wanted to get out of there.

"That's Marla in that photo," the woman said. She was in her forties, with short red hair. She had freckles even on her ears. "I can recognize her from here."

"Do you know her well?" Carver asked.

"Just talked to her a few times. She isn't very nice."

"Why do you say that?"

"She thinks her shit don't stink, is why."

The bartender smiled and shrugged at Carver.

"Know anything else about her?" Carver asked the redhead.

"No. Only that she isn't very nice. That's all I need to know about anybody."

"Seems a simple-enough philosophy," Carver said.

"It's one that works, anyway." She turned her attention back to her coffee cup, holding it with both hands as if it were a holy chalice and she feared harm might come to it.

Carver finished his beer, then tucked the photographs back into his pocket. He thanked the bartender and placed some bills on the bar, leaving a tip twice as generous as etiquette required.

"It's people like Marla that usually win the lottery," the red-head remarked bitterly as he was leaving.

28

A WAITRESS at Lip Gloss said she thought she recognized Marla, but not Willa Krull or Portia Brant, which left Carver still only 90 percent sure that Marla and Willa shared a romantic relationship.

There was no dance floor at Lip Gloss, and only soft, piped-in music that sounded vaguely Middle Eastern to Carver. Art Deco was the theme. In the corners were large, curved banquettes that looked as if they'd been bought when the Stork Club closed. There were Egyptian murals on the walls, and the bar was constructed of glass bricks with glimmers of light inside them. Centered on the ceiling was an ornate silver-and-crystal chandelier. Small silver candelabra sat in the center of each white-clothed table, echoes of the chandelier.

Carver walked over to the woman behind the bar, a petite blonde who was wearing brilliant red lipstick to exaggerate a cupid's-bow mouth and who looked like a 1930s Hollywood starlet.

"You look like Carole Lombard," he told her.

"Sometimes," she said, "I feel like Carole Lombard."

"I'm relieved," Carver said. "You're young and I was afraid you weren't going to know who she was."

"I like her old movies. She's sexy."

"Sure was."

"Is," she corrected. "Stars like that live forever through their films."

"That's what they say on the movie channel." He placed the photos on the bar's sleek gray surface. "Do you know any of these women?"

"That one used to come in here occasionally." She pointed to Marla's photo. "She's pretty enough to be a star herself, isn't she?"

"She has a certain appeal," Carver admitted uncomfortably. He did still find himself drawn to Marla, despite her apparent sexual preference.

"I never saw the other women," the bartender said.

"How long's it been since you've seen Marla?"

"So that's her name. Probably a good one for movies. I guess a month or so. She was usually with other people. I got the impression she was a journalist or something, doing interviews. I mean, the customers here are mostly from the east side of town and are pretty wealthy. We see more than a few designer originals in here on Saturday nights. Marla was usually stylishly dressed in a kind of funky way, but it was easy to tell her clothes weren't expensive. You develop an eye for that kind of thing working in a place like this."

"The other people she was with, were they usually women?"

The bartender smiled her starlet's smile. "Always. Sometimes we get men in here, but they're usually cops." She winked.

Carver wondered if she assumed he was with the police or had some kind of official authority. He decided not to ask.

"I'm not a vice cop," he said, "so I'm not clear on some things. Does Del Moray have a large lesbian or bisexual population?"

"Who knows for sure? It's large enough to keep us in business, along with a few other places across town on Victor. But there are plenty of women who are lesbian or bi and stay in the closet and never socialize, or who travel in circles too discreet for public places."

"Your clientele would be especially discreet, I suppose, among those who do frequent public places."

"Ha! People with their kind of money don't have to care as much as other folks about reputation or image. They don't have jobs to lose, and usually they have similar friends with plenty of money and time to get into bizarre stuff with them."

"What kind of bizarre stuff?"

"The kind straight people engage in, only with variation. Our customers aren't sex fiends, it's just that they're rich. You know, the devil and idle hands, idle this, idle that."

Carver said he knew, then ordered a beer. It was too early for happy hour and he was the only customer, so he didn't feel at all out of place.

"You a Marlins fan?" the bartender asked.

He said that he was, and she told him she enjoyed working in an upscale lounge, but that it wasn't the kind of place that featured a TV, and she missed seeing televised ball games and discussing them with the customers. He wondered if she was lesbian or bi herself, or if this was just a job to her. That was something else he decided not to ask.

It seemed odd to be talking baseball with Carole Lombard, but that's what he did until he finished his beer and went back outside into the heat and the straight world.

. . .

HE DROVE into Orlando and parked outside police headquarters on Hughey a little after five. Desoto didn't seem surprised to see him.

"I suppose you have questions," he said. He was seated behind his desk, listening to a Spanish music station as usual
while he did the paperwork that converted the chaos of crime
into the order of fact and law, so that an illusion of understanding was created and it could be dealt with like any other service
or commodity.

"I have information, too," Carver said. He told Desoto about
Marla and Willa Krull's probable sexual involvement.

"I don't know what that changes," Desoto said.

"That's what Beth said. I don't know, either, but maybe it
changes something."

"Hmm," Desoto said, and folded his hands on the desk, his
rings and gold cuff links sending light dancing over the walls.
Sometimes Carver wondered if he kept the office so bright
mainly so he could enjoy his jewelry, sitting there shooting his
cuffs and putting it all on display. No other cop Carver knew
dressed like Desoto, suave and handsome enough to be in the
movies with Carole Lombard.

"Anything fresh on Charley Spotto's murder?" Carver
asked.

"Nothing resembling a clue, *amigo*. Except that his neck
was broken by a powerful twisting motion, as if his head had
been gripped and rotated like a cap being unscrewed on a bottle. That's the M.E.'s description, not mine."

"He should write mysteries, the M.E."

"Speaking of mysteries, your giant attacker is still one. No
data bank anywhere in the country seems to contain anything
on an Achilles Jones. It's an a.k.a., no doubt, though he doesn't
seem the sort to be interested in Greek legend. It's possible,

| 1 8 5 |

even if unlikely, that nobody has anything on him. It happens, even in the era of the information highway. This guy might have avoided any priors and recently jockeyed his Harley here from Alaska or someplace."

"Or Atlantis," Carver said.

"Your friend in Miami, Lloyd Van Meter, is plenty pissed about Spotto being killed. He's leaning on us for action."

"He's probably frustrated. He has contacts outside the regular lanes of law enforcement, and apparently he's had the same luck as you when it comes to finding anything on the goon who worked me over." Carver thought about mentioning to Desoto that he'd glimpsed a huge motorcycle rider in his rearview mirror, but decided against it. There was probably nothing to it other than imagination and the fear that had been instilled in him when he was beaten. It would pass with time, like the pain in his ribs and his occasional headaches. "Are there any lesbian hangouts around Marla Cloy's old apartment on Graystone?" he asked.

"Sure. The corner of Graystone and Zella. Place called Lari's. Gays hang out there, too. Rough trade. It's kind of a dive. We get peace disturbance calls there every month or so. Nothing serious, just misunderstandings that turn into assaults." Desoto unclasped his hands and rested his elbows on the desk, releasing more shimmers of light. "Have you told McGregor about any of this?"

"Not yet. Maybe not ever."

Desoto rubbed his chin, thinking it over. "Wise choice," he said. "What's his take on the assault in your office? He come up with any information?"

"He'd probably thank the guy who beat me, if he could find him. Which he can't, because he's not looking very hard if at all. His latest slant is to view me as a possible accomplice if Brant actually kills Marla Cloy."

Carver was hoping Desoto would scoff at the idea, but he merely rubbed his chin again. Not very reassuring.

Someone knocked, then a sergeant Carver didn't recognize entered Desoto's office carrying a file folder beneath his arm and holding a plastic bag containing a knife. His uniform was impeccable and he wore an expression that suggested his stomach was upset and he was irritated.

"Crime marches on," Desoto said with a smile.

Carver stood up and thanked him for his help, then left him to busy himself with his paperwork and whatever grief the sergeant had brought.

Before returning to Del Moray, he decided to drive over to Lari's and see if Marla or Willa had been there. Their meeting that Carver had observed in the Holiday Inn lounge in Del Moray had carried no hint of romantic entanglement, and Willa had certainly been hesitant about any further public physical contact by the fountain outside her apartment building. It was possible that Willa, a religious woman whose sexual nature would almost certainly cause conflict and secrecy, would meet with Marla more openly here in a different city, where it was unlikely anyone would see them together and guess their relationship.

LARI'S WAS a dive that worked hard to look like one and capitalize on an outcast atmosphere. The tables were wooden and scarred, as was the long bar with its thick brass foot rail. The bar stools were red vinyl, some of them patched with black tape. An all-female band was milling about on a small stage toward the back, setting up sound equipment and tuning their instruments. There were half a dozen women at tables, singly and in pairs. Some of them cultivated the dyke look and wore items of male clothing or black shirts and studded jeans with black leather accoutrements. No one paid any attention to Carver except for one of three men seated at the bar. They all wore black T-shirts and boots and sported tattoos on their arms. The shirts were lettered WANDERBEASTS across the back. The man on the end glanced over at Carver with naked speculation in his eyes.

Carver fixed him with a firm, unreceptive look and clomped with his cane across the plank floor to where a male bartender with spiked brown hair and a painted-on black handlebar mustache was working a pencil on a clipboard.

Carver sat on a stool near him and waited. He noticed that the rest-room doors in Lari's had unmistakable male and female symbols on them. Beneath the symbol with the skirt, "Womyn" was scrawled in what looked like lipstick. There was a flurry of amplified sound from the stage, a drum roll and a shrieking guitar slide, then silence.

"Be with you in a minute," the bartender said in what might have been a feminine voice. Carver looked more carefully and decided he couldn't be sure of the bartender's gender. "We're gonna be mighty busy in about an hour, and I gotta make sure we can handle the crowd."

"Do you usually get busy around seven o'clock in here?" Carver asked.

"Yeah, but it's gonna be super crowded tonight. It's that band." He motioned toward the women setting up to play. "The Wolverines. They're great and they're on the way up and they draw big."

The electric guitar *ploiiinged* as one of the Wolverines fine-tuned her instrument. They favored the grunge look and were all tall, gaunt, and attractive, with straight, long blond hair. They might have been sisters from Sweden with the same consumptive disease.

Carver waited until the bartender was finished tallying figures on the paper clipped to his board, then laid the photos of

Marla, Portia, and Willa on the bar. "I'm looking for my sister Marla," he said. "She been in lately?"

The bartender glanced at the photos, then looked at him with savvy gray eyes, a young man or woman who recognized lies by instinct as well as by experience.

On the other hand, considering Lari's reputation, and the fact that the bartender didn't know who Carver was or what he represented, cooperation might be the wisest course. At least, cooperation within a certain range.

"She's not my sister, actually," Carver admitted. "But she's a friend and I mean her no harm, and I'd like to find out if she came in here with either of these other women."

"Marla's moved out of town," the bartender said. "To Miami, I think."

Uh-huh. "What about the other women?"

"Don't know them," the bartender said. "And I haven't seen Marla for a long time. Every now and then she and Gail used to come in here and drink and dance."

Carver was silent for a few seconds while he put it together. "Gail Rogers?"

"Sure. If you knew Marla, I figured you had to know Gail."

"Yeah. It was rough, Gail dying in the fire."

The bartender was studying the clipboard again. "It was a sad thing. Marla seemed to go a little crazy after Gail died."

Ploiiing! went the guitar again, this time accompanied by a light tap on the drums. "Marla ever spend time in here with anyone other than Gail?" Carver asked.

"A few times. There was a guy she used to come in with now and then. After Gail's death."

"Then Marla goes both ways?"

"Both ways?"

"Is she bisexual?"

Wrong question, coming from a guy who was supposed to know Marla. The bartender was staring at him again with those savvy gray eyes. The outrageous mustache made him or her look like a riverboat gambler.

"You said she spent time in here with a man," Carver explained.

"We all spend time in here together, you might say. There's lots of music, laughter. You should drop by some night." There was amusement in the gray gaze now. The game had ended and mental doors had closed.

Carver smiled. "I might if I feel like dancing," he said, setting the tip of his cane on the floor and swiveling down off the stool.

As he made his way to the door, the Wolverine with the guitar played a short, experimental riff that trailed away to a feedback whine. The end Wanderbeast at the bar caught his eye in the mirror behind the shelved liquor bottles but this time didn't change expression.

That made Carver feel better, but he wasn't sure why.

29

"HOW'S YOUR appetite?" he asked.

Carver and Beth were having dinner at the Happy Lobster, sitting next to the long, curved window and looking out at the failing light that merged the Atlantic with the sky at the horizon.

"Voracious," she said. She was wearing a yellow dress cut low enough to display generous cleavage and had her hair styled something like Tina Turner's in a sultry MTV video. The effect wasn't lost on Carver. "I'm sick sometimes in the mornings," she said, "but by the time noon rolls around, I'm OK. In fact, physically I've never felt healthier."

"Nature's way of preparing you and your offspring for the ordeal of pregnancy and birth," Carver said.

She smiled. "You been watching *Wild Kingdom,* Fred?"

He supposed he had sounded as if he were talking about her and their child being ready as soon as possible to move on with the herd. There were predators out there. "Have you given it more thought?" he asked.

"I guess by 'it' you mean the baby."

He sipped his martini and waited.

"I've thought a lot about our predicament," she said. He didn't like her describing it as a predicament. "I still haven't made up my mind. It isn't easy." She'd ordered a martini, too, then remembered her condition and changed it to iced tea. She added sugar to the tea and stirred, gazing at the miniature whirlpool she was creating as she said, "Either way I come down on this, Fred, are we gonna be OK? The two of us?"

"I think so," he said, but he wasn't so sure. It was something he hadn't allowed himself to consider, and something he didn't want to talk about. The conversation was making him uncomfortable; he felt the tug of strong currents and he feared the rocks. He told Beth about showing the photographs at lesbian bars.

"It appears now that Marla may have had an affair with her neighbor, Gail Rogers," he concluded.

Beth stared out the window at the blue-gray vastness. "Do you suspect Marla had something to do with the fire in the apartment building that killed Gail?"

"I don't know what to suspect. Marla's still an enigma. That's the problem. The way I saw her behave with Willa, then the bartender at Lari's saying she'd frequented the place with Gail Rogers, pretty well substantiates that she's a lesbian, or possibly bisexual. But I don't know what it means; or if it's relevant to her charges of harassment. I don't even know if her sexual orientation makes it less or more likely that she'd concoct a story or have delusions about a man she doesn't even know stalking her."

"You can't be sure she and Joel Brant don't know each other in some way you haven't discovered."

"True. But I keep uncovering information, and none of it suggests any previous connection between the two. I can't piece together the facts in any meaningful way."

She tested her tea, then added more sugar. "Maybe there is no meaningful way to piece them together," she said.

"No, I don't accept that."

"Oh, I know. You *can't* accept it. Because you can't accept that it's a random world out there. And you won't change, Fred. In twenty or thirty years you'll be the old guy sitting in a corner of the retirement home trying to figure out Rubik's Cube."

He thought he knew where she was going. "If you're suggesting I'm not good parent material and time's running short, maybe you're right."

"No, I didn't mean that at all."

He didn't believe her. Her pregnancy, in the first trimester, was tearing at their relationship already, and he felt helpless to do anything about it.

"While you were cruising alternative-lifestyle bars," she said, "I busied myself researching Portia Brant."

Carver used his red plastic sword to spear the olive in his martini.

"I talked to a lot of people about her," Beth went on, "from sorority sisters to charity contacts. Almost everyone remarked on how beautiful she was."

"No surprise there." He popped the olive into his mouth and chewed.

"Portia had plenty of male friends and admirers, and a college love affair with a star basketball player who died in his senior year of heart failure stemming from heroin use. There were other problems no one seemed willing to talk about. Two of her college friends said it was impossible for Portia to have children because of what might have been a botched abortion."

"The basketball player's child?"

"No one could say for sure. Portia went on to earn her degree in economics, then wandered through Europe for a while. When she returned to the States, she went to work at Eaton and Booth in Atlanta. They're a financial consulting and money management firm. Five years ago, Eaton and Booth were defendants in an account-churning lawsuit. They won, but legal fees and unfavorable publicity put them out of business, leaving Portia unemployed. About that time she met and married Joel Brant, and they moved to Florida. Joel somewhat regretted that they could never have children, but acquaintances say they seemed happy together. They were considering adopting and had visited an agency just before the accident. Joel stayed busy building a successful business while she became involved in fund-raising for charities."

"That was mentioned in her obituary, but not what kind of charities."

"There doesn't seem to be a pattern there. I'm not questioning her motives, but it seemed to be mostly a social thing for her. She worked for everything from AIDS research to saving the manatee."

"Balm for a guilty conscience, maybe."

"Could be. Whatever her motives, we oughta be grateful for people like her. There was some hint that she might have been a heavy drinker. Not in public, though. A secret alcoholic, like more than a few beautiful women who only *seem* to have the world by the ass."

Carver smiled at her, reaching across the table to touch the back of her hand. "You're my uncontested authority on beautiful women."

"Martini's getting to you, Fred. Next you'll be wanting to skip dinner."

"A possibility."

"Fraid not tonight. Food's about the extent of my physical craving lately. I've been famished all day."

The waiter arrived with steaming plates. Trout amandine for Carver, and a heaping and jumbled platter of boiled crab legs for Beth. The waiter asked Carver if he wanted another martini. Carver observed Beth already busy devouring her food and said that no, iced tea would be better.

When the waiter had gone, Carver said, "I've been replaced by crab legs."

"It would be going too far to say that," she assured him as she chewed.

When the waiter returned with the tea, Beth reminded him that he owed her a baked potato.

AFTER DINNER and coffee, they drove back to the cottage and found a message from Joel Brant on the answering machine. He wanted Carver to call him as soon as possible, and he sounded upset.

"I've gotten a couple of phone calls," he said when Carver contacted him. "I say hello and nobody answers. I can hear somebody breathing on the line, then they hang up."

"How many calls?" Carver asked, trying to digest this new piece of information. "And when did you receive them?"

"One this afternoon on my car phone. Two early this evening in my condo, only about an hour apart."

"Doesn't seem like Marla's style," Carver said. "She'd be more likely to claim *you've* been calling *her*."

"That's what I've been telling myself. And wondering who else it could be. Do the police ever do something like that? Phone a suspect?"

Carver was surprised. "Why do you ask that?"

"I went with my attorney this afternoon to try to convince the police that I'm the one being harassed. It didn't help. That Lieutenant McGregor is a horrible human being."

"Everyone who knows him would agree. I can't see him badgering you with anonymous phone calls, though. It takes the fun out of it for him if his victims don't know he's responsible for their misery."

"He seems capable of anything. He told my attorney we were wasting his time, that he doesn't care who's stalking who, and that his job begins when one of the players dies. My lawyer's so pissed off he's going to complain to McGregor's superiors and write the news media."

"It won't help," Carver said. "McGregor will deny the conversation. He's better at covering his backside than anyone you'll ever meet. It's his way of life. What did your lawyer tell you when he calmed down?"

"He advised me to leave the state, or at least the city, for a while. But I can't do that—I've got my business to run, and this would be a devastating time to ignore it. Anyway, that might not solve anything with Marla Cloy, only delay it. I haven't felt so trapped since Portia died. I've got a psychotic killer after me, and she's the one everybody believes."

"Not everybody."

"Listen, Carver, can you talk to McGregor?"

"I have talked to him. He threatened to charge me as your accomplice after you kill Marla."

"God! I tell you, I'm getting desperate!" He sure sounded desperate. "I'm convinced that woman's got me set up and might kill me at any time under circumstances that make it appear to be self-defense. Maybe then the police will question her more extensively and realize she's crazy, but by then it'll be too late."

"It doesn't have to come to that. Have you ever heard of a woman named Gail Rogers?"

"No."

"What about Achilles Jones?"

"Hercules, did you say?"

"No. Achilles. He of the vulnerable heel."

"Only in high school literature class. Why do you ask?"

"It doesn't matter. This whole business is tangled with wires that don't connect."

"What doesn't connect are the wires in Marla Cloy's head. She's deranged and dangerous, and I'm her target."

"There seems to be nothing in the past to link you and Marla," Carver said, "but what about Marla and your late wife?"

"Portia?" Brant was incredulous, but Carver had seen a lot of incredulous husbands. "Believe me, this can't have anything to do with Portia."

"Are you sure you never heard her mention Marla's name? Or any of the other names that have come up during the past week?"

"I'm sure. Portia's got nothing to do with this. If you knew her, you'd understand that. Women like Portia and Marla Cloy have absolutely nothing in common. It's impossible."

Carver didn't differ with him. He knew Brant wouldn't be receptive to dissent. Dead wives often attained sainthood status as time wore the rough spots from memory.

"I'll talk to a friend with the Orlando police," he said. "He has no jurisdiction in this instance, but he might know someone on a state level who can help."

"Help how?" Brant asked.

"Maybe put some pressure on McGregor to act more like a public servant."

"McGregor seems too much like a public parasite for that to work."

Carver agreed with that assessment but didn't say so. He assured Brant he'd keep working on Marla Cloy, and that often seemingly unrelated pieces of information fell into place to reveal pattern and motive.

"Those kinds of neat explanations only happen in movies

and mystery novels, not in real life," Brant said dismally before hanging up.

Carver thought he sounded remarkably like Beth, who was standing leaning on the open refrigerator door, gazing longingly at a shelf containing only beer, pickles, and yogurt.

Carver silently bet on the pickles and won.

30

"YOU KNOW the problem," Desoto said when Carver met him for lunch the next day in Orlando. "McGregor's right when he says there's a limit to what he can do to prevent stalking from becoming assault or murder. It's something law enforcement hasn't quite figured out how to deal with yet." He talked as if it were an administrative problem and not life or death.

They were in Ruggeri's, an Italian restaurant on Washington, not far from Church Street Station. It was small and cool, with red carpeting, lots of dark wood, and more booths than tables. It lent itself to private conversations and was a place where deals were struck over the pasta. Carver and Desoto were in a booth next to a window, but it was stained glass and they could see only vague, shadowy forms of passersby. "What I had in mind," Carver said, "was possibly familiarizing someone with the situation who might put pressure on McGregor by at least making him aware he's being watched."

Desoto paused in artfully coiling spaghetti strands around his fork. "But what exactly is the situation? Is it Marla Cloy trying to set up Brant for whatever action, for whatever reason? Or is it a simple case of a closet psychopath stalking a defenseless woman?"

"I wish I knew for sure," Carver said. He sipped his draft Budweiser. He'd ordered only a stuffed mushroom appetizer and a side salad and was finished eating. The pungent aroma of spices and cooked garlic in Rugerri's was almost enough by itself to satisfy his hunger. He watched Desoto fork in spaghetti and wondered how he stayed in such excellent physical condition. Desoto dined freely on sumptuous main dishes, with copious quantities of wine and rich desserts, and as far as Carver knew didn't exercise beyond vigorously brushing lint from his elegant clothes.

Pols from City Hall frequented Ruggeri's. One of them Carver recognized, an assistant to the mayor, noticed Desoto and nodded to him. A police lieutenant in a city the size of Orlando did have some political pull. Outside the city limits, it might be a different proposition. But Desoto wasn't a man to view as a handsome clothes horse and underestimate. Carver had seen him in action; he was hardly flash without substance.

"I do know a circuit court judge who might drop a word in the right ear," Desoto said. "But if McGregor is made aware that the Del Moray department's handling of Marla Cloy's complaint is being watched and evaluated, he's going to guess why. He might come down even harder on you if and when he can."

"He'll do everything possible anyway," Carver said, "so I don't see making him mad as much of a risk."

Desoto sipped Chianti and smiled. "You often have a purely pragmatic way of looking at things, *amigo*."

"It works with McGregor. He's a pure pragmatist who'll always act in his own best interest."

"True. But he might think destroying you is worth considerable inconvenience. You're only a pragmatist some of the time. You have an integrity that at times causes you to act in ways McGregor sees as irrational. In fact, you sometimes act in accordance with your heart or your gut and *are* irrational, not to mention obsessive. People like you puzzle and irritate Mc-Gregor because you're unpredictable. For instance, your client is Joel Brant, but you don't discount the possibility he might actually be stalking Marla Cloy just as she claims. It's inconceivable to McGregor that you might be genuinely concerned about Marla Cloy's fate as well as Brant's, because she's not paying you. Yet you sometimes appear to act in her behalf. He sees altruism as a dangerous imponderable."

"He's right about that," Carver said.

Desoto finished his spaghetti, sipped some more wine, then dabbed at his lips with his napkin. "You have never learned to be flexible, my friend."

Carver was becoming annoyed. "There's nothing wrong with having values. They give the world weight and worth. You talk as if they're some kind of affliction."

"People sink to the bottom of the sea clinging to their values. Are you going to have dessert?"

Carver told him no, but to go ahead and order and he'd have coffee.

Desoto settled on the spumoni, and when the waiter had left with the order said, "We managed to get a clear fingerprint from the trunk lid of Spotto's car. We've run it through local computers and VICAP for comparisons, but nothing matches. It isn't the print of any of the car rental agency employees, and we're going to see about comparing it with prints of previous drivers. But my guess is it belongs to Achilles Jones. Lab whizzes say the finger that left it is huge."

Carver thought about the attack in his office.

Desoto must have been thinking about it, too. "We'd like to dust your office for prints," he said. "We might be able to determine if Spotto's killer and your assailant are the same man."

"It should be done," Carver said, "but as soon as Jones came through the door he got right to work, and I don't think he touched anything other than me. He did snap my cane in half, but Beth threw it away when I was in the hospital. If this had happened earlier, we could have compared the prints from the car with my welts."

The waiter arrived with coffee and Desoto's spumoni. Desoto assured Carver he'd talk to the circuit court judge about the Marla Cloy case, then carefully laid his napkin back in his lap. Carver knew that if any sort of stain marred Desoto's clothes, there was a complete change of wardrobe waiting in a locker at police headquarters to restore him to his usual pristine condition.

"Are you still wearing the support around your ribs?" Desoto asked.

"No, I removed it yesterday."

Desoto seemed to savor his spumoni. "Time heals everything eventually."

"I'd like to think that," Carver said, "but I'm not so sure."

"Me neither, I suppose," Desoto said. "Having been raised Catholic."

They'd met at the restaurant and had separate cars, so Carver finished his coffee then left Desoto to enjoy the sin of gluttony.

Carver got into the Olds and started the engine, then the air conditioner. The meeting with Desoto hadn't been the only reason he'd driven into Orlando. Beth had told him which adoption agency the Brants had visited before the fatal accident, and it had an Orlando address.

It was only ten minutes away from the restaurant on Washington.

|31|

THE EDGEWORTH AGENCY was in a modern glass-and-steel building that reflected the sun with an eye-aching blue brilliance and whose lobby directory boasted several law offices. Carver supposed that juxtaposition of services made good sense, as he rode a gleaming steel elevator like a rocket to the fifth floor.

Despite the sleek modernity of the building, the offices of the Edgeworth Agency were comfortably cluttered. A young man with unruly dark hair and a harried expression sat behind a desk that was almost invisible beneath various pieces of electronic office equipment, fanned-out papers, and a sheet of crinkled aluminum foil on which rested a half-eaten turkey sandwich. His white shirt was rumpled, his tie was loosely knotted, and when he looked up and saw Carver he appeared startled.

"It's not always like this around here," he said, smiling uneasily as if he'd been caught reading pornography. "I'm, uh, trying to get some paperwork in order."

The name plaque on the desk said he was Jim Martinelli. Carver introduced himself.

"I'd like to ask some questions concerning a woman who came here about six months ago and inquired about adopting a child," he said.

Martinelli looked worried, then immediately relieved. "You'd want to talk to Ms. Atkinson. I've only been here a little over three months."

Carver nodded, waiting.

"Oh!" Martinelli said. "Just a moment. Please." He backed to a door, opened it, and disappeared into an inner office.

A minute later he came out. "She'll see you—Ms. Atkinson will." He stood aside, holding the door open for Carver but not leaving him much room to pass. Carver considered bearing down with the tip of his cane on Martinelli's toe, then decided there was probably nothing wrong with the flustered lad that a few years without a sore foot wouldn't cure.

Ms. Atkinson's brass desk plaque said her first name was Ellen. She was in her forties, with a tightly sprung blond hairdo, bright red lipstick, and a smile as wide as a clown's. As soon as Martinelli had closed the door and gone back to his wild paperwork, Ms. Atkinson shook her head with weary tolerance.

"Jim tells me you want to know about something that happened here six months ago," she said. She'd stood up when Carver entered. She was slender and wonderfully proportioned. Her crisp gray business suit, white blouse, and fluffy blue polka-dot bow tie seemed styled and tailored just for her and reminded Carver of Desoto. Now she sat back down. Her office was as neat as Martinelli's was sloppy. She motioned an invitation for Carver to sit in a light oak and brown leather Danish chair in front of her desk.

Carver sat leaning forward slightly with both hands resting

on the crook of his cane. He said he wondered if she remembered Portia Brant.

She studied him with bright and intelligent gray eyes. Though she wore little makeup other than the glaring lipstick, her complexion was smooth and unblemished except for a mole slightly off-center on the point of her jaw. "It's our policy not to reveal information about any of our clients," she said. "Confidentiality is taken seriously here."

"Here, too," Carver said. "But Portia Brant wasn't actually your client. I believe she came here and inquired about an adoption. If you're still concerned about confidentiality, I can tell you she's deceased."

Ellen Atkinson worried a pencil that was lying on her green felt desk pad, rolling it back and forth with alternating motions of the forefinger and middle finger of her right hand, as if pretending the fingers were legs and her hand was a miniature lumberjack logrolling on a tiny hexagonal log. "I remember Portia Brant," she said, "because of the accident."

"Have you seen her husband Joel since they were here?"

"She was never here with her husband, Mr. Carver. She came here twice, alone."

"Was she serious about adopting a child?"

The lumberjack stepped off the log. Ellen Atkinson forgot about playing with the pencil and sat back. "Who are you, Mr. Carver?"

Carver considered using the old insurance agent con. Or maybe dropping indirect hints that he was with the police. Neither seemed the right thing to do. With Ellen Atkinson, he decided on the truth.

"Interesting," she said, when he was finished.

"Was Portia Brant serious about adopting?" he asked again.

"Oh, quite serious. In fact, she wanted a child—an infant—

desperately. She was adopted herself, she told me, so she had insight. She said she knew what an adopted child needed."

"Why did she come here alone? Didn't she want her husband to know?"

"I never got that impression. She told me she was doing the preliminaries, and she'd bring him with her when they were actually ready to apply to adopt. It isn't easy, you know. And we're merely what you might call go-betweens in the process: we match prospective parents to child, provide legal advice, then counseling services after the adoption. It's rewarding work, Mr. Carver." Again her wide, infectious smile.

"I can imagine. When was the last time she was here?"

"Less than a week before she died. That's why I remember her so clearly. I was horrified when I read about the accident in the paper. A drunk driver . . . such a shame. She was a beautiful and kind woman. Very active in charity work, you know."

Carver agreed that it was a shame a woman like Portia Grant had to die because of a drunk driver, and he said he knew about the charity work.

"She'd told me she was bringing her husband next time," Ellen Atkinson said, "and that they were planning to begin the actual process of adoption." She shuddered as if she were chilled, burrowing her chin down into her voluminous silk bow tie until her mole was invisible. "They never kept the appointment, of course."

"Did she talk as if her own childhood had been difficult?"

"Yes and no. Her adoptive parents were quite well off, and there was plenty of love in the family. But it was a surprise to her when they told her in her teen years that she was adopted. I think one of the reasons she wanted to adopt so much was that her childhood was a happy one. She was grateful, and she felt she had a debt that she could repay by giving another unwanted child a home. It's not an uncommon reaction."

"Good," Carver said, smiling. "Did she say her husband was also enthusiastic about adopting?"

"Not directly that I can recall. But I assume he felt the same way, or she wouldn't have come to us." The many-lined phone on Ellen Atkinson's desk trilled, and she excused herself and answered it. She said, "Yes, yes, of course, just a minute," then covered the mouthpiece with her hand and started to say something to Carver.

He raised his hand in a goodbye, mouthed "Thank you," and stood up.

She nodded to him, then said, "Yes, yes, of course," into the phone again as he was leaving.

Martinelli grinned and waved a cheery good afternoon to him as he passed through the tumultuous outer office and stepped into the cool hall.

The stainless steel elevator dropped him smoothly to the warm lobby.

He'd left the Olds parked in the lot adjacent to the gleaming blue building. It seemed to have absorbed the reflected glare and grown unnaturally hot.

Carver cranked down the windows so the superheated air would swirl out as he drove, then switched the air conditioner on high. Within a few blocks, he should be able to raise the windows and stop sweating.

At the first red traffic light, he rolled up the windows while waiting for green. The light changed before he'd finished closing the passenger-side window.

As he straightened up and accelerated, he glanced in the rearview mirror to make sure he hadn't delayed anyone.

His seemed to be the only car around.

But the man on the motorcycle was behind him again, half a block back and keeping pace. Though there was little to lend them scale, both man and motorcycle appeared huge. Carver was certain it was the same cycle and rider he'd seen earlier.

His hands became slippery with sweat on the steering wheel. His eyes darting back and forth between the street ahead and the rearview mirror, he held the Olds's speed at thirty.

The motorcycle didn't turn onto a side street this time. Its front wheel broke from the pavement as it reared high with power.

It bloomed like a dark flower in the mirror as it came at Carver.

32

AS THE motorcycle pulled alongside the Olds with a roar like continuous thunder, Carver saw that it was a Harley-Davidson and had been crudely painted a lusterless gray. He had no time to take anything else in. The Harley shot even with the left front fender, then veered toward it.

It all happened so fast that Carver instinctively jerked the steering wheel to the right. The Olds's front tire jumped the curb, then wobbled back into the gutter, throwing the car out of control. The steering wheel came alive and writhed from his slippery grip, one of its cross-braces striking his thumb painfully. Tires squealed as the car swerved and rocked violently from side to side. His foot came off the accelerator, his body jerking with the force of the wild motion.

Finally he managed to regain his hold on the wheel. He wrestled it so that the car's course straightened and its rocking was less extreme.

When the Olds's speed had dropped somewhat, he jammed his foot down hard on the brake pedal. It responded sluggishly and he knew the engine had died and knocked out the power steering and brakes. The steering wheel's stiffness confirmed this. Carver braced his back against the seat and shoved his foot down on the pedal with all his strength, and gradually the car slowed to a halt.

The Harley had stopped about a hundred feet down the street. Before Carver could reach forward and try to restart the engine, the huge cyclist had dismounted, removed his helmet with its tinted plexiglass face guard, and was lumbering toward the car.

As Carver was desperately twisting the key and the starter was futilely grinding, Achilles Jones, outfitted as before in dirt-encrusted jeans and filthy, wool-lined leather vest, casually swung the helmet at the driver's-side window and smashed the glass. Carver's hand slipped from the ignition key as he jerked his body to the side to avoid the giant's grasp. A massive hand closed on his shirt, as his own hand gripped his cane, which had been leaning against the seat. He turned and saw the same mindless smile he'd seen in his office, the same pale blue eyes with the frightening void behind them.

He jabbed the tip of the cane into one of the eyes. The big man, whose actions were cramped by the window frame and what was left of the glass, couldn't fend off the cane. Or a second, more accurate jab. He released Carver's shirt and backed away a step.

As he stood there rubbing his eyes, Carver drove the tip of the cane hard into his throat. The giant gagged and leaped back out of his reach.

It gave Carver time to get the Olds started.

When Jones heard the sound of the engine turning over, he came at the car again immediately. But blindly this time. He bounced hard off the door as Carver jammed the accelerator down and the tires screamed and propelled the Olds forward with all the primitive power of its V-8 engine.

Carver glanced in the rearview mirror and saw Jones mounting his motorcycle, shaking his head from side to side to try to clear his mind and vision.

The Olds might have been able to outrun the Harley, but a large yellow Hertz rental truck entered the intersection directly in its path. Carver stomped hard on the brakes. The Olds's hood dipped and it screeched sideways in the street.

As Achilles Jones was larger than Carver, so the Olds was larger than the Harley. The dusk-colored bike slammed into the side of the car just behind the door, rocking it sideways. Carver heard something scrape across the canvas top, and he turned to see Achilles Jones land hard on his back in the street after the impact had flung him over the car. He hit so hard that dust flew.

The Hertz truck had stopped and two husky men climbed down from the cab. They began walking toward Jones and the wrecked Harley. Attracted by the *eeek!* of tires and the sound of the collision, people began to appear on the sidewalk.

Jones struggled up to his full height, and the men who'd been approaching to help him suddenly stopped and stood still, staring. Sirens began wailing frantic loops of sound, drawing nearer.

Limping heavily, Achilles Jones ran from the street and between two buildings.

Carver watched him, admiring his combination of size and speed despite his apparently injured leg. With time to think, it occurred to him that Jones might hold the key to understanding what really was going on between Brant and Marla Cloy. If Carver could discover who'd hired him to stymie the investigation, everything else might come clear. And Jones was hurt, maybe badly, from the accident. He could be controlled at least until the police reached the scene.

Maybe.

Ignoring the strong smell of gasoline that warned of possible fire, Carver twisted the ignition key and got the Olds started again. One of the men from the Hertz truck was yelling at him, but he couldn't understand what he was saying and didn't care. He backed the Olds away from the wrecked Harley, frantically maneuvering until it was pointed in the direction he'd just come from, then accelerated down the street, trying to get around the block in time to intercept Jones. If he had the chance, he wouldn't hesitate to knock the giant down with the car. He had no doubt that Jones had intended to kill him.

He jounced the Olds over the curb, rounding the corner and speeding to the next intersection so he could peer up the street.

Achilles Jones was nowhere in sight.

Carver hit the accelerator and the Olds roared up the street as he swiveled his head to glance from side to side, like a fighter pilot in enemy skies. He no longer smelled gasoline, so the fuel must have leaked from the motorcycle and not the Olds. Several pedestrians stared at him, but they were half the size of the man he was seeking.

The siren was much louder now and had been joined by another, but Carver knew that by the time he explained what had happened and talked the uniforms into searching for Jones, it would be too late.

In frustration, he made a right turn and drove down the next block. He was aware now of a rhythmic scuffing sound as the car gained speed, then the acrid scent of burning rubber; the big Harley must have bent the Olds's fender in so that the tire was rubbing.

He circled the block twice, slowly enough so that he no longer heard the scraping sound, before conceding that Jones had somehow disappeared.

A part of him couldn't help feeling relieved.

His heart was racing faster than the car's backed-off engine, and his hands were trembling as he returned to the scene of the accident.

33

CARVER SAT in Desoto's office and wished he had a cold beer. The run-in with Achilles Jones had been more than attempted assault and a fender-bender traffic accident: Jones was a suspected killer on the run.

Desoto surveyed the fan-fold computer paper on his desk, his chin propped in his hand, his dark eyes moving in short, rapid glides as he read. A guitar was playing softly on the radio behind him, deep, somber chords, and a woman was singing softly in Spanish; life was such a bittersweet, tragic affair.

He looked up at Carver and dropped the hand that had been cupping his chin down to the desk. His beige suit coat was draped on a wooden hanger slung over a brass hook on the wall. He moved his arm slightly and rested his French-cuffed white shirtsleeve on the papers he'd been reading. "Jones is such a common name," he said, "that it poses difficulties."

Carver agreed. He thought of Clive Jones at *Burrow*. The name was not as stupid an alias as it at first seemed.

"The Harley's license plate was stolen in Jacksonville," Desoto said. "The bike itself—a ninety-four Harley-Davidson Electra Glide Ultra—was traced by its identification number. They're huge motorcycles that cost as much as some cars and weigh almost eight hundred pounds. That's why after Jones's went over on its side, even he didn't try to right it. It was stolen three weeks ago from a man named Art Figenbaum in Rome, Georgia."

Carver was disappointed but not surprised. The Achilles Joneses of the world were marauders who lived off the land. Stolen motorcycle, stolen plates. "You mean this monster's faded away again as if he never existed? Like Big Foot?"

Desoto's lips curved in a brief smile. "Not exactly, *amigo*. We believe Jones exists. And the fingerprints from the wrecked Harley match the print on the trunk of Spotto's rental car. Your eyeball account connects Jones directly to the stolen bike, which connects him to the rental car and Spotto. Enough for a murder warrant, and once we fingerprint Jones and make the match for sure, he's good for the fall. Big Foot doesn't have the cops after him, right?"

"Right," Carver said. "Does this mean you're not going to dust my office?"

"No, we still want to lift a matching print there if we can. Best to lock this up tight." Desoto raised his arm and adjusted the white cuff. Gold glinted. "Jones might not be bright in the conventional sense, but simply by remaining anonymous despite his remarkable appearance, he's demonstrated a certain cunning. He's probably heard of fingerprints."

Carver understood Desoto's meaning.

"You're the witness that ties him into all this until he's caught and printed," Desoto said. "You're the witness that can make it all stick to him in court."

"I'm the witness he wants dead," Carver said.

"That's how it is, I'm afraid. And if Jones isn't smart enough to know it, the person he's working for probably is."

"Marla Cloy or Joel Brant," Carver said.

"Maybe. No way to know for sure precisely what his involvement with either of them is—or if there is an involvement—until we get him in the net."

"That won't be easy," Carver said. "He's injured, but not badly enough to slow him down much."

"Sometimes injuries from accidents aren't apparent at first, but they can still be serious. Even fatal. We can only hope, hey? He's dangerous to people. He's exactly what you called him, a monster. Inside and out."

"True. But I don't want him dead. I'd like for him to say who hired him to stop my investigation."

Desoto looked at Carver, then arched an eyebrow and shook his head. "And you're dangerous to yourself, my friend. It was foolish of you to chase a man like that after he tried to kill you."

"He knows something I need to know," Carver said.

"What you need," Desoto said, "is to stay alive. Does your car still run?"

"As well as ever, now that I've bent the fender back out with a tire tool so the tire doesn't scrape it."

"Then I take it you're driving directly back to Del Moray when you leave here."

"That's my plan."

"Remember Jones is on the loose, and if he's intelligent enough to be capable of anger, where you're concerned he'll be incensed. And an incensed Achilles Jones is a sleep-disturbing notion. I'm assuming you're not walking around armed, or you'd have shot him."

Carver mentally kicked himself for again neglecting to carry the Colt. It remained at the cottage, tucked beneath his underwear in his dresser drawer.

He knew the practical use of guns and knew how to use one, had used one more than once and without regret because the only alternative was his own death. But he remembered the shock and pain of being shot in the leg, and he didn't want to carry a gun, to have its bulk pressing constantly against him. Consciously and unconsciously, he fought against arming himself unless it was necessary.

Today had convinced him it was necessary. He wouldn't forget again.

"Remember to be careful, hey?" Desoto said.

"I always am," Carver said, "and look what still happens to me."

Desoto laughed in his rich baritone, in contrast to the rapid and tragic guitar strumming seeping from the little Sony on his windowsill.

"My saving grace is that I'm lucky," Carver said.

"No, no. Your saving grace, my friend, is that you're still alive."

NO MOTORCYCLE, no black van with tinted windows appeared in Carver's rearview mirror as he drove the sun-baked highway back to Del Moray.

Two police technicians from Orlando were waiting in a four-door unmarked Pontiac when he parked outside his office. He greeted them, then let them inside and busied himself with things that didn't really need doing while they went about their task of lifting fingerprints. The taller of the two worked silently, while the short one hummed constantly beneath his breath. They had some kind of aerosol cold fog and a special light that supplemented fingerprint powder. They were diligent professionals. Carver didn't think they'd make a match here, but he didn't have the heart to tell them.

When they were gone, he phoned Beth to see how she was and to let her know what had happened in Orlando.

"Jones will be out to kill you for sure now," she said. "Fingerprints and an eyewitness make a case."

"I'm not so sure he's smart enough to figure that out. If you could see his eyes . . . I think he's more the sort who either follows orders or simply reacts."

"He'll react by trying to kill you again," Beth said flatly.

"You're a comfort."

"I'm a realist."

"I love talking to you on the phone. So reassuring. Do you believe in telephone sex?"

"Sure. It's the reason for all those little walkie-talkies."

"Hmm. How are the two of you feeling today?"

Silence. Thicker and thicker.

Then, "Don't give me that stuff, Fred. You know I haven't made up my mind."

"Okay, it was only idle conversation."

"That kind of conversation doesn't make things any easier."

She was obviously moody today. Hormonal, maybe. Pregnant women got that way. Hormones ruled. He'd better not mention that possibility, though. She'd jump on him again, accuse him of male misunderstanding and insensitivity.

"I'm sorry," he said. "It's just that sometimes I feel left out of this entire pregnancy process. But I'm the father, remember?"

"Yes, but it has to be my decision, Fred."

"I know."

He did know, but he wished she'd stop reminding him. Had she forgotten about telling him she wanted to make him part of whatever she decided? Hormones.

"Anything else come up on Portia Brant?" he asked.

"No, Jeff's still using the *Burrow* computer to find whatever's out there on record. Not just on Portia, but on Marla Cloy and Joel Brant."

"What about Achilles Jones? And a Harley-Davidson Electra Glide Ultra stolen two weeks ago in Rome, Georgia?"

"I'll ask him," Beth said. "Jeff has ways. If it's in a data base anywhere, he can get to it."

"Legally?"

"I don't go into that with him. If he's an information high-wayman, I don't want to know about it and neither do you."

He paused a few beats. "Don't get mad when I ask about this, but have you been to the doctor lately?"

"No. Why?"

Carver stared out the window at the patch of blue sea visible between the buildings across Magellan. "Ever hear of the string test?" he asked.

"Test for what?"

"Gender. A pregnant woman dangles a length of string an inch above her wrist, holding it as still as possible. If the end of the string moves in a circle, that means she's going to have a girl. If it moves back and forth in a straight line, she's going to have a boy."

"Damn it, Fred! I told you, keep that kind of shit to yourself!"

"All right! Some of the women in my family believed in it. I mean, I was just sitting here and I remembered it for some reason."

"You didn't have to tell me about your family's superstitious nonsense. Or maybe you *did* have to. You've taken leave of your senses and you're acting out of compulsion. It's like you're god-damned hormonal!"

She slammed down the receiver.

Hormonal, she'd said. He sat there for a minute with the dead phone to his ear, amazed that she'd accuse him of precisely what he'd been thinking about her.

Maybe pregnant women were sometimes psychic.

34

CARVER DECIDED not to drive to the cottage to get the gun he'd forgotten this morning. It might be best if he gave Beth time to cool down. He understood her fear. The breech birth and umbilical-cord strangulation of her child by Roberto Gomez had a grip on her mind.

He drove instead to the taco stand on Magellan and had a burrito, diet Coke, and some sort of odd deep-fried dessert sprinkled with powdered sugar. When he was finished, he planned on driving to Jacaranda Lane to see what if anything was happening with Marla Cloy. Following Joel Brant had resulted mostly in further confusion.

He'd just fired up a Swisher Sweet cigar when a long shadow drifted across his legs and the tray on the table containing the remains of his early supper. A whiff of cheap lemon-scent deodorant and stale perspiration told him who'd cast the shadow even before he looked.

McGregor was standing with his fists on his hips, grinning and gazing over at the pleasure boats bobbing lazily at their moorings in the public marina. He'd cut himself shaving this morning, and from Carver's low angle a large bead of dried blood on the underside of his jaw could be seen still clinging stubbornly.

"Some day I'll be able to afford one of those babies," McGregor said, pointing to the expensive array of boats.

"Yours will be the only yacht with a lifeboat that seats one," Carver said.

McGregor probed between his front teeth with his tongue, still staring at the boats. "Women and children first, I always say. First into the drink, that is." Carver didn't doubt that he meant it. McGregor turned his mean little blue eyes on Carver, then carefully surveyed the cardboard plate and waxed wrappers on the table. "You really like that rat food?"

"Wouldn't eat here if I didn't. And it's a great place to be left alone—usually."

"Don't smart off with me, ass-face, or you'll be carting around a plasma bottle by the time you get the trots from this chow."

"A threat from a police officer?" Carver asked.

"Uh-huh. Direct threat."

Carver took a drag on the Swisher Sweet and watched the breeze play with the smoke. He appreciated the sharp scent of the cigar; it alleviated the odor of the habitually unclean McGregor. "How'd you know I was here?"

"I know everything about you, jerkoff. When you weren't at your office, I called your cottage. Dark meat said you weren't there and probably weren't gonna be home for supper. So I figured you'd be here at one of your favorite five-star restaurants stuffing your face, and sure enough, here you are."

"Do you have some reason to look me up," Carver asked, "or do you just want to sit around and talk about yachting?"

"I came to tell you that if you know where your client is, I'd better know right along with you. And I mean within ten seconds."

"Why should I know where he is?"

"Marla Cloy reported a car like Brant's almost ran her down, then sped away. She's sure Brant was at the wheel. That's attempted murder, not to mention violation of a restraining order. I sent a couple of uniforms to pick up Brant for questioning. He blew his cool in their presence and swore he'd kill Marla for what she's done to him—that's the way he expressed it, anyway."

"Then why isn't he in custody?" Carver asked.

McGregor looked uncomfortable, then angry. The breeze off the ocean whipped the tail of his suitcoat around, revealing his holstered nine-millimeter. He raised a hand and touched its checked butt lightly, as if he longed to draw the weapon and shoot Carver.

"Your client escaped, Carver. That makes things worse for the two of you. He's a fugitive now, and you're an accessory if you know where he is."

"Escaped how?"

"He walked into the kitchen to get his sport coat where it was draped over the back of a chair. The next thing my guys knew, they heard a car engine. By the time it occurred to them there was a door to the back stairs from the kitchen, Brant was hauling ass away in that high-powered sports car of his. Nobody's seen him since."

"Your officers give chase?"

"For about a block, then a tree stopped them."

"Some police work," Carver said. "Reflects on their immediate superior, don't you think?"

"What I think is that your ass is in more of a sling than those dumb-fuck uniforms I sent to pick up Brant."

"I don't see it that way," Carver said. "Brant's my client, not my brother. I can't tell you where to find him. What you should do, though, is watch Marla Cloy. You said he threatened to kill her."

"Not the first time," McGregor said.

"Maybe not. Have you got somebody over at her place on Jacaranda?"

"She's gone. I called ahead and told her what happened, told her to stay put. What we found when we got to her house was a note saying she'd left town and wasn't coming back until Joel Brant was in custody."

"More solid police work," Carver said, smiling around his cigar. "The way you're going, you're never going to be promoted out of your broom-closet office."

McGregor stuck out his long jaw, almost making the bead of blood fall off. He curled his upper lip up close to his nose. "It would behoove you to find Brant and give him to me, or you're gonna find yourself in a cell even smaller than a broom closet."

"I'm not on your payroll."

"But you are on my shit list. Doesn't pay as well, but it's more certain."

"What else was in Marla's note?" Carver asked.

"Why? You think if you find her you'll find Brant?"

"They'll come together eventually," Carver said. "We both know that."

McGregor turned his head to the side and spat between his teeth onto the pavement. A woman at a nearby table paused with her burrito near her mouth and glared furiously at him. "It was a simple typewritten note, nothing more in it than what I told you."

"Signed?"

"Not in pen or pencil. She typed her name at the bottom, left the note under a ketchup bottle on her kitchen table." McGregor spat again, near Carver's chair this time. "There is, of course, the possibility she wrote the note under duress, and your client abducted her."

"He said he wanted to kill her, not kidnap her."

McGregor flicked his tongue around between his teeth. "Maybe he wants to kill her slow and milk it for enjoyment. I would."

"You're not Joel Brant. You're not most people."

"Thank fucking God for that. But don't get too concerned about who I'm not. You got other worries. The wheels have come off this thing, Carver, and you better help get 'em back on."

Carver snuffed out his cigar in the hammered tin ashtray sitting on the table. It died hard, with a final, wavering curl of smoke. "I'll do everything I can," he said. It was a good thing to say for the record.

"You better do just that," McGregor said. He used the bulky sole of one of his huge brown wing tips to grind the glob of phlegm he'd expectorated into the concrete.

Carver was beginning to sweat heavily. The heat, McGregor's body odor and behavior, and the aftertaste of salsa and cigar were making him slightly nauseated. He sat quietly, very still, hoping McGregor wouldn't notice a sheen of perspiration on his forehead. McGregor homed in on signs of potential weakness like a carnivore on the prowl. Carver moved a hand with deliberate steadiness and took a sip of his cold but watered-down Coke.

"I hope Brant does kill the bitch," McGregor said. "Then all I gotta think about is how to nail the both of you." He turned and walked away, his long arms swinging apelike, his shoulders hunched so that his suit coat belled out in the wind.

Carver decided he'd wasted his time speaking for the record. There wasn't going to be any record of their conversation.

Or if there was, it would be pure fiction written by McGregor.

He piled the greasy wrapper and containers and remains of supper on his red plastic tray and dumped them in one of the trash receptacles.

Then he got in the Olds and drove to Jacaranda Lane.

THE HOUSE sat partially shaded by a neighbor's palm trees. It looked the same, sad and in disrepair, its green canvas awnings still drooping over the windows. The sun-browned lawn still hadn't been mowed and appeared ready to go to seed. The dead plants in their terra-cotta pots remained lined along the railing of the tiny front porch. The gravel driveway was empty.

Carver parked the Olds a few houses down, then climbed out and made his way down the sidewalk toward number 22. He didn't hesitate; if any of the neighbors happened to see him, they'd assume he had an honest reason for approaching Marla's house. He hoped.

On the porch, he leaned with a hand on the iron railing and pressed the doorbell button with the tip of his cane. He heard the chimes sound inside.

A full minute passed. He pressed the button again. He was going to take a chance here and had to be positive Marla hadn't returned.

As he waited he studied the door. It appeared thick and had four tiny, rectangular windows at eye level. Each time he'd seen Marla leave the house, it was by the front way. He could assume the door's lock was a dead lock, which the security-minded Marla would surely have thrown when she left.

He glanced impatiently at his wristwatch, as if he might be a salesman with appointments lined up and he was in a hurry. Then he went down the two concrete porch steps and walked along the driveway to the back of the house.

No one was out in the yards of the houses on Cenit Street, whose back property butted up to the yards of Jacaranda Lane.

Hoping Mildred Fain, whose house was directly behind Marla's, wasn't looking out her window, Carver limped up onto the small wooden back porch, sizing up the door as he went. It wasn't nearly as sturdy as the front door. Again he didn't hesitate. He held open the rickety screen door, then braced with his cane and stiff leg. He shot out his good leg so the flat of his sole hit the back door just above knee level.

It sprang open without making much noise, leaving a splintered door frame where the lock was ripped away. A brass chain dangled hardware from which protruded four screws that the force of Carver's kick had torn from the doorjamb.

He went in quickly and closed the door behind him, sure that it wouldn't reveal much damage from outside unless viewed close up.

The house's interior was stifling and smelled of rancid bacon grease. He was in the kitchen: New-looking linoleum made to emulate gray marble tiles; a small gray Formica table with stainless steel legs, a half-empty ketchup bottle and glass salt and pepper shakers forming a triangle in its center; a yellowed sink and a small gas stove with an iron frying pan on one of the back burners. Clean dishes were wedged into a pink, rubber-coated drainer on the sink's counter. The refrigerator, which was chugging along determinedly in the heat, was so old it had the motor and coils on top. Carver hadn't seen one of those in years. It often amazed him, what he found when he went where he shouldn't. Maybe that was really why he went.

He crossed the kitchen and continued into the small combination living and dining room. The overstuffed blue furniture was soiled and worn, he noticed. Marla's work table by the window held only the plastic in-out trays, the lamp with the dangerous extension cord, and a black rotary-dial phone. The trays were empty. Carver went to a small, maple kneehole desk against the wall with the bookcase shelving and examined its drawers' contents.

He found nothing of interest—some rent receipts, a few unpaid utility bills, a stack of grocery coupons, and some discount coupons from the fast-food restaurants in the neighborhood. The frayed wicker wastebasket next to the desk was empty except for a used Pepsi can and a frantic cockroach.

Carver glanced in the bathroom. It was tiled in black and white and had a white washbasin, a commode about the same age as the refrigerator, and a wooden vanity whose oak veneer was peeling from the humidity of baths and showers taken in the claw-footed tub with the white plastic curtain bunched at one end of the shower rod. Carver looked in the mirrored medicine cabinet above the basin and saw only an array of over-the-counter drugs, some of them outdated and obvious leftovers from previous tenants. There was a sliver of aqua-colored soap stuck to the bottom of the bathtub. The indentation that served as the washbasin's soap dish was empty but coated with an aqua residue that Carver touched and found moist.

After wiping soap from his forefinger on a towel, he went to the bedroom. It was small and contained only a single bed, a bureau, and a tall mahogany wardrobe in lieu of a closet. The bed was sloppily made and had a white spread over it that looked as if it had been in the wash with something pink. Carver suspected the wardrobe had some value as an antique. He opened it and found only a few items of clothing hanging from a retractable rod: a red blouse, a denim skirt, a business-like gray blazer. The clothes were separated by several wire hangers. He went through the blazer's pockets but found nothing other than lint. The left side of the wardrobe held drawers. They contained the usual assortment of lingerie, folded shirts and blouses, and a tangled wad of panty hose. The bottom drawer contained half a dozen pairs of shoes, some of which were almost worn out.

The bureau drawers also yielded little of interest. A few

neatly folded slacks and T-shirts, a coiled extension cord, and some old sweaters suitable for a cooler clime. One of the drawers was empty, and another contained only a milk-glass jar with a peeling cosmetic cream label. The cream was long gone and the jar was half full of pennies.

It seemed to Carver that some of Marla's clothes were missing. And there had been no toothbrush or soap in the bathroom other than the sliver of soap on the bottom of the tub. She might have packed the washbasin soap bar when she left. A financially struggling woman might do that, either to save money or because she used a particular brand of soap.

Carver returned to the living room. His rummaging through Marla's desk hadn't turned up a checkbook. And Marla's typewriter was missing. It was possible that the Del Moray police had confiscated both, but he doubted it. McGregor seemed sure that Marla had either left of her own volition or been abducted by Brant.

There was no way to be certain, but Carver figured her note was genuine, and that she'd left in a hurry on her own after loading her typewriter into the little Toyota and packing some clothes and incidentals, including her toothbrush.

An enraged and pursued Joel Brant wouldn't have been concerned about what Marla had to wear if he'd abducted her, and there would have been no reason to take her typewriter with them.

And cavities would have been the least of her problems.

Finding Marla or Brant was Carver's problem. He decided to start with Brant. Brant had a business to worry about.

A project where they were pouring concrete.

|35|

BETH WAS eating a tuna salad sandwich and drinking a glass of lemonade when Carver entered the cottage. She gave him a sideways glance, then took a vicious bite of sandwich and chewed.

"Chips would be good with that," Carver said.

"Don't make feeble small talk, Fred."

"OK."

He limped over to the sofa and sat down, leaning his cane against a cushion. "McGregor came to see me. Marla accused Brant of trying to run her down, told the law, and when they tried to pick up Brant he bolted. Marla's gone, too. She's afraid of Brant and left a note saying she was clearing out of the area until he's caught."

Beth stopped chewing and swallowed. "She left a note, but nobody actually saw her leave alone and by choice?"

It intrigued Carver that Beth's mind was working the same way as McGregor's, but he thought he'd keep that to himself.

"How do you know Brant didn't abduct her?" Beth asked.

"Before I came here, I let myself into her house. Indications are that she packed and left of her own volition, taking her toothbrush and probably a bar of soap. Her car is gone. And her typewriter's gone. Brant wouldn't have let her take that with her."

Beth nodded, then sipped some lemonade. Carver saw what looked like a sprig of parsley floating among the ice cubes in her glass. Well, maybe they always made lemonade that way where she'd grown up in the slums of Chicago.

"What about you?" he said. "You doing OK?"

He saw her fingers stiffen, then relax. It was still no good talking about the baby, about what, if anything, she'd decided. Carver felt a hot coal of anger start to glow in his gut. It was up to her, sure. She was the one who was pregnant. What was he, only the father. Damn it, he should have *some* say in the matter!

But he knew that if he were a woman he'd think differently. Beth was the one who had to carry the child to term or had to undergo an abortion. Beth was the one who carried the fear and burden of a previous pregnancy that ended tragically. And Beth was the one who had to live with her decision in a blood-and-body way Carver could only guess at.

His flush of anger had left him, and he felt ashamed. "Whichever side of the fence you come down on," he said, "I want you to know it's all right with me. We'll be OK."

She swiveled down from the stool at the breakfast counter. She was wearing a cream-colored shirt with net sleeves and faded Levi's, and had her hair pinned back. Not much makeup. She slid her feet into her white leather sandals, then bent gracefully and fastened the straps. Carver, who almost always wore shoes without straps or laces, wished he had that kind of mobility.

"I'm going to walk along the beach for a while," she said.

He thought she'd invite him to accompany her, but she

didn't. She didn't say anything else as he watched her stride across the room and walk outside into the hot night.

The wooden screen door slammed behind her like a gun-shot.

EARLY THE next morning, Carver drove the Olds along the curved main street of Brant Estates to where cement trucks were pouring driveways for framed-in houses in a cul-de-sac. Five of the bulky, dusty, and mud-caked trucks were lined up, waiting their turn. A dozen laborers and cement finishers were hard at work, either spreading and smoothing the freshly poured cement or using hammers and pry bars to remove wooden forms from driveways poured within the last few days.

Wade Schultz was standing off to the side watching the pro-ceedings, his red hard hat tucked beneath his arm like a foot-ball. He had on jeans and a white T-shirt with a breast pocket stuffed with one of those plastic pocket protectors full of pens and pencils. A cigarette pack was rolled into the left sleeve of his shirt, forming a neat rectangular lump on his shoulder, as if some sort of transmitter or receiver had been surgically im-planted beneath his skin.

When he saw Carver approaching, he casually plopped his hard hat on his head, as if preparing for trouble.

"Seen Joel Brant this morning?" Carver asked.

"No," Schultz said, turning his head to watch a gravelly mass of concrete slide down a metal chute into a driveway. Immediately, two muscular laborers began shoveling it out to the sides and up against the wooden forms. There was a me-tallic *chunk!* each time their shovel blades slid into the wet concrete. "Mr. Brant's not gonna be in today. The sales office over there is where you might wanna go. You *are* interested in buying a house, aren't you?" he said sarcastically. Apparently Schultz and Nancy Quartermain had talked.

"Right now I'm interested in talking to Joel Brant. It's only seven-thirty. How do you know he won't show up here today?"

"He told me last night on the phone. In fact, he said he was gonna be gone for a while. Left me instructions to keep this job running on schedule."

"He say where he was going?"

"Didn't say he was going anywhere. Just said he wasn't coming here." Schultz touched a hand to Carver's arm and motioned for him to step aside and make room for one of the huge mixers to maneuver in close so its swinging steel chute could reach the shallow driveway excavation. "Look at that," he said, pointing to a spot on the other side of the driveway. "Some asshole was riding around here on a motorcycle this morning. Left ruts across this yard, and tire marks on concrete that hadn't set yet on a driveway down the street."

Carver looked and saw deep tread marks from an obviously heavy motorcycle. He wondered if Achilles Jones had stolen another Harley. "Anybody see the cycle rider?"

"Naw, but it's sure obvious he was here. Or maybe there was more'n one of 'em. I never checked to find out. Don't make much difference now."

"If Joel Brant contacts you again," Carver said, "tell him he needs to phone Fred Carver immediately."

"Sure." Schultz began waving his sunburned arm in a wide circle, signaling for the mixer to ease back closer to the driveway. The truck's diesel engine roared and its air brakes hissed and squealed as the driver worked the vehicle backward in a series of lurches, no more than a foot each, eyes glued to Schultz's hand signals in the side mirror.

"Don't wait by the phone, though," Schultz said when the noise of the truck had subsided. The sound of the laborers hammering away the wooden forms seemed strangely soft and distant after the din of the truck. "Mr. Brant talked like we wouldn't be in contact again for quite a while."

Carver nodded his thanks to Schultz, then left him to supervise the creation of driveways.

A few minutes after he'd turned onto the highway, on his way to talk with Willa Krull, a Del Moray police car passed him traveling fast in the opposite direction. It was likely that Wade Schultz was going to be interrupted on the job again, and one of the first things he'd tell his questioners was that Carver had already talked to him.

That would make McGregor more unhappy.

And even happy, he was a man to avoid.

36

WILLA OPENED her apartment door on its chain and stared out at Carver with a reddened eye that was little more than a puffy slit in her pinched features.

"Mr. Carver," she said. "You were the one who was knocking." As if he didn't know and had asked.

"For the past five minutes," Carver said. He'd heard movement in the apartment even before he'd knocked the first time. He thought Willa might need a while to work up nerve before coming to the door.

She didn't move or say anything.

"Can I come in?" Carver asked. "I need to talk with you."

The eye suddenly opened wider, as if her mind had drifted and she'd abruptly realized where she was and what was going on.

The door closed and its chain lock rattled, a sound that must be a daily accompaniment to Willa Krull's life. Then it opened wide.

The scent of gin wafted out into the hall. Willa was wearing a pink rayon robe that made a pass at looking like silk, and pink, fuzzy slippers over a pink nightgown. All that pink only made her puffy eyes appear pinker. Her thin brown hair was uncombed, wildly mussed on one side as if she'd been plucking at it. As Carver made his way past her into the apartment the gin fumes became stronger and he saw a half-empty bottle standing on the floor beside the sofa.

"I didn't get much sleep last night," Willa said. She sniffled. "I feel like death warmed over."

"You look fine," Carver lied. He moved a *Target Shooter* magazine out of the way and sat down where she'd know it would be impossible for him to see the gin bottle.

She sat across from him in a spindly wooden chair that looked like something built by Puritans for discomfort. With an ashamed, crooked smile, she raised her thin arms then let them fall back to her lap. "I'd offer you some coffee, but I don't have any made."

"Marla Cloy's disappeared," Carver said. "She claims Joel Brant tried to run her down with his car."

Willa didn't seem surprised. "I don't know where Marla is."

"What about Brant?"

She stared at Carver with ferretlike, hostile eyes. "Why should I have any idea where he is? I never laid eyes on the man. All I know about him is what Marla told me. And believe me, that's enough."

"You didn't ask why Marla dropped out of sight."

"I assume it's because she's afraid of Brant—and with good reason." She stood up suddenly, as if her chair had grown hot. "I don't understand this. You're acting like Marla's some kind of criminal. Didn't you say Brant tried to run over her?"

"No. That's what she says."

"Then it's the truth." She remained standing, staring down at him. Her arms and hands were very still at her sides, but the tips of her fingers were vibrating.

Carver gave the closed bedroom door a lingering look. He'd seen it work in *Murder, She Wrote.* "Are you sure you don't know where to find Marla?"

Her eyes didn't follow his glance. "Positive." She made an obvious effort to relax, breathing in deeply and smoothing her uncooperative hair with the flat of her hand. "You don't think I'm hiding her here, do you?"

"It's possible. She's your friend."

"My friend," Willa repeated. She stared down at her fuzzy pink slippers. Then she sat back down, raised both hands to her face, and began to sob.

Carver gripped his cane and stood up. He went over to her and touched his fingertips to her quaking shoulder. She sucked in her breath and drew back away from him. Her sobbing racked her thin body. He was afraid she might drop from the chair onto the threadbare oriental rug and curl into the fetal position. Her despair was genuine and profound. Pity for her swelled in him and lumped in his throat.

He moved away from her, out in front of her, where if she opened her eyes and peeked between her fingers she could see him. But she didn't peek, didn't change position.

"You going to be OK?" he asked when her sobbing had subsided to the point where she might be able to answer.

"I think so," she said, her voice muted, her face still buried in her hands. She expelled air between her hands in a long hiss. "It's just that I'm worried about Marla. And I told you, I didn't get much sleep last night."

He laid his card on the sofa arm. "If you hear from her, will you call me?"

She didn't answer.

"It's the best thing for Marla," Carver said.

She began to cry again, her head bowed and her shoulders heaving with increasing violence, her gaunt body riding her out-of-control sobs. Carver glanced at the Russian handgun mounted in its case on the wall and wondered if he should leave her alone.

Then he decided he was being alarmist. The woman lived with the pain and sorrow of being a rape victim and she hadn't shot herself. It was unlikely she was in any danger now. He knew he could do nothing for her except perhaps leave. And there was the crucifix, mounted on the wall next to the gun. Her religion would sustain her.

"Call me if Marla contacts you," Carver said. "Please," he added, and went to the door.

He thought Willa nodded assent, but he couldn't be sure. She began sobbing louder, still completely out of control, as he stepped into the hall and closed the door behind him.

WILLA HAD been one possible lead in discovering Marla's whereabouts. Marla's parents were another.

It was 11:00 when Carver turned the Olds into Sleepy Hollow Mobile Home Park and drove down Crane to L Street.

The Cloys' car was parked in the driveway beside their clean white mobile home. The black kettle-style barbecue smoker and webbed aluminum chairs on the lawn at the end of the driveway hadn't moved. Even the beer can still rested in the coiled metal holder stuck in the hard ground next to one of the chairs. Sleepy Hollow was the kind of place where a barbecue might break out at any moment.

Sybil Cloy answered Carver's knock and smiled out at him. "Do come in out of the heat, Mr. Carver."

Her gray-streaked black hair was combed back off her forehead today, emphasizing her strong bone structure. She was wearing dark slacks and a red stretch shirt, black sandals something like Beth's white ones, with the soles treaded like tires. She had a trim, surprisingly good figure for a woman approaching sixty.

Carver climbed the steel steps and moved past her into the trailer's oak-paneled interior. It was cool inside. The scent of fresh-perked coffee was sharp and strong. From the kitchen came the relentless watery chugging of a dishwasher on wash or rinse. Now and then glass and utensils dinged together in the churning water with a high, bell-like tone.

Wallace Cloy walked in from the kitchen, holding a mug of coffee in his right hand.

"Mr. Carver again," Sybil said, as if Wallace might have difficulty identifying Carver.

"Finish your puzzle?" Carver asked. The kitchen table, which Wallace had littered with jigsaw puzzle pieces the last time Carver was there, was visible from where he stood and was bare.

"I never complete those puzzles," Wallace said. "I work on them until I get fed up, then say the hell with it and put everything back in the box. You can't do that with most things in life, but you sure as shit can with a jigsaw puzzle."

Carver felt a twinge of envy. "That's a healthy attitude."

The Cloys were both standing watching him, waiting patiently for him to get to the point.

"Your daughter reported that Joel Brant—the man I told you about last time I was here—tried to run her down with his car."

"She OK?" Wallace asked.

"Yes, she wasn't injured. She reported the incident to the police, then she went into hiding."

"Into hiding where?" Sybil asked. Wallace glared at her for asking what he obviously considered to be a stupid question.

"That's what I came here to ask you," Carver said. "Marla left a note saying she was leaving town. Do you have any idea where she might have gone?"

"If she's hiding," Wallace said, "why should we tell you where she might be?"

"For her own good. Brant's on the run from the police, maybe searching for Marla. She might need protection."

"Orlando," Sybil blurted out. "She used to live in Orlando, you know. She has friends there."

"Do you know anyone she might have gone to for help? Someone who'd give her a place to stay for a while?"

"No. We never talked much about her life in Orlando. Never talked much about anything the last few years." Now it was Sybil's turn to glare at her husband.

Carver decided to take a chance. "Mrs. Cloy, are you, uh, aware of your daughter's alternative lifestyle?"

Several seconds passed.

"Alternative lifestyle?" she echoed.

"Get out!" Wallace growled the words.

"It's a question that might be important," Carver said.

"Get out before I throw this hot coffee on you." Wallace took a threatening step toward Carver.

"Stop it!" Sybil yelled.

"Stop it hell!" Wallace took another step and drew back his arm, holding the mug level. Carver could see steam rising from it.

Carver set his cane on the plush blue carpet and backed away. Wallace stood motionless, glowering at him from beneath his hedgelike eyebrows. A vein on the side of his neck was protruding and pulsing out his rage like a primitive dark code.

As Carver made his way outside, Wallace advanced on him, the coffee mug held at his side now. "There was nothing wrong with the way Marla was raised! You understand that?"

Carver said nothing as he worked his way down the steel steps, then limped out into the front yard.

Wallace stopped and stood in the doorway, leaning from the waist so only his stocky upper body was outside. "It don't matter about Sybil's sister anyway! We raised Marla right!" He tossed the hot coffee in Carver's direction but down into the ground, where it sloshed onto the grass and steamed even in the heat. Sybil's arm snaked around Wallace's waist and gently pulled him back, easing him all the way inside the trailer. The white aluminum door slammed shut.

Carver walked down the driveway to where his car was parked at the curb.

He was about to open the door and get in when he looked up and saw Sybil coming toward him. She strode swiftly but gracefully, her handsome face creased with concern. "Mr. Carver!"

He braced with his forearm on the car's top and stood waiting. She came to the passenger's side of the car and stood staring across the expanse of the canvas top at him, as if it were a negotiating table that would give ideas and insults time to cool as they crossed.

"Please don't think too harshly of Wallace," she said. "He's sensitive about that subject. Just its mention makes him angry. A man his age, and he's from a small town in the Midwest. I guess you'd have to say he has a simplistic and bigoted view of people with different sex preferences. Alternative lifestyles, as you called them."

"I understand," Carver told her.

"My sister Grace lives in New York and is active in the gay and lesbian rights movement. That never has set well with Wallace."

"So that's what he meant when he said your sister didn't matter. Does he think she might have somehow influenced Marla?"

"Oh, no. Grace and Marla hardly know one another. What Wallace meant was that even if those scientific studies suggesting sexual orientation might be inherited are correct, it doesn't reflect on us—on him, really—because Marla was adopted. I told you, he's touchy on the subject."

"Does Marla know she was adopted?"

"Yes. We told her before she graduated high school. She was surprised, but she seemed to get over it. The truth is, she never had what you'd call a happy childhood. She was so unsettled all the time. And there was always trouble with Wallace, something between them."

Sybil paused, catching herself. Whatever had been between Wallace and Marla, she didn't want to discuss it.

Carver said, "Mrs. Cloy, are you afraid of Wallace?"

"No," she said defensively. "Not as long as we live life his way. If we do that, everything is all right."

"Is that why you have little contact with Marla, because Wallace doesn't want you to see her?"

She held her hands out and examined the backs of them, as if looking for new liver spots or wrinkles. "Wallace can be a violent man, Mr. Carver."

"Was he violent with Marla?"

"Marla had boyfriends in high school," Sybil said, as if Carver hadn't asked the question. "Dates with boys, anyway. Then the business with other girls started, and we—Marla and Wallace, actually—had a terrible falling out." Sybil looked back at the pristine white trailer like an infidel trying to recall paradise, then at Carver. "I'd like to think someday Wallace will come to his senses and love her like a daughter."

Carver smiled. "I'd like to think that, too." But he didn't believe it would ever happen.

Sybil returned his smile and straightened up to stand away from the car.

She remained standing motionless as he slid behind the steering wheel and drove away.

Near the main entrance to Sleepy Hollow he pulled the Olds to the curb and sat in the heat with the engine idling. He went over in his mind the newspaper accounts of Portia's fatal accident. Then he got out Marla's photograph and stared at it, along with the copy of Portia's newspaper photo.

What he suspected was possible, he decided, as he slipped the gearshift lever into drive and accelerated out onto the highway.

He wasn't sure what it might mean, but it was possible.

|37|

A FEW miles outside Orlando, at a combination souvenir shop, produce stand, and country and western restaurant called Citrustown, Carver stopped for lunch and to phone Beth.

While he was waiting for his order of chicken salad sandwich, french fries, and Gallopin' Grapefruit Freezy, he made his way to the public phone mounted on the wall over by an alcove crammed with a display of souvenirs.

He punched out the cottage's number and waited while the phone rang on the other end of the line, eyeing the miniature covered-wagon lamps, realistic plastic fruit, animals constructed of tiny sea shells, and waxed and polished slabs of genuine cypress with electric clocks (quartz movement) inlaid in their centers.

When Beth answered the phone, he knew better than to ask how she felt.

Instead he said, "Can you get your friend the *Burrow* computer hacker to try tracing the origins of Portia Brant and Marla Cloy?"

"Origins? You mean their childhoods?"

"Yes. As far back as possible."

"All I have to do is ask," Beth said. "Jeff already has a lot of information on them, from social security numbers to their credit ratings. Backtracking into their childhoods should be relatively easy. But why do you want to do it?"

"I just came from seeing Marla's parents. Turns out Marla was adopted."

"I don't see the significance," Beth said.

"I'm not sure I do, either, but it's worth exploring."

A young family came in from outside, Mom and Dad and three little preschool-age blond girls. Mom and Dad were sweaty and looked to be in mild shock. The girls looked irritable. One of them grabbed at the hair of another. They all screamed. Mom and Dad seemed not to have heard. Carver hoped they wouldn't sit near his table.

Beth must have heard the screaming over the phone. "Where are you, Fred?"

"Just outside Orlando, about to dine on Florida tourist cuisine."

He observed the waitress setting his food on his table, looking around for him. When her gaze slid his way, he waved to her. She smiled and nodded, finished laying out his lunch, then moved away toward the kitchen.

"I was hard on you this morning," Beth said. "I'm sorry."

"No need."

He watched the couple with the loud kids go to a table all the way in the back of the restaurant. No, wait. Only two kids. The third blond girl was sitting at the table behind Carver's, demanding that the family sit there. Mom and Dad looked at each other, shrugged, rose slowly from their chairs, and the girl at the table behind Carver's was joined by the rest of the family.

"Yes, there is a need," Beth said. "I apologize. I can be a bitch sometimes."

"You've been consistently swell before today."

"Don't be ironic, Fred. I appreciate what you told me this morning, that no matter what I decide you'll stand by me, and we'll be all right together."

"I meant it," Carver said. "Sometimes it takes me a while to get where I need to go. I have a hard time empathizing, putting myself in other people's skins unless I'm trying to figure them out in relation to my work."

"You got there, though," Beth said. "Most men don't."

One of the blond girls was turned around in her chair and had developed an interest in Carver's food.

"Speaking of going places," he said, "after lunch I'm driving over to talk with Gloria Bream. It's possible she knows where Brant is."

"Maybe he'll call and tell you himself," Beth said. "He's your client. Have you checked your answering machine at the office?"

"No. I'm going to as soon as I hang up."

The blond girl reached for Carver's sandwich but Mom clutched her wrist, stopping her just in time. Mom looked around, saw Carver on the phone, and smiled at him. *Kids*, said the smile. *What are you gonna do?*

"Want me to call you when Jeff gets the information on Portia and Marla?" Beth asked.

"I'll call you," Carver said. "Or I'll come by the cottage. I'll be back sometime late afternoon."

"If you get a chance, stop someplace and buy some lemons."

He looked over at the mountains of citrus fruit displayed in bins outside the restaurant and told her lemons would be no problem.

Then he hung up, fed more change into the phone, and

called his office. When his machine answered, he punched in the code that would play his messages.

A man wanting to sell him international mutual funds had called, and Desoto. No one else. Not Joel Brant.

Carver decided to drop in and see Desoto instead of returning his call. He hung up the phone then limped over to his table. He didn't give the international funds a thought; he had a difficult enough time figuring out Florida.

Lunch looked terrible but tasted good. Especially the Gallopin' Grapefruit Freezy. The little blond girl who wanted his sandwich swiveled around in her chair again and stared at him with eyes like laser beams.

He ate fast and got out of there, pausing only to buy lemons.

DESOTO LOOKED up from what he was working on and smiled at Carver. He was holding a round magnifying glass with a long handle in his left hand, the kind Sherlock Holmes used. Before him on his desk lay his gold wristwatch and an array of miniature tools. The watch's back had been removed. In Desoto's other hand was a tiny screwdriver with a yellow plastic handle.

"You ever try to replace a watch battery, *amigo?*" Desoto asked.

Carver leaned on his cane and shook his head no.

"You've got to remove these two minuscule screws you can hardly even see. Do it with this tiny screwdriver almost too small to pick up with your bare fingers, all the time watching what you're doing through a magnifying glass."

"You better take the watch to a jeweler."

"Yeah." He put down the magnifying glass and carefully moved everything to the side. "I thought it would be something like changing a battery in a flashlight." Wiping his hands with a white handkerchief he produced from a pocket, he leaned back in his chair. His windowsill stereo was silent today, maybe so his concentration on the watch wouldn't be broken. "I wanted to let you know we got a print from your office that matches the ones on the wrecked Harley and on the trunk lid of Spotto's rental car."

"Now all you need is Achilles Jones."

"That's another reason I wanted to talk to you. A nineteen ninety-four Harley-Davidson Electra Glide Ultra was stolen from in front of a biker bar over on Vermont Avenue late last night. The owner apparently tried to stop the thief."

"Apparently?"

"Nobody saw what happened. The guy who owned the bike went outside to get cigarettes from his saddlebag. When he didn't come back, one of his friends went to see what was keeping him. Found him dead behind a line of parked motorcycles. His nose and eye area had been smashed in hard enough to drive bone splinters into his brain. The M.E. says the fatal injury required incredible force and was done with a blunt instrument, possibly a huge fist."

Carver told Desoto about the motorcycle tire tracks Wade Schultz had pointed out this morning at Brant Estates.

"I'll get somebody out there and makes casts of the tread," Desoto said. "Something else. The dead biker—Rawley Everwatt was his name—was holding a knife with blood on the blade. Must have taken a run at the thief and got some of him. It's the same type as a blood sample we took off the wrecked motorcycle after its run-in with your car."

Carver grinned appreciatively. "You really are good at your work."

"So Jones is wounded beyond whatever injuries he received in the accident with your car. But there's no way to know how bad he's hurt from either incident. He might have superficial injuries from the accident, and Everwatt might only have managed to nick him with the knife before getting punched out of the world." Desoto's tanned features creased to form his handsome white smile, but there was nothing of humor there. "The case builds. When we get this Jones, we'll have him good."

"He's too large to go unnoticed forever," Carver said.

Desoto picked up his wristwatch and carefully snapped its back into place. He stared at the watch as if contemplating putting it on his wrist, then wrapped it in the white handkerchief and slipped it into an inside pocket of his pale yellow suit coat. "Why were you at Brant Estates this morning?" he asked.

"To talk to Brant's foreman, Wade Schultz."

Carver told Desoto about Marla's claim that Brant tried to run her down. About Brant's disappearance, then Marla's. About McGregor's repeated threat to nail him as Brant's accomplice.

Desoto's brown eyes darkened and seemed to lose depth, as if his attention had flagged and turned inward. Carver knew better. He'd seen Desoto angry before.

"This gets more serious," Desoto said. "And don't worry about McGregor. His Marla Cloy and Brant are part of my homicide case. I'm going to give him a call."

Carver wasn't so sure Desoto could hobble McGregor. "Don't expect professional courtesy."

"I don't. But McGregor can expect a professional reaming out if he doesn't stop playing personal games and cooperate. Where are you going when you leave here?"

"Red Feather Realty, to try to see Gloria Bream."

Desoto arched an eyebrow in puzzlement. "Who is?"

"A real estate agent. Red Feather handles the listings in the condo development where Brant lives. Gloria Bream and Brant are rumored to be in a personal relationship."

"Hmm. You better let us talk to her. Brant might have hired Achilles Jones to scare you off delving into his life when you were supposed to be investigating Marla Cloy. Questioning Gloria Bream might qualify as delving."

"Or Marla might have hired Jones to scare me off investigating her claims of harassment against Brant."

"That could be. Why do you think he killed Spotto?"

"He knew Spotto was working for me, but that doesn't tell us much. He might have thought Spotto's involvement was in regard to either Brant or Marla. If you find Jones, that's what I need to know from him, which of the two hired him."

"It might not have been either of them."

"There's that possibility," Carver admitted.

Desoto unconsciously caressed a gold cuff link with the very tip of his middle finger. "It's difficult," he said, "to know where the truth lies. Maybe we won't even know the truth for sure when this is over."

"That's what Beth says. You two think amazingly alike at times."

"About you, I expect we do. Where's Beth now?"

"My cottage."

"I think you better go to her. I'll send some of our people over to talk with this Gloria Bream. Achilles Jones might still be searching for you, and he might find Beth."

Carver knew he was right, and suddenly he was struck by a sense of urgency so strong that he almost felt he could dash from the office without his cane.

"Call me after you get Gloria Bream's statement," he said.

"Sure. And you remember to be careful," he heard Desoto say behind him as he headed for the door and the hot, fast drive back to Del Moray.

|38|

THEY'D MADE love within minutes after Carver arrived at the cottage, the Colt handgun within easy reach on his side of the bed. Though the breeze that found its way in through the screened window was warm, its whimsical movement kept the dim room comfortable.

Beth slept sprawled loosely on her back, while Carver lay awake, listening to the ocean continue its endless and ultimately victorious assault on the land. He tried to discern some primal truth in its hushed message, but failed. Something profound was always there, inches or seconds beyond reach and understanding. Carver had read somewhere that ancient philosophers believed the basic elements of all things, singly or in combination, were earth, fire, water, and air. Maybe, in a way that had little do with hard fact, they were right.

The phone by the bed trilled, and so alert was Carver to sound that he snatched it up before its first ring was completed.

He glanced over at Beth, who hadn't moved, then whispered a hello into the receiver.

Desoto said, "Isn't it early to be in bed?"

"How do you know I'm in bed?" Carver asked.

"Someone is, or you wouldn't be whispering, right?"

"Not necessarily."

"Besides, I heard bed springs squeak as you picked up the phone. I know that sound."

"All right. I'm in bed."

Desoto could probably guess why, at four in the afternoon, but he dropped the subject. "We were told at Red Feather Realty that Gloria Bream was on vacation, visiting her mother in Kansas City."

"You check on that?"

"Of course. We talked to her. Then we even had the Kansas City police make sure the woman who told us on the phone she was Gloria Bream was actually there and was who she claimed to be. And her vacation and visit had been planned for a month, according to some of the other Red Feather employees. It looks like Bream's out of the picture here."

"Unless Kansas City is where Brant's gone."

"The K.C. police are onto that possibility, but they say it's unlikely, given the situation there. They're keeping the Bream house, and Gloria Bream, under observation in case Brant does show up, but it's more a matter of touching all the bases than thinking in terms of a home run."

"There's always the possibility of a wild pitch," Carver said.

"Ah! Another baseball analogy. Very good, *amigo*, but I'd already changed seasons to football."

"Football?"

"Yes. I see your dilemma more as sudden-death overtime than extra innings."

"Is that your way of cautioning me?"

"It is, though I don't delude myself that it makes any difference. Still, one must try."

"One sure doesn't talk like a cop sometimes."

"Like a friend, I hope."

"Like a friend," Carver confirmed. "And it does make a difference."

"I'm assuming Beth's okay."

"She's never been better."

"Uh-huh."

Carver thanked Desoto and hung up, letting the back of his head sink deep into the pillow. For more than the obvious reasons, he'd been hoping Brant had run to Gloria Bream. It would mean he hadn't snapped entirely under the strain and frustration and been serious about his threat to kill Marla. Now Carver feared Brant was determined to thwart Marla by actually killing her, his judgment warped as he moved in a dream of vengeance. Carver knew how it was to be trapped in that dream, and how difficult it was to escape. Revenge could be as basic and powerful a craving as hunger or sex. He wondered how the ancient philosophers had regarded revenge. Fire, he decided.

Fire and then earth.

HE DIDN'T remember falling asleep. His mind and body lurched, and suddenly he realized the room was dark. The digital numerals on the clock near the bed said it was almost ten o'clock.

Beth's form was barely visible, but he could hear her snoring lightly. She didn't seem to have changed position. The crash of the surf on the beach was louder, with more time between incoming waves. Though it was probably cooler outside, the breeze had died and the bedroom was warm. Carver's nude body was perspiring, and he could feel heat emanating from Beth. The scent of their coupling was heavier in the air than when he'd fallen asleep, stirring desire in him again, but only faintly. He became aware of the pressure of his bladder and reached for his cane so he could make his way into the bathroom.

As he was standing at the commode relieving himself, he heard the phone trill again. It stopped after two rings. Beth must not have been sleeping as deeply as he'd thought.

By the time he'd returned to the bedroom, she was sitting cross-legged on his side of the bed with the reading lamp on, holding the receiver to her ear with a hunched shoulder while she wrote with a pencil on the back of a magazine she'd managed to find.

She said "Owe you" into the phone, then smiled and hung up.

She stared at the magazine in her lap for a few seconds, as if double checking her information, then looked up at Carver. "Marla and Portia Zahn," she said.

"What?"

"That was Jeff Mehling on the phone. He's been at his computer almost all day and worked his way back to Marla's and Portia's birth records. They were born within a year of each other in Winter Haven, Florida. Same mother and father. Jeff said the Zahns' car was struck broadside by a tractor-trailer when the girls were eighteen months and seven months old. They were the only survivors. Since they had no other family, they became wards of the state and were put up for adoption."

Then it was true.

Carver shifted weight over his cane and limped to the bed, but he didn't sit or lie down.

"Sisters," he said. "Jesus!"

He remembered again the alcohol level in Brant's blood after the accident that killed Portia. Marla, for that or for whatever reason, might blame Brant for her sister's death.

Brant was probably unaware that Portia had a sister. Maybe Portia had been unaware of Marla's existence. Adoption agencies invariably made the effort to begin their charges' lives anew, especially if they were infants, to sever the past from them the way the umbilical cord had been cut to detach them completely from life in the womb. Like a second birth. It might be a necessary policy, but it could later cause pain and problems.

Carver turned and moved to where his pants were folded over a chair.

"Where are you going?" Beth asked when she saw he intended getting dressed.

He sat down on the bed and quickly worked his legs into his pants, got them all the way on, then zipped them and fastened his belt. It was more of a struggle to get his socks on, but he was used to that, too.

"Fred?" Beth said.

He slipped his feet into black leather moccasins. "I'm going to see if Marla's returned home. If she has, I plan to confront her with the evidence that she's Portia Brant's sister, blames Joel Brant for the accident that killed Portia, and is setting him up for a vengeance killing."

He knew she was watching as he worked his muscular upper body into a black T-shirt, then used his fingers to smooth back the thick hair above his ears.

He went to the bed and picked up the Colt from beside the clock radio on the table. Oiled metal clucked and clacked smoothly as he jacked a round into the chamber. Then he showed Beth where the safety was located and how it worked. He knew she was familiar with firearms, but he wasn't sure she knew about this one. "I'm leaving this with you in case Achilles Jones happens to show up."

"I know how to use it," she said.

He almost told her not to hesitate if she had time to shoot, then he realized there was no need. She wouldn't hesitate, and her aim would be steady.

At least, the aim of the former, nonpregnant Beth would have been steady.

"What makes you think Marla might be home?" she asked.

"If what I suspect is true, she only pretended to leave town because that's what a terrified woman would do. She actually wants Joel Brant to find her. On her terms and home turf."

He made sure he had his wallet and keys, then he got a firm handhold on his cane and headed for the door.

Behind him Beth said, "None of it's going to be that simple, Fred."

He didn't look back. "Why not?"

"Because it never is. You know that."

He did know it, but not the way she did. His heart had never learned.

The night was warm and the stars were bright and seemed to float low and huge, like the diffuse globs of yellow that were stars in a Van Gogh painting. There was very little breeze now.

Finally, theory suited probability. As he gunned the Olds's engine to follow its headlight beams to Jacaranda Lane, he thought Beth might be wrong.

Sometimes, when you pulled the right lever or pushed the right button, it was precisely that simple.

Sometimes.

|39|

CARVER PARKED half a block away from Marla Cloy's house on Jacaranda. If she was home, he didn't want to chance her seeing him drive up. She might decide to leave by the back door.

He climbed out of the Olds and made his way along the uneven sidewalk, feeling the slant of its cracked and jagged planes of concrete through his cane. The air was thick and still. There weren't enough street lights on Jacaranda, and only a few of the houses showed light at their windows. People here went to bed early. Cicadas screamed and ratcheted in the dark yards behind the houses and in the shadowed palm fronds above Carver, but that was the only sound.

As he neared Marla's house, he noticed that the sidewalk and street were brighter there. And there was a strange orange cast to the light. He glanced up to see if it was coming from an overhead street lamp, but he saw only stars and a silhouetted palm tree.

Then he noticed that the orange glow was flickering.

Almost simultaneously, he realized something else. The cicadas had stopped their relentless mating scream and the night was quiet.

A slight sound or movement made him turn around just in time to see the massive, shadowed form of Achilles Jones emerge from the darkness of the bushes between two houses.

Carver stopped and stood still, gripping his cane tighter just below its crook, wishing he hadn't left the Colt with Beth.

Beth, who'd known it wouldn't be simple.

Jones said nothing as he advanced. He was limping badly, and when he got within ten feet of Carver the faint light shone on a white gauze bandage that covered one eye. There was a long gash across his forehead. Another was visible on his bare stomach where his wool-lined leather vest was ripped away to hang like a flap of skin. He looked like hell. He was hell.

He said nothing, only growled, as he launched himself at Carver.

Carver stuck the cane out like a spear then pulled it back, causing the giant to hesitate, allowing Carver to barely avoid the swipe of his huge arm. Injuries had slowed the big man, taken the edge off the smooth flow of his great strength, but he was still a dangerous force, like a grizzly bear on an off day.

Carver jabbed again, quickly, and felt the cane make contact with Jones's face. He pushed off Jones, reeled, and almost fell, but regained his balance. Jones stumbled on his bad leg and banged into the side of a parked car, leaving a shallow dent in its door and sinking to the ground. Carver thought inanely that Jones was death on vehicles.

Jones reached up with a plate-sized hand and grabbed a door handle to pull himself up. Before he could get completely to his feet, Carver moved toward him, jabbing at his face again with the cane, yanking it back just in time to avoid Jones's frantic attempts to grab it. The best Jones seemed able to do was brush the cane as if by accident. Carver realized that with one eye bandaged Jones had no depth perception. If he could spike the other eye, he'd blind the giant completely and have a chance to survive. He doubled his efforts, zeroing in on the unbandaged eye.

Jones realized what Carver was doing. He roared like a tortured beast in his frustration as he tried to protect his eye and figure out where the cane was so he could snatch it away from Carver. The cane's tip missed the good eye but bounced off the bridge of Jones's nose and struck the bandaged eye. Jones yelled in pain and instinctively raised his arms to shield his face. Carver whipped the cane hard across Jones's legs, hoping he'd hit the injured one, and Jones slid back down to a sitting position from where he'd been leaning with his back against the parked car.

Carver was breathing hard now, feeling the strain in his arms and good leg. Maintaining his balance after each strike with the cane took tremendous effort, and he was sweating heavily and tiring. He had to back up a step and try to catch his breath and regain a firm grip on the hard walnut cane.

Jones grinned, seeing that Carver was almost spent. He rolled to the side and gained his feet, listing to the left and teetering for a moment. Then, still with his eerie, vacuous grin, he lurched toward the exhausted and vulnerable Carver, risking a chance injury to the good eye, his arms spread wide so Carver couldn't avoid their terrible reach.

But Carver didn't jab at the eye. He faked with the cane as if to strike at the legs again, and Jones dropped his arms for a second. That was when Carver raised the level of the cane and lashed it sideways with all his might as if it were a baseball bat, knowing it was his last chance.

He felt the shock of the blow connecting and heard the cartilage-cracking sound of Jones's larynx being crushed.

Jones gave a ghastly, choking gurgle and stood very still except for both his huge hands fluttering with a weird delicacy at his throat, as if feeling for something that wasn't there. The slowly comprehending expression on his face said he knew he'd been badly hurt. Maybe he sensed already that it had been a death blow, the way fatally injured animals somehow knew.

The effort of the swing had caused Carver to lose his balance and fall. He raised himself to his feet with the cane and waited for Jones to drop, seeing behind him the flickering orange glare from the flames consuming Marla Cloy's house. He became aware of several people standing outside their houses, unmoving on porches and lawns. Sirens were screaming, drawing near. Flashing lights illuminated the end of the block, and a yellow Del Morray fire engine blasted its horn and roared around the corner.

At the sound of the sirens, then the blaring horn, Jones gazed incredulously at Carver with eyes like clouded glass. Instead of toppling like an ordinary man, the giant staggered into the street, trying to escape, his hands now clawing desperately at his ruined throat. He was a creature of raw will. He'd been dealt death, but life was a force in him.

With an undeniable admiration that he tried to ignore, Carver limped past him, toward Marla's house. His injured ribs were aching again, as if he'd just been struck there.

Above the wail of sirens he heard tires screech and air brakes hiss, and without slowing down he glanced to the side and saw Jones raise his arms high and go down beneath the gleaming front bumper of a huge yellow vehicle lettered 4TH DIST. LADDER. Voices shouted and there was a rush of activity behind Carver as he reached Marla's front yard and hobbled toward the tiny porch with its dead potted plants.

Every window in the house was illuminated, making it look oddly like a child's doll house lit by a single bulb. Flames were visible only on the driveway side. They licked at the overhang and roof shingles. One of the drooping canvas awnings was ablaze. Marla's old Toyota was parked in the drive, glowing embers scattered over its roof and hood and twinkling like Christmas decorations.

Marla must be inside, maybe still alive. Carver tried the front door and found it unlocked. Its tarnished brass doorknob was warm, but not painful to touch. He opened the door and limped inside, crouching awkwardly so he could get beneath the swirling black smoke that pressed against the ceiling and halfway down the walls. He knew the thick layer of smoke was moving lower; he didn't have much time. Heat grabbed at his right side with a pain like the brutal pinch of flesh. His bare right arm and the right side of his neck felt as if hot coals were being pressed to them. He saw flames glaring at him through the smoke.

Marla was easy enough to find.

So was Joel Brant.

They were lying side by side on the living room floor. Both looked dead, but Carver couldn't be sure. Marla was on her back, and Brant was curled on his side as if napping, his head cradled in the crook of his arm.

Carver got down on his hands and his good knee, his stiff leg trailing behind him, and crawled over to Marla. When he was a few feet from her, he stopped. Her eyes were open and not seeing anything. Brant's eyes were open, too. He seemed to be staring directly at Marla, but he wasn't.

The black pall was swirling lower, and Carver's breath rasped as he drew in smoke-tainted air that felt hot inside his chest. He could hear flames crackling, and the heat was searing. He reached out a hand to grab Brant's wrist, imagining with some strange reflexive responsibility to a client that he might be able to drag the body outside and save it from the fire. But he saw the hair on his own forearm sizzle and blacken, and he withdrew his hand and began crawling toward the door.

Something rolled painfully between his left palm and the floor, almost causing him to fold over onto his side. Then he realized it was his cane. He jammed its tip against the floor and tried to stand and make better time, but the air was much hotter even a few feet above the floor, the smoke so dense he began gagging and coughing immediately and had to drop back down. Holding the cane out in front of him, he dragged himself on his elbows and good knee toward where he thought the door must be, knowing that if he lost direction in the smoke, he was dead.

The cane jerked around in his hand, and at first he thought someone was trying to snatch it away from him. Achilles Jones, somehow still alive! Like in one of those protracted Hollywood thriller endings when the villain is presumed dead but keeps getting back up.

Then a voice said, "Come on! This way, goddamnit!"

Carver laced his fingers and held tight to the crook of the cane with both hands as a powerful force drew him forward. Hands clutched his shirt, then his upper arms, and he let himself be dragged outside. One of his moccasins came off, then the other.

He rolled onto his back, staring up at the stars and trying to suck in the sweet nectar of clear night air. But he couldn't seem to get any. He coughed three times, then he began to choke.

Something was placed over his mouth and nose. A figure in a yellow slicker was bending over him. "Easy now! Easy, bub! Breath in easy. . . ."

The tightness in Carver's throat slackened, and he began drawing cool oxygen into his lungs through the mask held by the firefighter staring calmly down at him with the dark, sad eyes of a martyr. More figures in yellow slickers were milling around him, and he saw streams of water being played over the fire. Several additional pieces of firefighting equipment had arrived, along with police cars. Marla's neighbors on Jacaranda Lane were clustered on the other side of the street, held back by a uniformed cop with his arms spread wide. The way Jones had spread his arms when he'd come at Carver for the kill.

"He's yours," the firefighter who'd been holding Carver's oxygen mask in place said. Then he stood up and passed from sight.

White-clad paramedics were over Carver now, working him onto a gurney. He tried to sit up and tell them he could walk, but they gently eased him back down. "This yours?" one of them asked, holding the cane out where he could see it while the other fastened the oxygen mask's strap behind his head. He nodded, and the paramedic placed the cane next to him on the gurney, beneath one of the straps that were now holding Carver fast, his arms at his sides. He felt himself levitating then, and being rolled feet first across the hard ground toward where bright lights were flashing red, blue, yellow . . .

Ambulance doors swung open wide, as if waiting to embrace him. The gurney jerked and tilted a few degrees as its wheels were folded up so it could become a simple stretcher again and be slid inside. Weakness rushed over Carver like a dark wave, and the ambulance seemed to swoop and whirl crazily, making him dizzy.

The hell with it, he thought. He closed his eyes and concentrated on drawing in sweet, sweet oxygen. He was addicted. It was impossible to get enough of it. Fire, earth, water . . . Didn't precious air have to be in there somewhere?

The hell with it, he thought again, hearing the ambulance doors slam shut somewhere off in the distance. He'd puzzle it all out later.

Breathing in.

Breathing out.

That was all that mattered now.

|40|

CARVER SAT in the hard oak chair in McGregor's office. It had been two days since the fire. His injured ribs were wrapped again, though this time not in a support but with a thousand yards of flesh-colored Ace elastic bandage fastened to itself with metal clips.

A multiline phone chirped and flashed yellow lights on McGregor's desk, but he ignored it and the calls were answered elsewhere.

Two detectives Carver had noticed when he'd walked past the booking area were joking and laughing loudly out in the hall. McGregor unwound from his desk chair, strode to the door, slammed it hard, then stalked back behind his desk and sat down.

The laughing and joking got softer then ceased altogether.

McGregor absently inserted a forefinger in his ear, rotated it for what seemed a full minute, then wiped the finger on his shirtsleeve. In the hot, confining office, his body odor was probably enough by itself to make a suspect confess.

"The deal was that we share information," Carver reminded him.

McGregor grinned and probed the gap between his teeth with his tongue. "Deal? Deals with shitheads like you don't count. They're like putting poison out for roaches. On the other hand, if I wasn't to tell you how this mess of yours wound up, you'd be sniffing around like a cur smells a bitch in heat, being a pest all the longer."

"You have a poetic way of putting things."

"Well, it ain't gonna rhyme, but here it is: Marla was shacked up in Orlando with a guy named Dan, fella who customizes vans so the suckers think they got a rolling Taj Mahal. She'd known him for a while and they had an on-again, off-again thing going. He knows nothing about her being stalked or anything else. Only knew she was a lively piece of tail. He says she left his apartment the evening of the fire but didn't say where she was going."

"What about the fire?"

"Arson squad says it was set with an accelerant, probably gasoline, since there was a metal gas can in the debris. There wasn't much left of the bodies. The autopsy report says each was shot, probably fatally, before the fire got to them. No way to know which of them started the fire, or who shot who first. My bet would be on Brant. Though the place *was* rented, so Marla might have torched it."

"What about the guns?" Carver asked, marveling at the idea of a penny-wise murderer-arsonist.

"We found only one gun, or what was left of it. A thirty-two revolver."

"Two corpses," Carver said, "only one gun."

"That's right. You pass the fucking math test."

"So where's the other gun?"

"Who knows and who gives a shit?"

"I don't and I do," Carver said. "Were all the bullets thirty-twos?"

"No way to say for sure. The heat of the fire melted them down. Messed up the gun, too. There was no way to run ballistics tests. Way I see it, there might have been only one gun to begin with, and Marla and Brant got shot when they were struggling over it. Or their deaths might have been the result of a murder-suicide pact. Anything's possible. After all, you never found out what the fuck was going on between them. If there ever was another gun, it must have got lost in the confusion of the fire. Or maybe it got stolen later. Lots of people at the scene, poking around."

Carver folded his hands over the crook of his cane and leaned forward in his chair, saying nothing.

"Like I said," McGregor told him, "anything's possible. And since we got nobody to charge, the case is fucking closed."

"The way you like them."

"Nothing wrong with that. I'm a cop."

"What about the other dead man?"

"The not-so-jolly green giant? He got mashed by a fire engine. We haven't identified him yet except by that silly a.k.a., Attila Jones."

"Achilles," Carver corrected.

"Whatever. It's all Greek to me. My guess is we never will know who he is. His prints don't match anything on record, and it's for sure his mommy's not gonna turn up and claim the carcass."

"No ID on him?" Carver asked.

"Weren't you listening?"

Carver stared at McGregor and waited.

"OK, OK. There was nothing in his pockets except twenty bucks and the keys to a motorcycle parked on the next block."

"A Harley-Davidson?"

"That's right. Stolen plates, stolen bike. No surprise there except that sometime somewhere somebody trained the geek to ride a motorcycle."

Frustration tightened like a fist in Carver's stomach. He'd never know who hired Jones, or whether it was Marla or Brant who wanted him to back away from the investigation. And if Marla knew she was Portia's sister, so Brant might have known and had some motive to harass Marla. Carver realized that now there was no way to sort out victim or perpetrator.

"Anything else?" he asked, but not with any real hope.

McGregor sneered. "Only if I can figure out a way to charge you with something."

Carver stood up and limped toward the door.

"And I'll think of a way eventually," McGregor added.

Neither man said good morning. Neither would have been sincere.

Without looking back, Carver went out the door. He needed fresh air almost as much as he had the night of the fire.

''WHAT DID McGregor say?" Beth asked when Carver returned to the cottage.

"That the case is closed."

He told her the details of his visit with McGregor. She listened carefully, all the while continuing making a sandwich at the breakfast bar. He glanced at his watch and saw that it was almost noon. Without asking if he was hungry, she began building another tuna salad sandwich. For him, he assumed.

"I'm not hungry," he said.

"Sure you are," she told him. "You only had coffee for breakfast. Eat this. You need it."

He didn't say no. It was best not to cross her these days.

On the cottage porch after lunch, sitting next to Beth and watching the sun spark off the sea, Carver said, "I'll never know the truth." He spoke more to a soaring gull than to Beth. "Who was the stalker and who was the intended victim? Who was the killer? And why?"

Beth turned her face in his direction and raised her sunglasses so the lenses rested above her forehead like a second pair of eyes. She was sweating in the afternoon heat. A bead of perspiration zigzagged from her hairline down her temple and cheek. "But you *do* know the truth now, lover. Which is that human nature's so complex the truth's hardly ever accessible."

"I have a problem with that," Carver said.

She laughed. Then she bent effortlessly, picked up one of her sandals from the porch floor, and swatted hard at an insect near her chair. "Only problem is, Fred, you don't accept it."

"Sometimes I do."

"No. Never. You keep flying at the light like a wasp at a window." She examined the sandal's rubber sole and made a face. "Why I love you, I guess."

He stood up and went inside for a cold beer.

Then he sat for a while longer, staring out at the sea.

|41|

WHEN CARVER parked the Olds in front of 22 Jacaranda Lane the next morning, he found half of Marla's house still standing. Her car remained where it had been parked in the driveway, tilting toward the house on two partly melted tires, its left side charred and blistered. No attempt had been made to board up any of the remaining windows; there would have been little point, with much of the house reduced to blackened, skeletal framework.

The police were finished there, and probably the insurance investigators, too. The tattered remains of a police-scene ribbon dangled from where it was tied in a bow around a porch rail, reminding Carver of when people put up yellow ribbons in support of political hostages. Partially protected from firefighter action by the railing, the dead potted plants on the porch looked virtually unchanged. One of the terra-cotta pots had been knocked about six inches out of line, but that was all.

Ignoring a NO TRESPASSING sign, Carver made his way along the walk to the front porch. The door was hanging open, black and alligatored from the fire. He stepped into what had been the living room. It was quite bright because that part of the roof had been burned away or removed by firefighters. Carver glanced up at a sky perfectly blue except for a very high, white vapor trail. The airliner that had left it was still visible as a slowly moving silver splinter, tracing a northerly course in a cold, pure world not at all like the one from which it had risen.

He picked his way through the blackened debris of furniture and the collapsed roof to stand near where he estimated Marla's and Brant's bodies had lain, then he began probing the ashes with his cane. It had rained late last night, leaving the wreckage a sodden black mess that soon saturated and darkened his socks and the cuffs of his khaki pants. The dampness kept the soot down, but it helped to create an acrid stench of ruin that stung the nostrils and back of the throat.

Half an hour of searching, widening the area to cover most of the living room, yielded nothing. He wasn't sure what he'd expected to find. The police had done their work.

But he told himself the police had been under McGregor's command, so they were hardly pressed to be thorough. He continued searching through the charred remains of the house.

After an hour, he gave up. He was satisfied that whatever clues might have been at the death site had been destroyed by flames, or by the turmoil and ruin created during the fighting of the fire.

Remembering what Beth had told him yesterday about being like a wasp at a window that kept flinging itself at the light with futile determination, he took a last look around, a part of him still unwilling to leave. Then he limped toward the door.

It was when he was out on the tiny porch that he noticed something: A faint gleam of brass among the earth and wet blackness of one of the pots containing the dead plants. The rain must have washed away enough of the ashes and soot to reveal it, as it had washed away most of the ash on the porch itself, now that the small wooden overhang was burned to nothing more than a few charred stubs.

Supporting himself carefully with his cane, Carver leaned down and picked up the object.

It was a brass casing from a fired bullet. McGregor had mentioned that the gun recovered from the scene was a revolver. They didn't eject shells after firing rounds of ammunition; the casings remained in the cylinder. So the police probably weren't searching very thoroughly for brass casings. And who could tell how such a tiny object had been moved around during the fire, blasted by powerful streams of water, stepped on and kicked by firefighters, swept aside with piles of debris?

There was also the possibility it had been in the terra-cotta pot for months or years and had nothing to do with the deaths of Marla and Brant. No way to prove otherwise now. Its discovery actually meant little in a case that was closed.

Carver wiped dampness and soot from the shell and held it up to the light in the manner of a man examining a rare gem. He couldn't place the caliber until he turned the brass casing at a certain angle to the slanted rays of the morning sun. Faintly lettered on the outer rim of its base was "7.62 mm." An uncommon-size shell ejected by an uncommon gun.

He'd dropped the casing in his pocket and was stepping down off the porch when he remembered.

He stood still for almost a full minute, frozen by realization, squeezing the brass shell through the material of his pants so hard that his fingers ached.

Then he got in the Olds and drove to see Willa Krull.

|42|

THE ROSES on the iron trellis that was the entrance arch to the old apartment building on Fourteenth Street looked vividly red and fresh after last night's rain. Carver noticed there was even a shallow, greenish layer of water on the bottom of the tile pond, as if the maimed and perpetually leaping concrete swordfish had at last found its element.

Willa Krull answered his knock in her usual fashion, by staring out through the crack available when she opened her door on the chain lock. Even through the narrow opening, Carver could smell the scent of gin. It wasn't yet noon and she'd obviously been drinking heavily. She'd apparently been crying, too. The single red-rimmed eye that peered out at him was open barely wide enough to see.

"Sorry, don' wanna talk to anyone today," she said.

He unobtrusively moved the tip of his cane forward so she wouldn't be able to close the door. She was going to hear what he had to say, even if he had to tell her standing there in the hall. "I just came from Marla Cloy's house."

"What's left of it, you mean."

"I know most of what happened," he said.

" 'Course. It was in the papers, on the TV news. And you were there, right?"

"You were there, too."

She didn't say anything. The eye didn't change.

"Am I coming in?" Carver asked.

She nodded. He moved the cane out of the way quickly as she closed the door to remove the chain, then opened it just wide enough for him to enter.

She looked even worse than she had the last time he'd seen her, like someone who'd gotten dressed in a hurry at gunpoint. She was wearing wrinkled jeans that made her bony figure appear even more angular, and a stained white blouse that was buttoned crookedly. Her mousy hair was in disarray as usual. She was barefoot and holding a cracked water tumbler with ice and gin in it.

Carver moved past her into the apartment. The place was a mess. Unfolded and creased newspapers were scattered on the floor, as if she'd been reading the news so frenetically she hadn't had time to refold the pages. Her gun magazines were littered over the coffee table, next to an almost empty gin bottle. Carver saw that the display case with the Russian handgun was gone from the wall. Only the plastic crucifix remained.

Willa closed the door and reattached the chain lock. Then she walked unsteadily to the center of the room, not seeming to notice that one foot was on the front page of the *Gazette-Dispatch*, and stood staring at him. She unconsciously waved the glass around as she talked, almost spilling out gin. "You said I was someplace you were last night." A note of fear rang in her voice; the booze couldn't insulate her from reality completely.

"Where's the Russian handgun?" he asked, motioning with

his head toward the faint, clean rectangle on the wall where the gun's case had been.

"What's the difference?"

He drew the 7.62-millimeter shell casing from his pocket and held it up for her to see. "I found this on Marla's front porch this morning."

She stared at it, her pinched features screwing up in fear, then in desperate defiance. "It doesn't mean anything. Not without the gun."

"That's true," Carver agreed. "Why don't you tell me what happened?"

"Why should I do that?"

"Three reasons. You're safe from the law. I need to know. And most of all, you need to tell somebody."

She stared at the floor, then tugged at a strand of her lank hair and laughed sadly. "She liked me, too, you know. No, it was much more than that. We were fond of each other as more than friends."

"I know."

"She told me she was going to leave me. For a man. She didn't tell me his name."

"You had to know it wasn't Brant."

"Of course."

"Then how did it happen?"

"The evening of—the evening after she told me she was going to Orlando so she'd be safe, Brant came here. I'd never seen him, didn't know who he was. But he was sneaky. He used a different name, acted as if he and Marla were close. He told me he was searching for her, had to find her. What was I supposed to think? I figured he was the one Marla was leaving me for. He wouldn't have known about us, wouldn't have dreamed he wasn't the only one with a relationship with Marla."

"You were jealous of him," Carver said.

"Oh, I was more than jealous. I wanted to kill him. To kill

both of them. I'm not—I mean, Marla was the first woman I'd ever been intimate with. She needed money and I worked free for her, did anything for her. Maybe she was only using me, but it killed me that she was deserting me for one of them . . . a man. I phoned her in Orlando and arranged to meet her at her house that night, told her it was important. I took Brant with me, still not knowing who he really was, thinking he was Marla's other lover. I didn't find out I was wrong until the next day."

"Wasn't Marla surprised to see Brant when she opened her door? Didn't she say anything?"

"She was astounded, but I thought it was the shock of seeing me with the man she was leaving me for. She just stood there with her mouth open, and as soon as we were in the house, I shot both of them to death before I could change my mind. She never really had time to do anything but stammer. I used the Tokarev because I knew it would be difficult to trace, and I could dispose of it without arousing suspicion or having to replace it. Then I fired some rounds with the gun I'd talked Marla into buying and knew she kept in her nightstand, hoping that in the aftermath of the fire it would appear the two of them had become locked in a struggle for it and killed each other in a burst of gunfire."

"The thirty-two-caliber revolver the police found," Carver said.

"Yes. I meant for them to find it. I thought if the fire was hot enough, the bullets would melt and become misshapen so there couldn't be any ballistic tests, and the police would think they all could have come from Marla's gun. After planting the gun, I went outside and got the spare gasoline can I kept in my car."

"You left the can behind, along with the brass casing from the Russian gun."

"I'm not an experienced arsonist, Mr. Carver. I was planning as I went. The flames shot up faster than I imagined and

I panicked and ran. I didn't realize until later I'd dropped the gas can in my flight. And I thought I'd picked up all the 7.62-millimeter shells ejected by the Tokarev. But I counted them later and realized I'd missed one."

"You're not an experienced killer, either," Carver said.

"Experienced now," she said sadly, and shivered.

"Tell me the truth about Marla and Brant," Carver said. "Was he really stalking her?"

Willa seemed to be talking to the floor, her head still bowed, her voice a dull monotone. "No. Marla was rejected by her adoptive family, especially her father, and it left a void and a restlessness in her, a yearning. She told me once she'd been molested by her father, but she never talked about it again. She's a journalist and knows how to do research, so she decided to find her real family. She contacted Portia Brant and identified herself as her sister shortly before Portia's death. Portia was frightened, and because Marla was her sister she confided in her. She told Marla she suspected Joel was planning to murder her for her life insurance money so he could pay off gambling debts."

"That's Marla's version. Did you believe her?"

"Of course. But before Marla could learn more, Portia was dead. Marla did some investigating. She was sure the air bag on the passenger side of the Brants' car had been tampered with so it inflated a precious second too late after impact. The driver would be relatively safe in a head-on collision, but the passenger would die."

"Why didn't she go to the police?"

"She probably would have, but while she was considering it, the salvage yard crushed the car and destroyed the evidence."

"So Marla decided to avenge her sister's death," Carver said. "She was going to murder Joel Brant by setting him up, convincing the police he was fixated on her and stalking her, so she could make it look as if she'd killed him in self-defense."

"Marla was the one with the fixation," Willa said. "She lived with the conviction that Joel Brant had murdered her sister, but she did nothing about it. Then, three months ago, a woman named Gail she was involved with in Orlando died in a fire. First her sister, then her lover, gone. I think that's when Marla became mentally unhinged with grief and obsessed with Joel Brant's execution. She never called it murder. She was going to shoot him. I gave her the gun, taught her how to use it. I guess I was going to be a murderer either way." She raised her head and stared at him beseechingly, as if she craved absolution. He couldn't give it to her. "Do you understand now?" she asked.

He nodded silently.

She saw that he wasn't going to forgive her. "I'm basically a good person," she said, her voice an agony of guilt and a plea for understanding if not mercy. "Deeply religious." She glanced with a terrible longing at the crucifix on the wall. "A good person. Nothing like any of this ever happened to me before. I lost my way. I only made one, horrible mistake that I'll never be free of inside. But I disposed of the murder gun, and the shell casing you found doesn't mean anything by itself. There's no way you can prove what I just told you. No way a jury could convict me even I did have to go to trial."

He knew she was right.

About everything but justice.

"In your case," he said, "I don't think it matters about the law or the jury."

He gently removed from her hand the half-full glass of gin that was tilting sharply and about to spill, then he placed it next to the bottle on the table. On a glossy copy of *Shooter's World*.

Then he left her to the truth.

43

''I TALKED to the detective in charge of the Portia Brant accident investigation," Carver said. "He told me there was no reason for Marla Cloy to think Joel had tampered with the passenger-side air bag. Portia's death was an accident."

"He could be wrong," Beth said.

"It's possible."

They were sitting side by side on the plank steps of the cottage's front porch, watching sky and ocean darken as the sun set behind them. Far offshore the lights of a cruise ship became faintly visible in the void, a distant, self-contained world of soothing delusion.

"You think she was paranoid about Joel?" Beth asked.

"I don't know. A lonely woman, forsaken by her adoptive family, a victim of childhood molestation. Then she discovers she has a sister. A lifeline. Then she suddenly loses the sister. Easy to understand how she might have blamed Joel Brant." Carver stared out at the distant lights that seemed motionless. "Or maybe she really did have some reason to suspect him."

"Might she have lied to Willa Krull?" Beth asked.

"Anyone might lie to anyone."

"Then Willa might have lied to you."

"Yes," Carver said, "you can call this one whichever way you choose, however your mind colors it. You were right. Sometimes the truth's impossible to discover. Life's about irresolution, and learning to live with it."

"But you," Beth said, "you discover some of the truth, then you figure out the rest as accurately as possible. You find a faint thread woven through the tapestry and you follow wherever it goes, no matter the consequences. That makes you special, Fred."

Special? Or simply good at his work? Or maybe it was the same thing. He knew the only kind of proof he had was Willa Krull. He'd believed her story, believed her pain. She was living with the truth.

"You solved your case," Beth said. "You found the killer and the motive. The rest is always shadow."

Carver's stiff leg was extended so the heel of his moccasin dug into the sandy earth beyond the steps. He and Beth were sitting so close together that their arms touched. In the dying heat they continued to watch the darkness close in. The wavering snarl of a speedboat drifted in on the night, then faded as the boat made its way south along the shoreline.

"I've been thinking some more about the baby," Beth said. "Trying to come to a decision."

"It's your call," Carver said. It sounded lame, but he didn't know what else to tell her. He was with her either way. And either way, it wasn't the kind of decision a woman made then walked away whistling. Whatever she decided, he knew he might lose her if she thought he'd pressured her into it. She'd talked to the doctor, who'd quoted her the odds on giving birth to another dead child. She knew her chances but hadn't told Carver. With something like that, what did the odds mean, anyway, if you were the one taking the risk?

"Let's try it," she said.

He couldn't quite believe what he'd heard. "You sure it's what you want?"

"No. But I've made up my mind."

He touched her hand in the dark and she squeezed his fingers hard, digging her nails into his flesh. Then her grip loosened and he heard her quiet sobs and felt their subtle vibrations.

Carver knew the truth now. She needed him.

The cruise ship's lights had disappeared. A cool breeze came out of the night with a sound like a sudden intake of breath. Gazing into unbroken blackness, he thought of Portia and Joel Brant, of Charley Spotto and Achilles Jones, of Willa Krull sitting alone in her apartment with her gin and her *Shooter's World* subscription, her guilt and her guns. With her time running out.

He pulled Beth to him and held her close.

Death was in the air, and she was life.